PENGUIN CLASSICS

# THE POWER AND THE GLORY

Graham Greene, whose long life (1904–1991) nearly spanned the twentieth century, was one of its greatest novelists. Educated at Berkhamsted School and Balliol College, Oxford, he started his career as sub-editor on *The Times*. He began to attract notice as a novelist with his fourth book, *Stamboul Train*, in 1932. In 1935 he trekked across northern Liberia, his first experience of Africa, told in *Journey Without Maps*. He converted to Catholicism in 1926 and reported on religious persecution in Mexico in 1938 in *The Lawless Roads*, which served as background for his famous *The Power and the Glory*, one of several "Catholic" novels (*Brighton Rock*, *The Heart of the Matter*, *The End of the Affair*). During the war he worked for the British secret service in Sierra Leone; afterward, he began wide-ranging travels as a journalist, reflected in novels such as *The Quiet American*, *Our Man in Havana*, *The Comedians*, *Travels with My Aunt*, *The Honorary Consul*, *The Human Factor*, *Monsignor Quixote*, and *The Captain and the Enemy*. As well as his many novels, Graham Greene wrote several collections of short stories, four travel books, six plays, two books of autobiography, *A Sort of Life* and *Ways of Escape*, two of biography, and four books for children. He also contributed hundreds of essays and film and book reviews to *The Spectator* and other journals, many of which appear in the late collection *Reflections*. Most of his novels have been filmed, including *The Third Man*, which was first written as a film treatment. Graham Greene was named Companion of Honour and received the Order of Merit and many other awards.

WORKS BY GRAHAM GREENE

NOVELS

The Man Within    Stamboul Train
It's a Battlefield    England Made Me
A Gun for Sale    Brighton Rock
The Confidential Agent    The Power and the Glory
The Ministry of Fear    The Heart of the Matter
The Third Man    The Fallen Idol
The End of the Affair    Loser Takes All
The Quiet American    Our Man in Havana    A Burnt-Out Case
The Comedians    Travels With My Aunt
The Honorary Consul    The Human Factor
Doctor Fischer of Geneva or The Bomb Party
Monsignor Quixote    The Tenth Man
The Captain and the Enemy

SHORT STORIES

Collected Short Stories (*including* Twenty-One Stories, A Sense of
Reality *and* May We Borrow Your Husband?)
The Last Word and Other Stories

TRAVEL

Journey Without Maps    The Lawless Roads
In Search of a Character    Getting to Know the General

ESSAYS AND REVIEWS

Collected Essays    Reflections
Yours Etc.    Mornings in the Dark

PLAYS

Collected Plays (*including* The Living Room, The Potting Shed, The
Complaisant Lover, Carving a Statue, The Return of A. J. Raffles,
The Great Jowett, Yes and No *and* For Whom the Bell Chimes)

AUTOBIOGRAPHY

A Sort of Life    Way of Escape
Fragments of Autobiography    A World of My Own

BIOGRAPHY

Lord Rochester's Monkey    An Impossible Woman

CHILDREN'S BOOKS

The Little Train    The Little Horse-Bus
The Little Steamroller    The Little Fire Engine

# GRAHAM GREENE

# The Power and the Glory

PENGUIN BOOKS
*in association with* William Heinemann Ltd

PENGUIN BOOKS

Published by the Penguin Group

Penguin Group (USA) Inc., 375 Hudson Street, New York, New York 10014, U.S.A.
Penguin Group (Canada), 90 Eglinton Avenue East, Suite 700, Toronto, Ontario,
Canada M4P 2Y3 (a division of Pearson Penguin Canada Inc.)
Penguin Books Ltd, 80 Strand, London WC2R 0RL, England
Penguin Ireland, 25 St Stephen's Green, Dublin 2, Ireland (a division of Penguin Books Ltd)
Penguin Group (Australia), 250 Camberwell Road, Camberwell,
Victoria 3124, Australia (a division of Pearson Australia Group Pty Ltd)
Penguin Books India Pvt Ltd, 11 Community Centre, Panchsheel Park,
New Delhi – 110 017, India
Penguin Group (NZ), 67 Apollo Drive, Rosedale, North Shore 0632, New Zealand
(a division of Pearson New Zealand Ltd)
Penguin Books (South Africa) (Pty) Ltd, 24 Sturdee Avenue, Rosebank,
Johannesburg 2196, South Africa

Penguin Books Ltd, Registered Offices: 80 Strand, London WC2R 0RL, England

First published in Great Britain under the title
*The Power and the Glory* by William Heinemann Ltd 1940
First published in the United States of America under the title
*The Labyrinthine Ways* by The Viking Press 1940
Reissued under its original title by The Viking Press 1946
Viking Compass Edition published 1958
Reprinted with a new Introduction 1962
Published in Penguin Books (U.K.) 1962
Reset and reprinted from the Collected Edition, without an Introduction,
in Great Britain 1971 and in the USA 1977
Reprinted in Penguin Books with an Introduction by John Updike 1991
This edition published 2003

15   17   19   20   18   16   14

The Introduction by John Updike was first published in a special fiftieth-anniversary edition,
reset and reprinted from the pre-Collected Edition text, in the USA by Viking Penguin 1990

Copyright 1940 by Graham Greene
Copyright © Graham Greene, 1968, 1971
Introduction copyright © John Updike, 1990
All rights reserved

LIBRARY OF CONGRESS CATALOGING IN PUBLICATION DATA
Greene, Graham, 1904–1991
The power and the glory / Graham Greene.
p.  cm.—(Penguin classics)
ISBN 978-0-14-243730-8
1. Anti-clericalism—Fiction.   2. Catholic Church—Fiction.
3. Mexico—Fiction.   4. Clergy—Fiction.   I. Title.   II. Series.
PR6013.R44 P6 2003
823'.912—dc21       2002034604

Printed in the United States of America

# INTRODUCTION

*by John Updike*

*The Power and the Glory*, first published fifty years ago in a modest English edition of 3,500 copies, is generally agreed to be Graham Greene's masterpiece, the book of his held highest in popular as well as critical esteem. Based upon less than two months spent in Mexico in March and April of 1938, including five weeks of gruelling, solitary travel in the southern provinces of Tabasco and Chiapas, the novel is Greene's least English, containing only a few minor English characters. Perhaps it succeeds so resoundingly because there is something un-English about the Roman Catholicism which infuses, with its Manichaean darkness and tortured literalism, his most ambitious fiction. The three novels (as opposed to 'entertainments') composed before and after *The Power and the Glory* – *Brighton Rock* (1938), *The Heart of the Matter* (1948), and *The End of the Affair* (1951) – all have claims to greatness; they are as intense and penetrating and disturbing as an inquisitor's gaze. After his modest start as a novelist under the influence of Joseph Conrad and John Buchan, Greene's masterly facility at concocting thriller plots and his rather blithely morbid sensibility had come together, at a high level of intelligence and passion, with the strict terms of an inner religious debate that had not yet wearied him. Yet the Roman Catholicism, in these three novels, has something faintly stuck-on about it – there is a dreamlike feeling of stretch, of contortion. This murderous teen-age gang-leader with his bitter belief in hell and his habit of quoting choir-boy Latin to himself, this mild-mannered colonial policeman pulled by a terrible pity into the sure damnation of suicide, and this blithely unfaithful housewife drawn by a happenstance baptism of which she is unaware into a sainthood that works posthumous miracles – these are moral grotesques, shaped in some other world; they refuse to attach to the worlds around them, the so sharply and expertly evoked milieux of Brighton, British West Africa, London. Whereas *The Power and the Glory*'s nameless whisky priest blends seamlessly with his tropical, crooked, anti-clerical Mexico.

Roman Catholicism is intrinsic to the character and terrain both; Greene's imaginative immersion in both is triumphant. A Mexican priest in 1978 told Greene's biographer, Norman Sherry: 'As a Mexican I travel in those regions. The first three paragraphs, where he gives you camera shots of the place, why it is astounding. You are *in* the place.' In 1960, a Catholic teacher in California wrote Greene:

> One day I gave *The Power and the Glory* to . . . a native of Mexico who had lived through the worst persecutions . . . She confessed that your descriptions were so vivid, your priest so real, that she found herself praying for him at Mass. I understand how she felt. Last year, on a trip through Mexico, I found myself peering into mud huts, through village streets, and across impassable mountain ranges, half-believing that I would glimpse a dim figure stumbling in the rain on his way to the border. There is no greater tribute possible to your creation of this character – he lives.

Greene's identification with his anonymous hero – 'a small man dressed in a shabby dark city suit, carrying a small attaché case' – burns away the educated upper-middle-class skepticism and ennui which shadow even the most ardently spiritual of his other novels. Mr Tench, the dentist, and the complicated Fellows family are English, and may have been intended to play a bigger part than they do; as is, they exist marginally, like little figures introduced to give a landscape its grandeur. The abysses and heights of the whisky priest's descent into darkness and simultaneous ascent into martyrdom so dominate the canvas that even his pursuer and ideological antagonist, the fanatically atheistic lieutenant, is rather crowded out, flattened to seem a mere foil. Only the extraordinary apparition of the mestizo, with his yellow fangs and wriggling exposed toe and fawning, clinging, inexorable treachery, exists in the same oversized realm of transcendent paradox as the dogged, doomed priest.

Edith Sitwell wrote Greene in 1945 that he would have made a great priest. His conversion, in Nottingham at the age of twenty-two in 1926, was at the hands of a priest, Father Trollope, who, after his own conversion, had been – according to Greene's memoir *A Sort of Life* – 'driven further by some inner compulsion to the priesthood.' But Greene was in little such danger; he was converted in order to marry a Roman Catholic, and in any case, he wrote in 1938, 'chastity would have been beyond my powers.' Yet his serious novels usually have a priest in them, portrayed as fallibly human but in his priestly function beyond reproach. In his second book of autobiography, *Ways of Escape*, Greene writes, 'I think *The Power and the Glory* is the only novel I have written to a thesis . . . I had always, even when I was a schoolboy, listened with impatience to the scandalous stories of tourists concerning the priests they had encountered in remote Latin villages (this priest had a mistress, another was constantly drunk), for I had been adequately taught in my Protestant history books what Catholics believed; I could distinguish even then between the man and the office.' The distinction between sinful behaviour and sacramental function is clear also to the debased priests of *The Power and the Glory*. Father José, compelled by the state and his cowardice to marry, remembers 'the gift he had been given which nobody could take away. That was what made him worthy of damnation – the power he still had of turning the wafer into the flesh and blood of God.' The whisky priest can no longer find meaning in prayer but to him 'the Host was different: to lay that between a dying man's lips was to lay God.' Greene says of his hero what he might say of himself: 'Curious pedantries moved him.'

In the unrelenting succession of harrowing scenes as the hunted man tries to keep performing his priestly offices, none is more harrowing, more grisly in its irony and corrosive earthy dialogue, than the episode wherein he must watch a trio of local lowlife, including the police chief, drink up a bottle of wine he had bought with his last pesos for sacramental purposes. But almost every stage of the priest's ragged pilgrimage, between Mr Tench's two glimpses of him in the stultifying capital of the hellish state (Tabasco, but unnamed), grips us with sorrow and pity. Greene, as a reviewer, saw a lot of movies in the thirties, and his scenes are abrupt, cinematic, built of brilliant, artfully lit images: the 'big whitewashed building,' for instance, which the priest does not recognize as a church and mistakes for a barracks, at the end of Part II, and the mountaintop grove of tall, crazily leaning crosses 'like trees that had been left to seed,' which marks the Indian cemetery and the boundary of the less intolerant, safe state (Chiapas, also unnamed). The preceding climb, in the company of the Indian woman carrying her dead child on her back, is as grandly silent as a pageant in Eisenstein, and there is a touch of surreal Buñuel horror in the priest's discovery, when he returns to the cemetery, of the dead child's exposed body, with a lump of sugar in its mouth. In *A Sort of Life*, Greene, thinking back upon his many novels for 'passages, even chapters, which gave me at the time I wrote them a sense of satisfaction,' named 'the prison dialogue in *The Power and the Glory*,' and indeed this scene, in which the priest, at the nadir of his abasement and peril, sits up all night in a crowded dark cell listening to the varied voices – the disembodied souls – of the other inmates, is, in its depth, directness, and strange comedy, worthy of Dostoevsky, another problematical believer.

Greene's conversion to Catholicism, as he describes it in *A Sort of Life*, was rather diffident. He was walking his dog past a church that 'possessed for me a certain gloomy power because it represented the inconceivable and the incredible. Inside, there was a wooden box for inquiries and I dropped into it a note asking for instruction . . . I had no intention of being received into the Church. For such a thing to happen I would need to be convinced of its truth and that was not even a remote possibility.' But, after a few sessions of vigorously arguing the case for atheism with Father Trollope, something happened: 'I can only remember that in January 1926 I became convinced of the probable existence of something we call God, though I now dislike the word with all its anthropomorphic associations.' Early the next month, he made his first general confession, was baptized, and received. 'I remember very clearly the nature of my emotion as I walked away from the Cathedral: there was no joy in it at all, only a sombre apprehension.' The entire swift surrender reminds us of another, which occurred a bit earlier during his four months of living alone in Nottingham and being terribly bored.

> Once on my free day I walked over the hills to Chesterfield and found a dentist. I described to him the symptoms, which I knew well, of an abscess. He tapped a perfectly good tooth with his little mirror and I reacted in the correct way. 'Better have it out,' he advised.
>
> 'Yes,' I said, 'but with ether.'
>
> A few minutes' unconsciousness was like a holiday from the world. I had lost a good tooth, but the boredom was for the time being dispersed.

While still an Oxford undergraduate, he had repeatedly played Russian roulette, in search of a permanent holiday from the world. The world gets a grim report in his fiction. For Pinkie in *Brighton Rock*, 'the world never moved: it lay there always, the ravaged and disputed territory between two eternities.' In *The Power and the Glory*, the priest, looking at the stars, cannot believe that 'this world could shine with such brilliance: it would roll heavily in space under its fog like a burning and abandoned ship.' Looking at his illegitimate child, he sees that 'the world was in her heart already, like the small spot of decay in a fruit.' In the prison cell, he reflects, 'This place was very like the world: overcrowded with lust and crime and unhappy love, it stank to heaven; but he realized that after all it was possible to find peace there, when you knew for certain that the time was short.' An ascetic, reckless, life-despising streak in Greene's temperament characterized, among other precipitate ventures, his 1938 trip to Mexico.

He had been angling since 1936 for a way to travel on assignment to Mexico, to write about 'the fiercest persecution of religion anywhere since the reign of Elizabeth.' The persecution had peaked a few years earlier, under President Calles, elected in 1924, and the infamous atheist Governor of Tabasco, Garrido Canabal. Greene finally got his backing, from Longman's in England and Viking in the United States, survived his trip, and produced his book, called *The Lawless Roads* in England and *Another Country* here. (Such trans-atlantic title-changes were once common; *The Power and the Glory* was first issued by Doubleday under what Greene called 'the difficult and misleading title of *The Labyrinthine Ways*.') *Another Country* still reads well, though episodic and in spots carelessly written. Greene has a charming way of tossing into its text passages from Trollope and Cobbett, as he was reading them on the move, and also accounts of his dreams. Many elements of the novel are easily recognizable: the geography, the vultures, the layout and torpor of Villa-hermosa, the amiably corrupt police chief, the officious village schoolteacher trying to replace the banished priest, the Euro-pean *finca* whose proprietors bathe in the stream with nib-bling fish, the lump of sugar, the fanged mestizo (encountered behind a typewriter in the village of Yajalon), and the germ of the whisky priest in several rumours, even to his drunken insistence on baptizing a son Brigitta. But it was all marvel-lously transposed and edited: the priest's mule-riding flights from capture in the Tabasco-like state were based upon agonizingly long rides that Greene took in Chiapas, on the way to Las Casas, which his fictional priest never reaches. Had the air service between Yajalon and Las Casas not been cancelled by rain, his novel might have lacked its most mem-orable and Biblical mode of transportation.

The tone, too, is transformed; in *Another Country* Greene is very much the exasperated tourist, hating Mexican food, manners, hotels, rats, mosquitoes, mule rides, souvenirs, and ruins. He even inveighs against the 'hideous inexpressiveness of brown eyes.' In the novel, as it shows a Mexican moving among Mexicans, and these generally the most lowly and im-poverished, all querulousness has vanished, swallowed by matters of life and death and beyond. There are hints of a redeeming mood even in *Another Country*: 'What had exhausted me in Chiapas was simply physical exertion, unfriendliness, boredom; life among the dark groves of leaning crosses was at any rate concerned with eternal values.' The whisky priest, who before *The Power and the Glory* opens has been stripped of his livelihood and the flattery of the pious, in the course of the novel loses his attaché case and suit; he is stripped down to his eternal value, or valuelessness. Greene, at a low ebb in his Chiapas travels, took shelter in a roadside hut, 'a storehouse for corn, but it contained what you seldom find in Mexico, the feel of human goodness.' The old man living there gave up his bed – 'a dais of earth covered with a straw mat set against the mound of corn where the rats were burrowing' – to Greene, who wrote of the moment, 'All that was left was an old man on the verge of starvation living in a hut with the rats, welcoming the strangers without a word of payment, gossiping gently in the dark. I felt myself back with the population of heaven.' *Blessed are the poor in spirit: for theirs is the kingdom of heaven.*

Graham Greene's sympathy with the poor in spirit, with the world's underdogs, preceded his religious conversion and survives it, apparently: he doubted to Norman Sherry that he still believes in God and in *A Sort of Life* tells how 'many of us abandon Confession and Communion to join the Foreign Legion of the Church and fight for a city of which we are no longer full citizens.' His religious faith always included a conviction that, as he put it in an essay on Eric Gill in 1941, 'Conservatism and Catholicism should be . . . impossible bedfellows.' Reflecting again upon Mexico in *Ways of Escape* (where he describes how *The Power and the Glory* was written, back in London, in the afternoons, slowly, on Benzedrine, after mornings of racing through *The Confidential Agent*), he complains not that the present government is left-wing but that it is not left-wing enough, compared to Cuba's. His sympathies have led him into a stout postwar anti-Americanism and a rather awkward pleading for the likes of Castro and Kim Philby. But the energy and grandeur of his finest novel derive from the same will toward compassion, an ideal communism even more Christian than Communist. Its unit is the individual, not any class. The priest sees in the dark prison cell that 'When you visualized a man or woman carefully, you could always begin to feel pity – that was a quality God's image carried with it.'

John Updike

# THE POWER
# AND THE GLORY

FOR GERVASE

Th' inclosure narrow'd; the sagacious power
Of hounds and death drew nearer every hour.
                                    DRYDEN

# PART ONE

## *Chapter 1:* THE PORT

MR TENCH went out to look for his ether cylinder, into the blazing Mexican sun and the bleaching dust. A few vultures looked down from the roof with shabby indifference: he wasn't carrion yet. A faint feeling of rebellion stirred in Mr Tench's heart, and he wrenched up a piece of the road with splintering finger-nails and tossed it feebly towards them. One rose and flapped across the town: over the tiny plaza, over the bust of an ex-president, ex-general, ex-human being, over the two stalls which sold mineral water, towards the river and the sea. It wouldn't find anything there: the sharks looked after the carrion on that side. Mr Tench went on across the plaza.

He said '*Buenos días*' to a man with a gun who sat in a small patch of shade against a wall. But it wasn't like England: the man said nothing at all, just stared malevolently up at Mr Tench, as if he had never had any dealings with the foreigner, as if Mr Tench were not responsible for his two gold bicuspid teeth. Mr Tench went sweating by, past the Treasury which had once been a church, towards the quay. Half-way across he suddenly forgot what he had come out for – a glass of mineral water? That was all there was to drink in this prohibition state – except beer, but that was a government monopoly and too expensive except on special occasions. An awful feeling of nausea gripped Mr Tench in the stomach – it couldn't have been mineral water he wanted. Of course his ether cylinder . . . the boat was in. He had heard its exultant piping while he lay on his bed after lunch. He passed the barbers' and two dentists' and came out between a warehouse and the customs on to the river bank.

The river went heavily by towards the sea between the banana plantations; the *General Obregon* was tied up to the bank, and beer was being unloaded – a hundred cases were already stacked upon the quay. Mr Tench stood in the shade of the customs house and thought: what am I here for? Memory drained out of him in the heat. He gathered his bile together and spat forlornly into the sun. Then he sat down on a case and waited. Nothing to do. Nobody would come to see him before five.

The *General Obregon* was about thirty yards long. A few feet of damaged rail, one lifeboat, a bell hanging on a rotten cord, an oil-lamp in the bow, she looked as if she might weather two or three more Atlantic years, if she didn't strike a Norther in the gulf. That, of course, would be the end of her. It didn't really matter: everybody was insured when he bought a ticket, automatically. Half a dozen passengers leant on the rail, among the hobbled turkeys, and stared at the port, the warehouse, the empty baked street with the dentists and the barbers.

Mr Tench heard a revolver holster creak just behind him and turned his head. A customs officer was watching him angrily. He said something which Mr Tench did not catch. 'Pardon me,' Mr Tench said.

'My teeth,' the customs man said indistinctly.

'Oh,' Mr Tench said, 'yes, your teeth.' The man had none: that was why he couldn't talk clearly. Mr Tench had removed them all. He was shaken with nausea – something was wrong – worms, dysentery ... He said, 'The set is nearly finished. Tonight,' he promised wildly. It was, of course, quite impossible; but that was how one lived, putting off everything. The man was satisfied: he might forget, and in any case what could he *do*? He had paid in advance. That was the whole world to Mr Tench: the heat and the forgetting, the putting off till tomorrow, if possible cash down – for what? He stared out over the slow river: the fin of a shark moved like a periscope at the river's mouth. In the course of years several ships had stranded and they now helped to prop up the bank, the smoke-stacks leaning over like guns pointing at some distant objective across the banana trees and the swamps.

Mr Tench thought: ether cylinder: I nearly forgot. His mouth fell open and he began moodily to count the bottles of

8

Cerveza Moctezuma. A hundred and forty cases. Twelve times a hundred and forty: the heavy phlegm gathered in his mouth: twelve fours are forty-eight. He said aloud in English, 'My God, a pretty one': twelve hundred, sixteen hundred and eighty: he spat, staring with vague interest at a girl in the bows of the *General Obregon* – a fine thin figure, they were generally so thick, brown eyes, of course, and the inevitable gleam of the gold tooth, but something fresh and young. . . . Sixteen hundred and eighty bottles at a peso a bottle.

Somebody whispered in English, 'What did you say?'

Mr Tench swivelled round. 'You English?' he asked in astonishment, but at the sight of the round and hollow face charred with a three-days' beard, he altered his question: 'You speak English?'

Yes, the man said, he spoke a little English. He stood stiffly in the shade, a small man dressed in a shabby dark city suit, carrying a small attaché case. He had a novel under his arm: bits of an amorous scene stuck out, crudely coloured. He said, 'Excuse me. I thought just now you were talking to me.' He had protuberant eyes; he gave an impression of unstable hilarity, as if perhaps he had been celebrating a birthday, alone.

Mr Tench cleared his mouth of phlegm. 'What did I say?' He couldn't remember a thing.

'You said my God a pretty one.'

'Now what could I have meant by that?' He stared up at the merciless sky. A vulture hung there, an observer. 'What? Oh just the girl I suppose. You don't often see a pretty piece round here. Just one or two a year worth looking at.'

'She is very young.'

'Oh, I don't have intentions,' Mr Tench said wearily. 'A man may look. I've lived alone for fifteen years.'

'Here?'

'Hereabouts.'

They fell silent and time passed, the shadow of the customs house shifted a few inches farther towards the river: the vulture moved a little, like the black hand of a clock.

'You came in *her*?' Mr Tench asked.

'No.'

9

'Going in her?'

The little man seemed to evade the question, but then as if some explanation were required: 'I was just looking,' he said. 'I suppose she'll be sailing quite soon?'

'To Vera Cruz,' Mr Tench said. 'In a few hours.'

'Without calling anywhere?'

'Where could she call?' He asked, 'How did you get here?'

The stranger said vaguely, 'A canoe.'

'Got a plantation, eh?'

'No.'

'It's good hearing English spoken,' Mr Tench said. 'Now you learnt yours in the States?'

The man agreed. He wasn't very garrulous.

'Ah, what wouldn't I give,' Mr Tench said, 'to be there now.' He said in a low anxious voice, 'You don't happen, do you, to have a drink in that case of yours? Some of you people back there – I've known one or two – a little for medical purposes.'

'Only medicine,' the man said.

'You a doctor?'

The bloodshot eyes looked slyly out of their corners at Mr Tench. 'You would call me perhaps a – quack?'

'Patent medicines? Live and let live,' Mr Tench said.

'Are *you* sailing?'

'No, I came down here for – . . . oh well, it doesn't matter anyway.' He put his hand on his stomach and said, 'You haven't got any medicine, have you, for – oh hell. I don't know what. It's just this bloody land. You can't cure me of that. No one can.'

'You want to go home?'

'Home,' Mr Tench said, 'my home's here. Did you see what the peso stands at in Mexico City? Four to the dollar. Four. O God. *Ora pro nobis*.'

'Are you a Catholic?'

'No, no. Just an expression. I don't believe in anything like that.' He said irrelevantly, 'It's too hot anyway.'

'I think I must find somewhere to sit.'

'Come up to my place,' Mr Tench said. 'I've got a spare

hammock. The boat won't leave for hours – if you want to watch it go.'

The stranger said, 'I was expecting to see someone. The name was Lopez.'

'Oh, they shot him weeks ago,' Mr Tench said.

'Dead?'

'You know how it is round here. Friend of yours?'

'No, no,' the man protested hurriedly. 'Just a friend of a friend.'

'Well, that's how it is,' Mr Tench said. He brought up his bile again and spat it out into the hard sunlight. 'They say he used to help . . . oh, undesirables . . . well, to get out. His girl's living with the Chief of Police now.'

'His girl? Do you mean his daughter?'

'He wasn't married. I mean the girl he lived with.' Mr Tench was momentarily surprised by an expression on the stranger's face. He said again, 'You know how it is.' He looked across at the *General Obregon*. 'She's a pretty bit. Of course, in two years she'll be like all the rest. Fat and stupid. O God, I'd like a drink. *Ora pro nobis.*'

'I have a little brandy,' the stranger said.

Mr Tench regarded him sharply. 'Where?'

The hollow man put his hand to his hip – he might have been indicating the source of his odd nervous hilarity. Mr Tench seized his wrist. 'Careful,' he said. 'Not here.' He looked down the carpet of shadow: a sentry sat on an empty crate asleep beside his rifle. 'Come to my place,' Mr Tench said.

'I meant,' the little man said reluctantly, 'just to see her go.'

'Oh, it will be hours yet,' Mr Tench assured him again.

'Hours? Are you certain? It's very hot in the sun.'

'You'd better come home.'

Home: it was a phrase one used to mean four walls behind which one slept. There had never been a home. They moved across the little burnt plaza where the dead General grew green in the damp and the gaseosa stalls stood under the palms. Home lay like a picture postcard on a pile of other postcards: shuffle the pack and you had Nottingham, a Metroland birthplace, an interlude in Southend. Mr Tench's father had been a dentist too -- his first memory was finding a discarded cast in a wastepaper basket -- the rough toothless gaping mouth of clay, like something dug up in Dorset -- Neanderthal or Pithecanthropus. It had been his favourite toy: they tried to tempt him with Meccano, but fate had struck. There is always one moment in childhood when the door opens and lets the future in. The hot wet river-port and the vultures lay in the wastepaper basket, and he picked them out. We should be thankful we cannot see the horrors and degradations lying around our childhood, in cupboards and bookshelves, everywhere.

There was no paving; during the rains the village (it was really no more) slipped into the mud. Now the ground was hard under the feet like stone. The two men walked in silence past barbers' shops and dentists'; the vultures on the roofs looked contented, like domestic fowls: they searched under wide dusty wings for parasites. Mr Tench said, 'Excuse me,' stopping at a little wooden hut, one storey high, with a veranda where a hammock swung. The hut was a little larger than the others in the narrow street which petered out two hundred yards away in swamp. He said, nervously, 'Would you like to take a look around? I don't want to boast, but I'm the best dentist here. It's not a bad place. As places go.' Pride wavered in his voice like a plant with shallow roots.

He led the way inside, locking the door behind him, through a dining-room where two rocking-chairs stood on either side of a bare table: an oil lamp, some copies of old American papers, a cupboard. He said, 'I'll get the glasses out, but first I'd like to show you -- you're an educated man ...' The dentist's operating-room looked out on a yard where a few turkeys moved with shabby nervous pomp: a drill which worked with a pedal, a dentist's chair gaudy in bright red plush, a glass cupboard in which instruments were dustily jumbled. A forceps stood in a cup, a broken spirit-lamp was pushed into a corner, and gags of cotton-wool lay on all the shelves.

'Very fine,' the stranger commented.

'It's not so bad, is it,' Mr Tench said, 'for this town. You can't imagine the difficulties. That drill,' he continued bitterly, 'is made in Japan. I've only had it a month and it's wearing out already. But I can't afford American drills.'

'The window,' the stranger said, 'is very beautiful.'

One pane of stained glass had been let in: a Madonna gazed out through the mosquito wire at the turkeys in the yard. 'I got it,' Mr Tench said, 'when they sacked the church. It didn't feel right – a dentist's room without some stained glass. Not civilized. At home – I mean in England – it was generally the Laughing Cavalier – I don't know why – or else a Tudor rose. But one can't pick and choose.'

He opened another door and said, 'My workroom.' The first thing one saw was a bed under a mosquito tent. Mr Tench said, 'You understand – I'm pressed for room.' A ewer and basin stood at one end of a carpenter's bench, and a soap-dish: at the other a blow-pipe, a tray of sand, pliers, a little furnace. 'I cast in sand,' Mr Tench said. 'What else can I do in this place?' He picked up the case of a lower jaw. 'You can't always get them accurate,' he said. 'Of course, they complain.' He laid it down, and nodded at another object on the bench – something stringy and intestinal in appearance, with two little bladders of rubber. 'Congenital fissure,' he said. 'It's the first time I've tried. The Kingsley cast. I doubt if I can do it. But a man must try to keep abreast of things.' His mouth fell open: the look of vacancy returned: the heat in the small room was overpowering. He stood there like a man lost in a cavern among the fossils and instruments of an age of which he knows very little. The stranger said, 'If we could sit down . . .'

Mr Tench stared at him blankly.

'We could open the brandy.'

'Oh yes, the brandy.'

Mr Tench got two glasses out of a cupboard under the bench, and wiped off traces of sand. Then they went and sat in rocking-chairs in the front room. Mr Tench poured out.

'Water?' the stranger asked.

'You can't trust the water,' Mr Tench said. 'It's got me here.' He put his hand on his stomach and took a long

13

draught. 'You don't look too well yourself,' he said. He took a longer look. 'Your teeth.' One canine had gone, and the front teeth were yellow with tartar and carious. He said, 'You want to pay attention to them.'

'What is the good?' the stranger said. He held a small spot of brandy in his glass warily – as if it was an animal to which he gave shelter, but not trust. He had the air, in his hollowness and neglect, of somebody of no account who had been beaten up incidentally, by ill-health or restlessness. He sat on the very edge of the rocking-chair, with his small attaché case balanced on his knee and the brandy staved off with guilty affection.

'Drink up,' Mr Tench encouraged him (it wasn't his brandy). 'It will do you good.' The man's dark suit and sloping shoulders reminded him uncomfortably of a coffin, and death was in his carious mouth already. Mr Tench poured himself out another glass. He said, 'It gets lonely here. It's good to talk English, even to a foreigner. I wonder if you'd like to see a picture of my kids.' He drew a yellow snapshot out of his note-case and handed it over. Two small children struggled over the handle of a watering-can in a back garden. 'Of course,' he said, 'that was sixteen years ago.'

'They are young men now.'

'One died.'

'Oh, well,' the other replied gently, 'in a Christian country.' He took a gulp of his brandy and smiled at Mr Tench rather foolishly.

'Yes, I suppose so,' Mr Tench said with surprise. He got rid of his phlegm and said, 'It doesn't seem to me, of course, to matter much.' He fell silent, his thoughts ambling away; his mouth fell open, he looked grey and vacant, until he was recalled by a pain in the stomach and helped himself to some more brandy. 'Let me see. What was it we were talking about? The kids . . . oh yes, the kids. It's funny what a man remembers. You know, I can remember that watering-can better than I can remember the kids. It cost three and elevenpence three farthings, green; I could lead you to the shop where I bought it. But as for the kids,' he brooded over his glass into the past, 'I can't remember much else but them crying.'

14

'Do you get news?'

'Oh, I gave up writing before I came here. What was the use? I couldn't send any money. It wouldn't surprise me if the wife had married again. Her mother would like it – the old sour bitch: she never cared for me.'

The stranger said in a low voice, 'It is awful.'

Mr Tench examined his companion again with surprise. He sat there like a black question mark, ready to go, ready to stay, poised on his chair. He looked disreputable in his grey three-days' beard, and weak: somebody you could command to do anything. He said, 'I mean the world. The way things happen.'

'Drink up your brandy.'

He sipped at it. It was like an indulgence. He said, 'You remember this place before – before the Red Shirts came?'

'I suppose I do.'

'How happy it was then.'

'Was it? I didn't notice.'

'They had at any rate – God.'

'There's no difference in the teeth,' Mr Tench said. He gave himself some more of the stranger's brandy. 'It was always an awful place. Lonely. My God. People at home would have said romance. I thought: five years here, and then I'll go. There was plenty of work. Gold teeth. But then the peso dropped. And now I can't get out. One day I will.' He said, 'I'll retire. Go home. Live as a gentleman ought to live. This' – he gestured at the bare base room – 'I'll forget all this. Oh, it won't be long now. I'm an optimist,' Mr Tench said.

The stranger asked suddenly, 'How long will she take to Vera Cruz?'

'Who?'

'The boat.'

Mr Tench said gloomily, 'Forty hours from now and we'd be there. The Diligencia. A good hotel. Dance places too. A gay town.'

'It makes it seem close,' the stranger said. 'And a ticket, how much would that be?'

'You'd have to ask Lopez,' Mr Tench said. 'He's the agent.'

'But Lopez . . .'

15

'Oh yes, I forgot. They shot him.'

Somebody knocked on the door. The stranger slipped the attaché case under his chair, and Mr Tench went cautiously up towards the window. 'Can't be too careful,' he said. 'Any dentist who's worth the name has enemies.'

A faint voice implored them, 'A friend,' and Mr Tench opened up. Immediately the sun came in like a white-hot bar.

A child stood in the doorway asking for a doctor. He wore a big hat and had stupid brown eyes. Behind him two mules stamped and whistled on the hot beaten road. Mr Tench said he was not a doctor: he was a dentist. Looking round he saw the stranger crouched in the rocking-chair, gazing with an effect of prayer, entreaty. . . . The child said there was a new doctor in town: the old one had fever and wouldn't stir. His mother was sick.

A vague memory stirred in Mr Tench's brain. He said with an air of discovery, 'Why, you're a doctor, aren't you?'

'No, no. I've got to catch that boat.'

'I thought you said . . .'

'I've changed my mind.'

'Oh well, it won't leave for hours yet,' Mr Tench said. 'They're never on time.' He asked the child how far. The child said it was six leagues away.

'Too far,' Mr Tench said. 'Go away. Find someone else.' He said to the stranger, 'How things get around. Everyone must know you are in town.'

'I could do no good,' the stranger said anxiously: he seemed to be asking for Mr Tench's opinion, humbly.

'Go away,' Mr Tench commanded. The child did not stir. He stood in the hard sunlight looking in with infinite patience. He said his mother was dying. The brown eyes expressed no emotion: it was a fact. You were born, your parents died, you grew old, you died yourself.

'If she's dying,' Mr Tench said, 'there's no point in a doctor seeing her.'

But the stranger got up as though unwillingly he had been summoned to an occasion he couldn't pass by. He said sadly, 'It always seems to happen. Like this.'

16

'You'll have a job not to miss the boat.'

'I shall miss it,' he said. 'I am meant to miss it.' He was shaken by a tiny rage. 'Give me my brandy.' He took a long pull at it, with his eyes on the impassive child, the baked street, the vultures moving in the sky like indigestion spots.

'But if she's dying . . .' Mr Tench said.

'I know these people. She will be no more dying than I am.'

'You can do no good.'

The child watched them as if he didn't care. The argument in a foreign language going on in there was something abstract: He wasn't concerned. He would just wait here till the doctor came.

'You know nothing,' the stranger said fiercely. 'That is what everyone says all the time – you do no good.' The brandy had affected him. He said with monstrous bitterness, 'I can hear them saying it all over the world.'

'Anyway,' Mr Tench said, 'there'll be another boat. In a fortnight. Or three weeks. You are lucky. You can get out. You haven't got your capital here.' He thought of his capital: the Japanese drill, the dentist's chair, the spirit-lamp and the pliers and the little oven for the gold fillings: a stake in the country.

'Vamos,' the man said to the child. He turned back to Mr Tench and told him that he was grateful for the rest out of the sun. He had the kind of dwarfed dignity Mr Tench was accustomed to – the dignity of people afraid of a little pain and yet sitting down with some firmness in his chair. Perhaps he didn't care for mule travel. He said with an effect of old-fashioned ways, 'I will pray for you.'

'You were welcome,' Mr Tench said. The man got up on to the mule, and the child led the way, very slowly under the bright glare, towards the swamp, the interior. It was from there the man had emerged this morning to take a look at the *General Obregon*: now he was going back. He swayed very slightly in his saddle from the effect of the brandy. He became a minute disappointed figure at the end of the street.

It had been good to talk to a stranger, Mr Tench thought, going back into his room, locking the door behind him (one

17

never knew). Loneliness faced him there, vacancy. But he was as accustomed to both as to his own face in the glass. He sat down in the rocking-chair and moved up and down, creating a faint breeze in the heavy air. A narrow column of ants moved across the room to the little patch on the floor where the stranger had spilt some brandy: they milled in it, then moved on in an orderly line to the opposite wall and disappeared. Down in the river the *General Obregon* whistled twice, he didn't know why.

The stranger had left his book behind. It lay under his rocking-chair: a woman in Edwardian dress crouched sobbing upon a rug embracing a man's brown polished pointed shoes. He stood above her disdainfully with a little waxed moustache. The book was called *La Eterna Mártir*. After a time Mr Tench picked it up. When he opened it he was taken aback – what was printed inside didn't seem to belong; it was Latin. Mr Tench grew thoughtful: he shut the book up and carried it into his workroom. You couldn't burn a book, but it might be as well to hide it if you were not sure – sure, that is, of what it was all about. He put it inside the little oven for gold alloy. Then he stood by the carpenter's bench, his mouth hanging open: he had remembered what had taken him to the quay – the ether cylinder which should have come down-river in the *General Obregon*. Again the whistle blew from the river, and Mr Tench ran without his hat into the sun. He had said the boat would not go before morning, but you could never trust these people *not* to keep to time-table, and sure enough, when he came out on to the bank between the customs and the warehouse, the *General Obregon* was already ten feet off in the sluggish river, making for the sea. He bellowed after it, but it wasn't any good: there was no sign of a cylinder anywhere on the quay. He shouted once again, and then didn't trouble any more. It didn't matter so much after all: a little additional pain was hardly noticeable in the huge abandonment.

On the *General Obregon* a faint breeze became evident: banana plantations on either side, a few wireless aerials on a point, the port slipped behind. When you looked back you could not have told that it had ever existed at all. The wide

Atlantic opened up; the great grey cylindrical waves lifted the bows, and the hobbled turkeys shifted on the deck. The captain stood in the tiny deck-house with a toothpick in his hair. The land went backward at a low even roll, and the dark came quite suddenly, with a sky of low and brilliant stars. One oil-lamp was lit in the bows, and the girl whom Mr Tench had spotted from the bank began to sing gently – a melancholy, sentimental, and contented song about a rose which had been stained with true love's blood. There was an enormous sense of freedom and air upon the gulf with the low tropical shore-line buried in darkness as deeply as any mummy in a tomb. I am happy, the young girl said to herself without considering why, I am happy.

Far back inside the darkness the mules plodded on. The effect of the brandy had long ago worn off, and the man bore in his brain along the marshy tract, which, when the rains came, would be quite impassable, the sound of the *General Obregon*'s siren. He knew what it meant: the ship had kept to timetable: he was abandoned. He felt an unwilling hatred of the child ahead of him and the sick woman – he was unworthy of what he carried. A smell of damp came up all round him; it was as if this part of the world had never been dried in the flame when the world spun off into space: it had absorbed only the mist and cloud of those awful regions. He began to pray, bouncing up and down to the lurching slithering mule's stride, with his brandied tongue: 'Let me be caught soon. . . . Let me be caught.' He had tried to escape, but he was like the King of a West African tribe, the slave of his people, who may not even lie down in case the winds should fail.


## Chapter 2: THE CAPITAL

THE squad of police made their way back to the station. They walked raggedly with rifles slung anyhow: ends of cotton where buttons should have been: a puttee slipping down over the ankle: small men with black secret Indian eyes. The little plaza on the hill-top was lighted with globes strung together in threes and joined by trailing overhead wires. The Treasury, the Presidencia, a dentist's, the prison – a low white colonnaded building which dated back three hundred years – and then the steep street down past the back wall of a ruined church: whichever way you went you came ultimately to water and to river. Pink classical façades peeled off and showed the mud beneath, and the mud slowly reverted to mud. Round the plaza the evening parade went on – women in one direction, men in the other; young men in red shirts milled boisterously round the gaseosa stalls.

The lieutenant walked in front of his men with an air of bitter distaste. He might have been chained to them unwillingly – perhaps the scar on his jaw was the relic of an escape. His gaiters were polished, and his pistol-holster: his buttons were all sewn on. He had a sharp crooked nose jutting out of a lean dancer's face; his neatness gave an effect of inordinate ambition in the shabby city. A sour smell came up to the plaza from the river and the vultures were bedded on the roofs, under the tent of their rough black wings. Sometimes, a little moron head peered out and down and a claw shifted. At nine-thirty exactly all the lights in the plaza went out.

A policeman clumsily presented arms and the squad marched into barracks; they waited for no order, hanging up their rifles by the officers' room, lurching on into the court-yard, to their hammocks or the excusados. Some of them kicked off their boots and lay down. Plaster was peeling off the mud walls; a generation of policemen had scrawled messages on the whitewash. A few peasants waited on a bench, hands between their knees. Nobody paid them any attention. Two men were fighting in the lavatory.

'Where is the jefe?' the lieutenant asked. No one knew for certain: they thought he was playing billiards somewhere in the town. The lieutenant sat down with dapper irritation at the chief's table; behind his head two hearts were entwined in pencil on the whitewash. 'All right,' he said, 'what are you waiting for? Bring in the prisoners.' They came in bowing, hat in hand, one behind the other. 'So-and-so drunk and disorderly.' 'Fined five pesos.' 'But I can't pay, your excellency.'

'Let him clean out the lavatory and the cells then.' 'So-and-so. Defaced an election poster.' 'Fined five pesos.' 'So-and-so found wearing a holy medal under his shirt.' 'Fined five pesos.' The duty drew to a close: there was nothing of importance. Through the open door the mosquitoes came whirring in.

Outside the sentry could be heard presenting arms. The Chief of Police came breezily in, a stout man with a pink fat face, dressed in white flannels with a wide-awake hat and a cartridge-belt and a big pistol clapping his thigh. He held a handkerchief to his mouth: he was in distress. 'Toothache again,' he said, 'toothache.'

'Nothing to report,' the lieutenant said with contempt.

'The Governor was at me again today,' the chief complained.

'Liquor?'

'No, a priest.'

'The last was shot weeks ago.'

'He doesn't think so.'

'The devil of it is,' the lieutenant said, 'we haven't photographs.' He glanced along the wall to the picture of James Calver, wanted in the United States for bank robbery and homicide: a tough uneven face taken at two angles: description circulated to every station in Central America: the low forehead and the fanatic bent-on-one-thing eyes. He looked at it with regret: there was so little chance that he would ever get south; he would be picked up in some dive at the border – in Juarez or Piedras Negras or Nogales.

'He says we have,' the chief complained. 'My tooth, oh, my tooth.' He tried to find something in his hip-pocket, but the holster got in the way. The lieutenant tapped his polished boot impatiently. 'There,' the chief said. A large number of people sat round a table: young girls in white muslin: older women with untidy hair and harassed expressions: a few men peered shyly and solicitously out of the background. All the faces were made up of small dots. It was a newspaper photograph of a first communion party taken years ago; a youngish man in a Roman collar sat among the women. You could imagine him petted with small delicacies, preserved for their

21

use in the stifling atmosphere of intimacy and respect. He sat there, plump, with protuberant eyes, bubbling with harmless feminine jokes. 'It was taken years ago.'

'He looks like all the rest,' the lieutenant said. It was obscure, but you could read into the smudgy photograph a well-shaved, well-powdered jowl much too developed for his age. The good things of life had come to him too early – the respect of his contemporaries, a safe livelihood. The trite religious word upon the tongue, the joke to ease the way, the ready acceptance of other people's homage ... a happy man. A natural hatred as between dog and dog stirred in the lieutenant's bowels. 'We've shot him half a dozen times,' he said.

'The Governor has had a report ... he tried to get away last week to Vera Cruz.'

'What are the Red Shirts doing that he comes to *us*?'

'Oh, they missed him, of course. It was just luck that he didn't catch the boat.'

'What happened to him?'

'They found his mule. The Governor says he must have him this month. Before the rains come.'

'Where was his parish?'

'Concepción and the villages around. But he left there years ago.'

'Is anything known?'

'He can pass as a gringo. He spent six years at some American seminary. I don't know what else. He was born in Carmen – the son of a storekeeper. Not that that helps.'

'They all look alike to me,' the lieutenant said. Something you could almost have called horror moved him when he looked at the white muslin dresses – he remembered the smell of incense in the churches of his boyhood, the candles and the laciness and the self-esteem, the immense demands made from the altar steps by men who didn't know the meaning of sacrifice. The old peasants knelt there before the holy images with their arms held out in the attitude of the cross: tired by the long day's labour in the plantations they squeezed out a further mortification. And the priest came round with the collecting-bag taking their centavos, abusing them for their small comforting sins, and sacrificing nothing at all in return – except a little sexual indulgence. And that was easy, the lieutenant thought, easy. Himself he felt no need of women. He said, 'We will catch him. It is only a question of time.'

'My tooth,' the chief wailed again. He said, 'It poisons the whole of life. Today my biggest break was twenty-five.'

'You will have to change your dentist.'

'They are all the same.'

The lieutenant took the photograph and pinned it on the wall. James Calver, bank robber and homicide, stared in harsh profile towards the first communion party. 'He is a man at any rate,' the lieutenant said with approval.

'Who?'

'The gringo.'

The chief said, 'You heard what he did in Houston. Got away with ten thousand dollars. Two G men were shot.'

'G men?'

'It's an honour – in a way – to deal with such people.' He slapped furiously out at a mosquito.

'A man like that,' the lieutenant said, 'does no real harm. A few men dead. We all have to die. The money – somebody has to spend it. We do more good when we catch one of these.' He had the dignity of an idea, standing in the little whitewashed room with his polished boots and his venom. There was something disinterested in his ambition: a kind of virtue in his desire to catch the sleek respected guest of the first communion party.

The chief said mournfully, 'He must be devilishly cunning if he's been going on for years.'

'Anybody could do it,' the lieutenant said. 'We haven't really troubled about them – unless they put themselves in our hands. Why, I could guarantee to fetch this man in, inside a month if . . .'

'If what?'

'If I had the power.'

'It's easy to talk,' the chief said. 'What would you do?'

'This is a small state. Mountains on the north, the sea on the south. I'd beat it as you beat a street, house by house.'

'Oh, it sounds easy,' the chief moaned indistinctly with his handkerchief against his mouth.

The lieutenant said suddenly, 'I will tell you what I'd do. I would take a man from every village in the state as a hostage. If the villagers didn't report the man when he came, the hostage would be shot – and then we'd take another.'

'A lot of them would die, of course.'

'Wouldn't it be worth it?' the lieutenant demanded. 'To be rid of those people for ever.'

'You know,' the chief said, 'you've got something there.'

The lieutenant walked home through the shuttered town. All his life had lain here: the Syndicate of Workers and Peasants had once been a school. He had helped to wipe out that unhappy memory. The whole town was changed: the cement playground up the hill near the cemetery where iron swings stood like gallows in the moony darkness was the site of the cathedral. The new children would have new memories: nothing would ever be as it was. There was something of a priest in his intent observant walk – a theologian going back over the errors of the past to destroy them again.

He reached his own lodging. The houses were all one-storeyed, whitewashed, built round small patios, with a well and a few flowers. The windows on the street were barred. Inside the lieutenant's room there was a bed made of old packing-cases with a straw mat laid on top, a cushion and a sheet. There was a picture of the President on the wall, a calendar, and on the tiled floor a table and a rocking-chair. In the light of a candle it looked as comfortless as a prison or a monastic cell.

The lieutenant sat down upon his bed and began to take off his boots. It was the hour of prayer. Black-beetles exploded against the walls like crackers. More than a dozen crawled over the tiles with injured wings. It infuriated him to think that there were still people in the state who believed in a loving and merciful God. There are mystics who are said to have experienced God directly. He was a mystic, too, and what he had experienced was vacancy – a complete certainty in the

24

existence of a dying, cooling world, of human beings who had evolved from animals for no purpose at all. He knew.

He lay down in his shirt and breeches on the bed and blew out the candle. Heat stood in the room like an enemy. But he believed against the evidence of his senses in the cold empty ether spaces. A radio was playing somewhere: music from Mexico City, or perhaps even from London or New York, filtered into this obscure neglected state. It seemed to him like a weakness: this was his own land, and he would have walled it in if he could with steel until he had eradicated from it everything which reminded him of how it had once appeared to a miserable child. He wanted to destroy everything: to be alone without any memories at all. Life began five years ago.

The lieutenant lay on his back with his eyes open while the beetles detonated on the ceiling. He remembered the priest the Red Shirts had shot against the wall of the cemetery up the hill, another little fat man with popping eyes. He was a monsignor, and he thought that would protect him. He had a sort of contempt for the lower clergy, and right up to the last he was explaining his rank. Only at the very end had he remembered his prayers. He knelt down and they had given him time for a short act of contrition. The lieutenant had watched: he wasn't directly concerned. Altogether they had shot about five priests – two or three had escaped, the bishop was safely in Mexico City, and one man had conformed to the Governor's law that all priests must marry. He lived now near the river with his housekeeper. That, of course, was the best solution of all, to leave the living witness to the weakness of their faith. It showed the deception they had practised all these years. For if they really believed in heaven or hell, they wouldn't mind a little pain now, in return for what immensities ... The lieutenant, lying on his hard bed, in the damp hot dark, felt no sympathy at all with the weakness of the flesh.

In the back room of the Academia Commercial a woman was reading to her family. Two small girls of six and ten sat on the edge of their bed, and a boy of fourteen leant against the wall with an expression of intense weariness.

25

'Young Juan,' the mother read, 'from his earliest years was noted for his humility and piety. Other boys might be rough and revengeful; young Juan followed the precept of Our Lord and turned the other cheek. One day his father thought that he had told a lie and beat him. Later he learnt that his son had told the truth, and he apologized to Juan. But Juan said to him, "Dear father, just as our Father in heaven has the right to chastise when he pleases . . ."'

The boy rubbed his face impatiently against the whitewash and the mild voice droned on. The two little girls sat with beady intense eyes, drinking in the sweet piety.

'We must not think that young Juan did not laugh and play like other children, though there were times when he would creep away with a holy picture-book to his father's cow-house from a circle of his merry playmates.'

The boy squashed a beetle with his bare foot and thought gloomily that after all everything had an end – some day they would reach the last chapter and young Juan would die against a wall shouting, 'Viva el Christo Rey.' But then, he supposed, there would be another book; they were smuggled in every month from Mexico City: if only the customs men had known where to look.

'No, young Juan was a true young Mexican boy, and if he was more thoughtful than his fellows, he was also always the first when any play-acting was afoot. One year his class acted a little play before the bishop, based on the persecution of the early Christians, and no one was more amused than Juan when he was chosen to play the part of Nero. And what comic spirit he put into his acting – this child, whose young manhood was to be cut short by a ruler far worse than Nero. His class-mate, who later became Father Miguel Cerra, S.J., writes: "None of us who were there will ever forget that day . . ."'

One of the little girls licked her lips secretively. This was life.

'The curtain rose on Juan wearing his mother's best bath-robe, a charcoal moustache and a crown made from a tin biscuit-box. Even the good old bishop smiled when Juan strode to the front of the little home-made stage and began to declaim . . .'

The boy strangled a yawn against the whitewashed wall. He said wearily, 'Is he really a saint?'

'He will be, one day soon, when the Holy Father pleases.'

'And are they all like that?'

'Who?'

'The martyrs.'

'Yes. All.'

'Even Padre José?'

'Don't mention him,' the mother said. 'How dare you? That despicable man. A traitor to God.'

'He told me he was more of a martyr than the rest.'

'I've told you many times not to speak to him. My dear child, oh, my dear child . . .'

'And the other one – the one who came to see us?'

'No, he is not – exactly – like Juan.'

'Is he despicable?'

'No, no. Not despicable.'

The smallest girl said suddenly, 'He smelt funny.'

The mother went on reading: 'Did any premonition touch young Juan that night that he, too, in a few short years, would be numbered among the martyrs? We cannot say, but Father Miguel Cerra tells how that evening Juan spent longer than usual upon his knees, and when his class-mates teased him a little, as boys will . . .'

The voice went on and on, mild and deliberate, inflexibly gentle; the small girls listened intently, framing in their minds little pious sentences with which to surprise their parents, and the boy yawned against the whitewash. Everything has an end.

Presently the mother went in to her husband. She said, 'I am so worried about the boy.'

'Why not about the girls? There is worry everywhere.'

'They are two little saints already. But the boy – he asks such questions – about that whisky priest. I wish we had never had him in the house.'

'They would have caught him if we hadn't, and then he would have been one of your martyrs. They would write a book about him and you would read it to the children.'

'That man – never.'

27

'Well, after all,' her husband said, 'he carries on. I don't believe all that they write in these books. We are all human.'

'You know what I heard today? About a poor woman who took to him her son to be baptized. She wanted him called Pedro – but he was drunk that he took no notice at all and baptized the boy Brigitta. Brigitta!'

'Well, it's a good saint's name.'

'There are times,' the mother said, 'when I lose all patience with you. And now the boy has been talking to Padre José.'

'This is a small town,' her husband said. 'And there is no use pretending. We have been abandoned here. We must get along as best we can. As for the Church – the Church is Padre José and the whisky priest – I don't know of any other. If we don't like the Church, well, we must leave it.'

He watched her with patience. He had more education than his wife; he could use a typewriter and knew the elements of book-keeping: once he had been to Mexico City: he could read a map. He knew the extent of their abandonment – the ten hours down-river to the port, the forty-two hours on the Gulf to Vera Cruz – that was one way out. To the north the swamps and rivers petering out against the mountains which divided them from the next state. And on the other side no roads – only mule-tracks and an occasional unreliable plane: Indian villages and the huts of herds: two hundred miles away, the Pacific.

She said, 'I would rather die.'

'Oh,' he said, 'of course. That goes without saying. But we have to go on living.'

The old man sat on a packing-case in the little dry patio. He was very fat and short of breath; he panted a little as if after great exertion in the heat. Once he had been something of an astronomer and now he tried to pick out the constellations, staring up into the night sky. He wore only a shirt and trousers; his feet were bare, but there remained something unmistakably clerical in his manner. Forty years of the priesthood had branded him. There was complete silence over the town: everybody was asleep.

The glittering worlds lay there in space like a promise – the world was not the universe. Somewhere Christ might not have died. He could not believe that to a watcher there *this* world could shine with such brilliance: it would roll heavily in space under its fog like a burning and abandoned ship. The whole globe was blanketed with his own sin.

A woman called from the only room he possessed, 'José, José.' He crouched like a galley-slave at the sound; his eyes left the sky, and the constellations fled upwards: the beetles crawled over the patio. 'José, José.' He thought with envy of the men who had died: it was over so soon. They were taken up there to the cemetery and shot against the wall: in two minutes life was extinct. And they called that martyrdom. Here life went on and on; he was only sixty-two. He might live to ninety. Twenty-eight years – that immeasurable period between his birth and his first parish: all childhood and youth and the seminary lay there.

'José. Come to bed.' He shivered: he knew that he was a buffoon. An old man who married was grotesque enough, but an old priest. ... He stood outside himself and wondered whether he was even fit for hell. He was just a fat old impotent man mocked and taunted between the sheets. But then he remembered the gift he had been given which nobody could take away. That was what made him worthy of damnation – the power he still had of turning the wafer into the flesh and blood of God. He was a sacrilege. Wherever he went, whatever he did, he defiled God. Some mad renegade Catholic, puffed up with the Governor's politics, had once broken into a church (in the days when there were still churches) and seized the Host. He had spat on it, trampled it, and then the people had got him and hung him as they did the stuffed Judas on Holy Thursday from the belfry. He wasn't so bad a man, Padre José thought – he would be forgiven, he was just a politician; but he himself, he was worse than that – he was like an obscene picture hung here every day to corrupt children with.

He belched on his packing-case shaken by wind. 'José. What are you doing? You come to bed.' There was never

anything to do at all – no daily Office, no Masses, no Confessions, and it was no good praying any longer at all: a
prayer demanded an act and he had no intention of acting.
He had lived for two years now in a continuous state of mortal
sin with no one to hear his Confession: nothing to do at all
but to sit and eat – eat far too much; she fed him and fattened
him and preserved him like a prize boar. 'José.' He began to
hiccup with nerves at the thought of facing for the seven
hundred and thirty-eighth time his harsh housekeeper – his
wife. There she would be lying in the big shameless bed that
filled half the room, a bony shadow within the mosquito-tent,
a lanky jaw and a short grey pigtail and an absurd bonnet.
She thought she had a position to keep up: a Government
pensioner: the wife of the only married priest. She was proud
of it. 'José.' 'I'm – hic – coming, my love,' he said and lifted
himself from the crate. Somebody somewhere laughed.

He lifted little pink eyes like those of a pig conscious of the
slaughter-room. A high child's voice said, 'José.' He stared in
a bewildered way around the patio. At a barred window
opposite three children watched him with deep gravity. He
turned his back and took a step or two towards his door,
moving very slowly because of his bulk. 'José,' somebody
squeaked again. 'José.' He looked back over his shoulder and
caught the faces out in expressions of wild glee; his little pink
eyes showed no anger – he had no right to be angry: he
moved his mouth into a ragged, baffled, disintegrated smile,
and as if that sign of weakness gave them all the licence they
needed, they squealed back at him without disguise, 'José,
José. Come to bed, José.' Their little shameless voices filled
the patio, and he smiled humbly and sketched small gestures
for silence, and there was no respect anywhere left for him in
his home, in the town, in the whole abandoned star.

## Chapter 3: THE RIVER

CAPTAIN FELLOWS sang loudly to himself, while the little
motor chugged in the bows of the canoe. His big sunburned

face was like the map of a mountain region – patches of varying brown with two small blue lakes that were his eyes. He composed his songs as he went, and his voice was quite tuneless. 'Going home, going home, the food will be good for me-e-e. I don't like the food in the bloody citee.' He turned out of the main stream into a tributary: a few alligators lay on the sandy margin. 'I don't like your snouts, O trouts. I don't like your snouts, O trouts.' He was a happy man.

The banana plantations came down on either bank: his voice boomed under the hard sun: that and the churr of the motor were the only sounds anywhere – he was completely alone. He was borne up on a big tide of boyish joy – doing a man's job, the heart of the wild: he felt no responsibility for anyone. In only one other country had he felt more happy, and that was in wartime France, in the ravaged landscape of trenches. The tributary cork-screwed farther into the marshy overgrown state, and a vulture lay spread out in the sky; Captain Fellows opened a tin box and ate a sandwich – food never tasted so good as out of doors. A monkey made a sudden chatter at him as he went by, and Captain Fellows felt happily at one with nature – a wide shallow kinship with all the world moved with the blood-stream through the veins: he was at home anywhere. The artful little devil, he thought, the artful little devil. He began to sing again – somebody else's words a little jumbled in his friendly unretentive memory. 'Give to me the life I love, bread I dip in the river, under the wide and starry sky, the hunter's home from the sea.' The plantations petered out, and far behind the mountains came into view, heavy black lines drawn low-down across the sky. A few bungalows rose out of the mud. He was home. A very slight cloud marred his happiness.

He thought: after all, a man likes to be welcomed.

He walked up to his bungalow; it was distinguished from the others which lay along the bank by a tiled roof, a flagpost without a flag, a plate on the door with the title 'Central American Banana Company'. Two hammocks were strung up on the veranda, but there was nobody about. Captain Fellows knew where to find his wife. He burst boisterously

31

through a door and shouted, 'Daddy's home.' A scared thin face peeked at him through a mosquito-net; his boots ground peace into the floor; Mrs Fellows flinched away into the white muslin tent. He said, 'Pleased to see me, Trix?' and she drew rapidly on her face the outline of her frightened welcome. It was like a trick you do with a blackboard. Draw a dog in one line without lifting the chalk – and the answer, of course, is a sausage.

'I'm glad to be home,' Captain Fellows said, and he believed it. It was his one firm conviction – that he really felt the correct emotions of love and joy and grief and hate. He had always been a good man at zero hour.

'All well at the office?'

'Fine,' Fellows said, 'fine.'

'I had a bit of fever yesterday.'

'Ah, you need looking after. You'll be all right now,' he said vaguely, 'that I'm home.' He shied merrily away from the subject of fever – clapping his hands, a big laugh, while she trembled in her tent. 'Where's Coral?'

'She's with the policeman,' Mrs Fellows said.

'I hoped she'd meet me,' he said, roaming aimlessly about the little interior room, full of boot-trees, while his brain caught up with her. 'Policeman? What policeman?'

'He came last night and Coral let him sleep on the veranda. He's looking for somebody, she says.'

'What an extraordinary thing. *Here?*'

'He's not an ordinary policeman. He's an officer. He left his men in the village – Coral says.'

'I do think you ought to be up,' he said. 'I mean – these fellows, you can't trust them.' He felt no conviction when he added, 'She's just a kid.'

'I tell you I had fever,' Mrs Fellows wailed, 'I felt so terribly ill.'

'You'll be all right. Just a touch of the sun. You'll see – now *I'm* home.'

'I had such a headache. I couldn't read or sew. And then this man . . .'

Terror was always just behind her shoulder: she was wasted

by the effort of not turning round. She dressed up her fear, so that she could look at it – in the form of fever, rats, unemployment. The real thing was taboo – death coming nearer every year in the strange place: everybody packing up and leaving, while she stayed in a cemetery no one visited, in a big above-ground tomb.

He said, 'I suppose I ought to go and see the man.' He sat down on the bed and put his hand upon her arm. They had something in common – a kind of diffidence. He said absent-mindedly, 'That dago secretary of the boss has gone.'

'Where?'

'West.' He could feel her arm go stiff: she strained away from him towards the wall. He had touched the taboo – the bond was broken, he couldn't tell why. 'Headache, darling?'

'Hadn't you better see the man?'

'Oh yes, yes. I'll be off.' But he didn't stir: it was the child who came to him.

She stood in the doorway watching them with a look of immense responsibility. Before her serious gaze they became a boy you couldn't trust and a ghost you could almost puff away, a piece of frightened air. She was very young – about thirteen – and at that age you are not afraid of many things, age and death, all the things which may turn up, snake-bite and fever and rats and a bad smell. Life hadn't got at her yet; she had a false air of impregnability. But she had been reduced already, as it were, to the smallest terms – everything was there but on the thinnest lines. That was what the sun did to a child, reduced it to a framework. The gold bangle on the bony wrist was like a padlock on a canvas door which a fist could break. She said, 'I told the policeman you were home.'

'Oh yes, yes,' Captain Fellows said. 'Got a kiss for your old dad?'

She came solemnly across the room and kissed him formally upon the forehead – he could feel the lack of meaning. She had other things to think about. She said, 'I told cook that Mother would not be getting up for dinner.'

'I think you ought to make the effort, dear,' Captain Fellows said.

'Why?' Coral asked.

'Oh, well . . .'

Coral said, 'I want to talk to you alone.' Mrs Fellows shifted inside her tent. Common sense was a horrifying quality she had never possessed: it was common sense which said, 'The dead can't hear' or 'She can't know now' or 'Tin flowers are more practical'.

'I don't understand,' Captain Fellows said uneasily, 'why your mother shouldn't hear.'

'She wouldn't want to. It would only scare her.'

Coral – he was accustomed to it by now – had an answer to everything. She never spoke without deliberation; she was prepared – but sometimes the answers she had prepared seemed to him of a wildness . . . They were based on the only life she could remember, the swamp and vultures and no children anywhere, except a few in the village with bellies swollen by worms who ate dirt from the bank, inhumanly. A child is said to draw parents together, and certainly he felt an immense unwillingness to entrust himself to this child. Her answers might carry him anywhere. He felt through the net for his wife's hand, secretively: they were adults together. This was the stranger in their house. He said boisterously, 'You're frightening us.'

'I don't think,' the child said, with care, 'that *you'll* be frightened.'

He said weakly, pressing his wife's hand, 'Well, my dear, our daughter seems to have decided . . .'

'First you must see the policeman. I want him to go. I don't like him.'

'Then he must go, of course,' Captain Fellows said, with a hollow unconfident laugh.

'I told him that. I said we couldn't refuse him a hammock for the night when he arrived so late. But now he must go.'

'And he disobeyed you?'

'He said he wanted to speak to you.'

'He little knew,' Captain Fellows said, 'he little knew.' Irony was his only defence, but it was not understood; nothing was understood which was not clear – like an alphabet or a

34

simple sum or a date in history. He relinquished his wife's hand and allowed himself to be led unwillingly into the afternoon sun. The police officer stood in front of the veranda, a motionless olive figure; he wouldn't stir a foot to meet Captain Fellows.

'Well, lieutenant?' Captain Fellows said breezily. It occurred to him that Coral had more in common with the policeman than with himself.

'I am looking for a man,' the lieutenant said. 'He has been reported in this district.'

'He can't be here.'

'Your daughter tells me the same.'

'She knows.'

'He is wanted on a very serious charge.'

'Murder?'

'No. Treason.'

'Oh, treason,' Captain Fellows said, all his interest dropping; there was so much treason everywhere – it was like petty larceny in a barracks.

'He is a priest. I trust you will report at once if he is seen.' The lieutenant paused. 'You are a foreigner living under the protection of our laws. We expect you to make a proper return for our hospitality. You are not a Catholic?'

'No.'

'Then I can trust you to report?' the lieutenant said.

'I suppose so.'

The lieutenant stood there like a little dark menacing question-mark in the sun: his attitude seemed to indicate that he wouldn't even accept the benefit of shade from a foreigner. But he had used a hammock; that, Captain Fellows supposed, he must have regarded as a requisition. 'Have a glass of gaseosa?'

'No. No, thank you.'

'Well,' Captain Fellows said, 'I can't offer you anything else, can I? It's treason to drink spirits.'

The lieutenant suddenly turned on his heel as if he could no longer bear the sight of them and strode away along the path which led to the village: his gaiters and his pistol holster

35

winked in the sunlight. When he had gone some way they could see him pause and spit; he had not been discourteous, he had waited till he supposed that they no longer watched him before he got rid of his hatred and contempt for a different way of life, for ease, safety, toleration, and complacency.

'I wouldn't want to be up against him,' Captain Fellows said.

'Of course he doesn't trust us.'

'They don't trust anyone.'

'I think,' Coral said, 'he smelt a rat.'

'They smell them everywhere.'

'You see, I wouldn't let him search the place.'

'Why ever not?' Captain Fellows asked, and then his vague mind went off at a tangent. 'How did you stop him?'

'I said I'd loose the dogs on him – and complain to the Minister. He hadn't any right . . .'

'Oh, right,' Captain Fellows said. 'They carry their right on their hips. It wouldn't have done any harm to let him look.'

'I gave him my word.' She was as inflexible as the lieutenant: small and black and out of place among the banana groves. Her candour made allowances for nobody: the future, full of compromises, anxieties, and shame, lay outside. But at any moment now a word, a gesture, the most trivial act might be her sesame – to what? Captain Fellows was touched with fear; he was aware of an inordinate love which robbed him of authority. You cannot control what you love – you watch it driving recklessly towards the broken bridge, the torn-up track, the horror of seventy years ahead. He closed his eyes – he was a happy man – and hummed a tune.

Coral said, 'I shouldn't have liked a man like that to catch me out – lying, I mean.'

'Lying? Good God,' Captain Fellows said, 'you don't mean he's here.'

'Of course he's here,' Coral said.

'Where?'

'In the big barn,' she explained gently. 'We couldn't let them catch him.'

'Does your mother know about this?'

She said with devastating honesty, 'Oh no. I couldn't trust

*her.*' She was independent of both of them: they belonged together in the past. In forty years' time they would be dead as last year's dog. He said, 'You'd better show me.'

He walked slowly; happiness drained out of him more quickly and completely than out of an unhappy man: an unhappy man is always prepared. As she walked in front of him, her two meagre tails of hair bleaching in the sunlight, it occurred to him for the first time that she was of an age when Mexican girls were ready for their first man. What was to happen? He flinched away from problems which he had never dared to confront. As they passed the window of his bedroom he caught sight of a thin shape lying bunched and bony and alone in a mosquito-net. He remembered with self-pity and nostalgia his happiness on the river, doing a man's job without thinking of other people. If I had never married. . . . He wailed like a child at the merciless immature back, 'We've no business interfering with politics.'

'This isn't politics,' she said gently. 'I know about politics. Mother and I are doing the Reform Bill.' She took a key out of her pocket and unlocked the big barn in which they stored bananas before sending them down the river to the port. It was very dark inside after the glare. There was a scuffle in a corner. Captain Fellows picked up an electric torch and shone it on somebody in a torn dark suit – a small man who blinked and needed a shave.

'*Quién es usted?*' Captain Fellows said.

'I speak English.' He clutched a small attaché case to his side, as if he were waiting to catch a train he must on no account miss.

'You've no business here.'

'No,' the man said, 'no.'

'It's nothing to do with us,' Captain Fellows said. 'We are foreigners.'

The man said, 'Of course. I will go.' He stood with his head a little bent like a man in an orderly-room listening to an officer's decision. Captain Fellows relented a little. He said, 'You'd better wait till dark. You don't want to be caught.'

'No.'

'Hungry?'

'A little. It does not matter.' He said with a rather repulsive humility, 'If you would do me a favour . . .'

'What?'

'A little brandy.'

'I'm breaking the law enough for you as it is,' Captain Fellows said. He strode out of the barn, feeling twice the size, leaving the small bowed figure in the darkness among the bananas. Coral locked the door and followed him. 'What a religion,' Captain Fellows said. 'Begging for brandy. Shameless.'

'But you drink it sometimes.'

'My dear,' Captain Fellows said, 'when you are older you'll understand the difference between drinking a little brandy after dinner and – well, needing it.'

'Can I take him some beer?'

'*You* won't take him anything.'

'The servants wouldn't be safe.'

He was powerless and furious. He said, 'You see what a hole you've put us in.' He stumped back into the house and into his bedroom, roaming aimlessly among the boot-trees. Mrs Fellows slept uneasily, dreaming of weddings. Once she said aloud, 'My train. Be careful of my train.'

'What's that?' he asked petulantly. 'What's that?'

Dark fell like a curtain: one moment the sun was there, the next it had gone. Mrs Fellows woke to another night. 'Did you speak, dear?'

'It was you who spoke,' he said. 'Something about trains.'

'I must have been dreaming.'

'It will be a long time before they have trains here,' he said, with gloomy satisfaction. He came and sat on the bed, keeping away from the window; out of sight, out of mind. The crickets were beginning to chatter and beyond the mosquito wire fireflies moved like globes. He put his heavy, cheery, needing-to-be-reassured hand on the shape under the sheet and said, 'It's not such a bad life, Trixy. Is it now? Not a bad life?' But he could feel her stiffen: the word 'life' was taboo: it reminded you of death. She turned her face away from him towards the

38

wall and then hopelessly back again – the phrase 'turn to the wall' was taboo too. She lay panic-stricken, while the boundaries of her fear widened to include every relationship and the whole world of inanimate things: it was like an infection. You could look at nothing for long without becoming aware that it, too, carried the germ . . . the word 'sheet' even. She threw the sheet off her and said, 'It's so hot, it's so hot.' The usually happy and the always unhappy one watched the night thicken from the bed with distrust. They were companions cut off from all the world: there was no meaning anywhere outside their own hearts: they were carried like children in a coach through the huge spaces without any knowledge of their destination. He began to hum with desperate cheerfulness a song of the war years; he wouldn't listen to the footfall in the yard outside, going in the direction of the barn.

Coral put down the chicken legs and tortillas on the ground and unlocked the door. She carried a bottle of Cerveza Moctezuma under her arm. There was the same scuffle in the dark: the noise of a frightened man. She said, 'It's me,' to quieten him, but she didn't turn on the torch. She said, 'There's a bottle of beer here, and some food.'

'Thank you. Thank you.'

'The police have gone from the village – south. You had better go north.'

He said nothing.

She asked, with the cold curiosity of a child, 'What would they do to you if they found you?'

'Shoot me.'

'You must be very frightened,' she said with interest.

He felt his way across the barn towards the door and the pale starlight. He said, 'I *am* frightened,' and stumbled on a bunch of bananas.

'Can't you escape from here?'

'I tried. A month ago. The boat was leaving and then I was summoned.'

'Somebody needed you?'

'She didn't need me,' he said bitterly. She could just see his

39

face now, as the world swung among the stars: what her father would call an untrustworthy face. He said, 'You see how unworthy I am. Talking like this.'

'Unworthy of what?'

He clasped his little attaché case closely and said, 'Could you tell me what month it is. Is it still February?'

'No. It's the seventh of March.'

'I don't often meet people who know. That means another month – six weeks – before the rains.' He went on, 'When the rains come I am nearly safe. You see, the police can't get about.'

'The rains are best for you?' she asked: she had a keen desire to learn. The Reform Bill and Senlac and a little French lay like treasure-trove in her brain. She expected answers to every question, and she absorbed them hungrily.

'Oh no, no. They mean another six months living like this.' He tore at a chicken leg. She could smell his breath: it was disagreeable, like something which has lain about too long in the heat. He said, 'I'd rather be caught.'

'But can't you,' she said logically, 'just give yourself up?'

He had answers as plain and understandable as her questions. He said, 'There's the pain. To choose pain like that – it's not possible. And it's my duty not to be caught. You see, my bishop is no longer here.' Curious pedantries moved him. 'This is my parish.' He found a tortilla and began to eat ravenously.

She said solemnly, 'It's a problem.' She could hear a gurgle as he drank out of the bottle. He said, 'I try to remember how happy I was once.' A firefly lit his face like a torch and then went out – a tramp's face: what could ever have made it happy? He said, 'In Mexico City now they are saying Benediction. The Bishop's there. . . . Do you imagine he ever thinks . . .? They don't even know I'm alive.'

She said, 'Of course you could – renounce.'

'I don't understand.'

'Renounce your faith,' she explained, using the words of her European History.

He said, 'It's impossible. There's no way. I'm a priest. It's out of my power.'

40

The child listened intently. She said, 'Like a birthmark.'
She could hear him sucking desperately at the bottle. She said,
'I think I could find my father's brandy.'

'Oh no, you mustn't steal.' He drained the beer: a long
glassy whistle in the darkness: the last drop must have gone.
He said, 'I must leave. At once.'

'You can always come back here.'

'Your father would not like it.'

'He needn't know,' she said. 'I could look after you. My
room is just opposite this door. You would just tap at my
window. Perhaps,' she went seriously on, 'it would be better
to have a code. You see, somebody else might tap.'

He said in a horrified voice, 'Not a man?'

'Yes. You never know. Another fugitive from justice.'

'Surely,' he asked in bewilderment, 'that is not likely?'

She said airily, 'These things do happen.'

'Before today?'

'No, but I expect they will again. I want to be prepared.
You must tap three times. Two long taps and a short one.'

He giggled suddenly like a child. 'How do you tap a long
tap?'

'Like this.'

'Oh, you mean a loud one?'

'I call them long taps – because of Morse.' He was hopelessly out of his depth. He said, 'You are very good. Will you
pray for me?'

'Oh,' she said, 'I don't believe in that.'

'Not in praying?'

'You see, I don't believe in God. I lost my faith when I
was ten.'

'Well, well,' he said. 'Then I will pray for you.'

'You can,' she said patronizingly, 'if you like. If you come
again I shall teach you the Morse code. It would be useful to
you.'

'How?'

'If you were hiding in the plantation I could flash to you
with my mirror news of the enemy's movements.'

He listened seriously. 'But wouldn't they see you?'

41

'Oh,' she said, 'I would invent an explanation.' She moved logically forward a step at a time, eliminating all objections.

'Good-bye, my child,' he said.

He lingered by the door. 'Perhaps – you do not care for prayers. Perhaps you would like . . . I know a good conjuring trick.'

'I like tricks.'

'You do it with cards. Have you any cards?'

'No.'

He sighed, 'Then that's no good,' and giggled – she could smell the beer on his breath – 'I shall just have to pray for you.'

She said, 'You don't sound afraid.'

'A little drink,' he said, 'will work wonders in a cowardly man. With a little brandy, why, I'd defy – the devil.' He stumbled in the doorway.

'Good-bye,' she said. 'I hope you'll escape.' A faint sigh came out of the darkness. She said gently, 'If they kill you I shan't forgive them – ever.' She was ready to accept any responsibility, even that of vengeance, without a second thought. It was her life.

Half a dozen huts of mud and wattle stood in a clearing; two were in ruins. A few pigs routed round, and an old woman carried a burning ember from hut to hut, lighting a little fire on the centre of each floor to fill the hut with smoke and keep mosquitoes away. Women lived in two of the huts, the pigs in another; in the last unruined hut where maize was stored, an old man and a boy and a tribe of rats. The old man stood in the clearing watching the fire being carried round; it flickered through the darkness like a ritual repeated at the same hour for a lifetime. White hair, a white stubbly beard, and hands brown and fragile as last year's leaves, he gave an effect of immense permanence. Living on the edge of subsistence nothing much could ever change him. He had been old for years.

The stranger came into the clearing. He wore what used to be town shoes, black and pointed; only the uppers were left, so that he walked to all intents barefoot. The shoes were symbolic, like the cobwebbed flags in churches. He wore a shirt and a pair of black torn trousers and he carried his attaché case, as if he were a season-ticket holder. He had nearly reached the state of permanency too, but he carried about with him the scars of time – the damaged shoes implied a different past, the lines of his face suggested hopes and fears of the future. The old woman with the ember stopped between two huts and watched him. He came on into the clearing with his eyes on the ground and his shoulders hunched, as if he felt exposed. The old man advanced to meet him; he took the stranger's hand and kissed it.

'Can you let me have a hammock for the night?'

'Ah, father, for a hammock you must go to a town. Here you must take only the luck of the road.'

'Never mind. Anywhere to lie down. Can you give me – a little spirit?'

'Coffee, father. We have nothing else.'

'Some food.'

'We have no food.'

'Never mind.'

The boy came out of the hut and watched them: everybody watched. It was like a bull-fight. The animal was tired and they waited for the next move. They were not hard-hearted; they were watching the rare spectacle of something worse off than themselves. He limped on towards the hut. Inside it was dark from the knees upwards; there was no flame on the floor, just a slow burning away. The place was half filled by a stack of maize, and rats rustled among the dry outer leaves. There was a bed made of earth with a straw mat on it, and two packing-cases made a table. The stranger lay down, and the old man closed the door on them both.

'Is it safe?'

'The boy will watch. He knows.'

'Were you expecting me?'

'No, father. But it is five years since we have seen a priest ... it was bound to happen one day.'

He fell uneasily asleep, and the old man crouched on the floor, fanning the fire with his breath. Somebody tapped on the door and the priest jerked upright. 'It is all right,' the old man said. 'Just your coffee, father.' He brought it to him – grey maize coffee smoking in a tin mug, but the priest was too tired to drink. He lay on his side perfectly still: a rat watched him from the maize.

'The soldiers were here yesterday,' the old man said. He blew on the fire. The smoke poured up and filled the hut. The priest began to cough, and the rat moved quickly like the shadow of a hand into the stack.

'The boy, father, has not been baptized. The last priest who was here wanted two pesos. I had only one peso. Now I have only fifty centavos.'

'Tomorrow,' the priest said wearily.

'Will you say Mass, father, in the morning?'

'Yes, yes.'

'And confession, father, will you hear our confessions?'

'Yes, but let me sleep first.' He turned on his back and closed his eyes to keep out the smoke.

'We have no money, father, to give you. The other priest, Padre José . . .'

'Give me some clothes instead,' he said impatiently.

'But we have only what we wear.'

'Take mine in exchange.'

The old man hummed dubiously to himself, glancing sideways at what the fire showed of the black torn cloth. 'If I must, father,' he said. He blew quietly at the fire for a few minutes. The priest's eyes closed again.

'After five years there is so much to confess.'

The priest sat up quickly. 'What was that?' he said.

'You were dreaming, father. The boy will warn us if the soldiers come. I was only saying – '

'Can't you let me sleep for five minutes?' He lay down again. Somewhere, in one of the women's huts, someone was singing – 'I went down to my field and there I found a rose.'

The old man said softly, 'It would be a pity if the soldiers came before we had time . . . such a burden on poor souls, father . . .' The priest shouldered himself upright against the wall and said furiously, 'Very well. Begin. I will hear your

44

confession.' The rats scuffled in the maize. 'Go on then,' he said. 'Don't waste time. Hurry. When did you last ...?' The old man knelt beside the fire, and across the clearing the woman sang: 'I went down to my field and the rose was withered.'

'Five years ago.' He paused and blew at the fire. 'It's hard to remember, father.'

'Have you sinned against purity?'

The priest leant against the wall with his legs drawn up beneath him, and the rats accustomed to the voices moved again in the maize. The old man picked out his sins with difficulty, blowing at the fire. 'Make a good act of contrition,' the priest said, 'and say – say – have you a rosary? – then say the Joyful Mysteries.' His eyes closed, his lips and tongue stumbled over the absolution, failed to finish ... he sprang awake again.

'Can I bring the women?' the old man was saying. 'It is five years ...'

'Oh, let them come. Let them all come,' the priest cried angrily. 'I am your servant.' He put his hand over his eyes and began to weep. The old man opened the door: it was not completely dark outside under the enormous arc of starry ill-lit sky. He went across to the women's huts and knocked. 'Come,' he said. 'You must say your confessions. It is only polite to the father.' They wailed at him that they were tired ... the morning would do. 'Would you insult him?' he said. 'What do you think he has come here for? He is a very holy father. There he is in my hut now weeping for our sins.' He hustled them out; one by one they picked their way across the clearing towards the hut, and the old man set off down the path towards the river to take the place of the boy who watched the ford for soldiers.

## Chapter 4: THE BYSTANDERS

IT was years since Mr Tench had written a letter. He sat before the work-table sucking at a steel nib; an odd impulse had come to him to project this stray letter towards the last address he had – in Southend. Who knew who was alive still? He tried to begin. It was like breaking the ice at a party where you knew nobody. He started to write the envelope – Mrs Henry Tench, care of Mrs Marsdyke, 3 The Avenue, Westcliff. It was her mother's house: the dominating interfering creature who had induced him to set up his place in Southend for a fatal while. 'Please forward,' he wrote. She wouldn't do it if she knew, but she had probably forgotten his handwriting by this time.

He sucked the inky nib – how to go on? It would have been easier if there had been some purpose behind it other than the vague desire to put on record to somebody that he was still alive. It might prove awkward if she had married again, but in that case she wouldn't hesitate to tear the letter up. He wrote: *Dear Sylvia*, in a big clear immature script, listening to the furnace purring on the bench. He was making a gold alloy – there were no depots here where he could buy his material ready-made. Besides, the depots didn't favour 14-carat gold for dental work, and he couldn't afford finer material.

The trouble was – nothing ever happened here. His life was as sober, respectable, regular as even Mrs Marsdyke could require.

He took a look at the crucible. The gold was on the point of fusion with the alloy, so he flung in a spoonful of vegetable charcoal to protect the mixture from the air, took up his pen again and sat mooning over the paper. He couldn't remember his wife clearly – only the hats she wore. How surprised she would be at hearing from him after this long while; there had been one letter written by each of them since the little boy died. The years really meant nothing to him – they drifted fairly rapidly by without changing a habit. He had meant to leave six years ago, but the peso dropped with a revolution, and so he had come south. Now he had more money saved, but a month ago the peso dropped again – another revolution somewhere. There was nothing to do but wait ... the nib went back between his teeth and memory melted in the little hot room. Why write at all? He couldn't remember now what had given him the odd idea. Somebody knocked at the outer door and he left the letter on the bench – *Dear Sylvia*, staring up, big and bold and hopeless. A boat's bell rang by the riverside: it was the *General Obregon* back from Vera Cruz. A memory stirred. It was as if something alive and in pain moved in the little front room among the rocking-chairs – 'an interesting afternoon: what happened to him, I wonder, when' – then died, or got away. Mr Tench was used to pain: it was his profession. He waited cautiously till a hand beat on the door again and a voice said, *'Con amistad'* – there was no trust anywhere – before he drew the bolts and opened up, to admit a patient.

Padre José went in, under the big classical gateway marked in black letters 'Silencio' to what people used to call the Garden of God. It was like a building estate where nobody had paid attention to the architecture of the next house. The big stone tombs of above-ground burial were any height and any shape; sometimes an angel stood on the roof with lichenous wings: sometimes through a glass window you could see some rusting metal flowers upon a shelf – it was like looking into the kitchen of a house whose owners have moved on, forgetting to clean the vases out. There was a sense of intimacy – you could go anywhere and see anything. Life here had withdrawn altogether.

He walked very slowly because of his bulk among the tombs; he could be alone here, there were no children about, and he could waken a faint sense of homesickness which was better than no feeling at all. He had buried some of these people. His small inflamed eyes turned here and there. Coming round the huge grey bulk of the Lopez tomb – a merchant family which fifty years ago had owned the only hotel in the capital – he found he was not alone. A grave was being dug at the edge of the cemetery next the wall: two men were rapidly at work: a woman stood by and an old man. A child's coffin lay at their feet – it took no time at all in the spongy soil to get down far enough. A little water collected. That was why those who could afford it lay above ground.

They all paused a moment and looked at Padre José, and he sidled back towards the Lopez tomb as if he were an intruder. There was no sign of grief anywhere in the bright hot day: a vulture sat on a roof outside the cemetery. Somebody said, 'Father.'

Padre José put up his hand deprecatingly as if he were trying to indicate that he was not there, that he was gone, away, out of sight.

The old man said, 'Padre José.' They all watched him hungrily; they had been quite resigned until he had appeared, but now they were anxious, eager. . . . He ducked and dodged away from them. 'Padre José,' the old man repeated. 'A prayer?' They smiled at him, waiting. They were quite accustomed to people dying, but an unforeseen hope of happiness had bobbed up among the tombs: they could boast after this that one at least of their family had gone into the ground with an official prayer.

'It's impossible,' Padre José said.

'Yesterday was her saint's day,' the woman said, as if that made a difference. 'She was five.' She was one of those garrulous women who show to strangers the photographs of their children, but all she had to show was a coffin.

'I am sorry.'

The old man pushed the coffin aside with his foot the better to approach Padre José; it was small and light and might have contained nothing but bones. 'Not a whole service, you understand – just a prayer. She was – innocent,' he said. The word in the little stony town sounded odd and archaic and local, outdated like the Lopez tomb, belonging only here.

'It is against the law.'

'Her name,' the woman went on, 'was Anita. I was sick when I had her,' she explained, as if to excuse the child's delicacy which had led to all this inconvenience.

'The law . . .'

The old man put his finger to his nose. 'You can trust us. It is just the case of a short prayer. I am her grandfather. This is her mother, her father, her uncle. You can trust us.'

But that was the trouble – he could trust no one. As soon as they got back home one or other of them would certainly begin to boast. He walked backwards all the time, weaving his

48

plump fingers, shaking his head, nearly bumping into the Lopez tomb. He was scared, and yet a curious pride bubbled in his throat because he was being treated as a priest again, with respect. 'If I could,' he said, 'my children . . .'

Suddenly and unexpectedly there was agony in the cemetery. They had been used to losing children, but they hadn't been used to what the rest of the world knows best of all – the hope which peters out. The woman began to cry, dryly, without tears, the trapped noise of something wanting to be released; the old man fell on his knees with his hands held out. 'Padre José,' he said, 'there is no one else . . .' He looked as if he were asking for a miracle. An enormous temptation came to Padre José to take the risk and say a prayer over the grave. He felt the wild attraction of doing one's duty and stretched a sign of the cross in the air; then fear came back, like a drug. Contempt and safety waited for him down by the quay: he wanted to get away. He sank hopelessly down on his knees and entreated them: 'Leave me alone.' He said, 'I am unworthy. Can't you see? – I am a coward.' The two old men faced each other on their knees among the tombs, the small coffin shoved aside like a pretext – an absurd spectacle. He knew it was absurd: a lifetime of self-analysis enabled him to see himself as he was, fat and ugly and old and humiliated. It was as if a whole seducing choir of angels had silently withdrawn and left the voices of the children in the patio – 'Come to bed, José, come to bed,' sharp and shrill and worse than they had ever been. He knew he was in the grip of the unforgivable sin, despair.

'At last the blessed day arrived,' the mother read aloud, 'when the days of Juan's novitiate were over. Oh, what a joyful day was that for his mother and sisters. And a little sad too, for the flesh cannot always be strong, and how could they help mourning a while in their hearts for the loss of a small son and an elder brother? Ah, if they had known that they were gaining that day a saint in heaven to pray for them.'

The younger girl on the bed said, 'Have *we* got a saint?'

'Of course.'

'Why did they want another saint?'

The mother went on reading: 'Next day the whole family received communion from the hands of a son and brother. Then they said a fond good-bye – they little knew that it was the last – to the new soldier of Christ and returned to their homes in Morelos. Already clouds were darkening the heavens, and President Calles was discussing the anti-Catholic laws in the Palace at Chapultepec. The devil was ready to assail poor Mexico.'

'Is the shooting going to begin soon?' the boy asked, moving restlessly against the wall. His mother went relentlessly on: 'Juan unknown to all but his confessor was preparing himself for the evil days ahead with the most rigorous mortifications. His companions suspected nothing, for he was always the heart and soul of every merry conversation, and on the feast-day of the founder of the Order it was he . . .'

'I know, I know,' the boy said. 'He acted a play.'

The little girls opened astounded eyes.

'And why not, Luis?' the mother said, pausing with her finger on the prohibited book. He stared sullenly back at her. 'And why not, Luis?' she repeated. She waited a while, and then read on; the little girls watched their brother with horror and admiration. 'It was he,' she said, 'who obtained permission to perform a little one-act play founded on . . .'

'I know, I know,' the boy said, 'the catacombs.'

The mother, compressing her lips, continued: '. . . the persecution of the early Christians. Perhaps he remembered that occasion in his boyhood when he acted Nero before the good old bishop, but this time he insisted on taking the comic part of a Roman fishmonger . . .'

'I don't believe a word of it,' the boy said, with sullen fury, 'not a word of it.'

'How dare you!'

'Nobody could be such a fool.'

The little girls sat motionless, their eyes large and brown and pious.

'Go to your father.'

'Anything to get away from this – this – ' the boy said.

'Tell him what you've told me.'

'This . . .'

'Leave the room.'

He slammed the door behind him. His father stood at the barred window of the *sala*, looking out; the beetles detonated against the oil-lamp and crawled with broken wings across the stone floor. The boy said, 'My mother told me to tell you that I told her that I didn't believe that the book she's reading . . .'

'What book?'

'The holy book.'

He said sadly, 'Oh that.' Nobody passed in the street, nothing happened; it was after nine-thirty and all the lights were out. He said, 'You must make allowances. For us, you know, everything seems over. That book – it is like our own childhood.'

'It sounds so silly.'

'You don't remember the time when the Church was here. I was a bad Catholic, but it meant – well, music, lights, a place where you could sit out of this heat – and for your mother, well, there was always something for her to do. If we had a theatre, anything at all instead, we shouldn't feel so – left.'

'But this Juan,' the boy said. 'He sounds so silly.'

'He was killed, wasn't he?'

'Oh, so were Villa, Obregon, Madero . . .'

'Who tells you about them?'

'We all of us play them. Yesterday I was Madero. They shot me in the plaza – the law of flight.' Somewhere in the heavy night a drum beat. The sour river smell filled the room: it was familiar like the taste of soot in cities. 'We tossed up. I was Madero: Pedro had to be Huerta. He fled to Vera Cruz down by the river. Manuel chased him – he was Carranza.' His father struck a beetle off his shirt, staring into the street: the sound of marching feet came nearer. He said, 'I suppose your mother's angry.'

'You aren't,' the boy said.

'What's the good? It's not your fault. We have been deserted.'

The soldiers went by, returning to barracks, up the hill near

51

what had once been the cathedral; they marched out of step in spite of the drum-beat, they looked undernourished, they hadn't yet made much of war. They passed lethargically by in the dark street and the boy watched them out of sight with excited and hopeful eyes.

Mrs Fellows rocked backwards and forwards, backwards and forwards. 'And so Lord Palmerston said if the Greek Government didn't do right to Don Pacifico ...' She said, 'My darling, I've got such a headache I think we must stop today.'

'Of course. I have a little one too.'

'I expect yours will be better soon. Would you mind putting the books away?' The little shabby books had come by post from a firm in Paternoster Row called Private Tutorials, Ltd – a whole education which began with 'Reading Without Tears' and went methodically on to the Reform Bill and Lord Palmerston and the poems of Victor Hugo. Once every six months an examination paper was delivered, and Mrs Fellows laboriously worked through the answers and awarded marks. These she sent back to Paternoster Row, and there, weeks later, they were filed: once she had forgotten her duty when there was shooting in Zapata, and had received a printed slip beginning: 'Dear Parent, I regret to see ...' The trouble was they were years ahead of schedule by now – there were so few other books to read – and so the examination papers were years behind. Sometimes the firm sent embossed certificates for framing, announcing that Miss Coral Fellows had passed third with honours into the second grade, signed with a rubber stamp Henry Beckley, B.A., Director of Private Tutorials, Ltd, and sometimes there would be little personal letters typewritten, with the same blue smudgy signature, saying: *Dear Pupil, I think you should pay more attention this week to....* The letters were always six weeks out of date.

'My darling,' Mrs Fellows said, 'will you see the cook and order lunch? Just yourself. I can't eat a thing, and your father's out on the plantation.'

'Mother,' the child said, 'do you believe there's a God?'

52

The question scared Mrs Fellows. She rocked furiously up and down and said, 'Of course.'

'I mean the Virgin Birth – and everything.'

'My dear, what a thing to ask: Who have you been talking to?'

'Oh,' she said. 'I've been thinking, that's all.' She didn't wait for any further answer; she knew quite well there would be none – it was always her job to make decisions. Henry Beckley, B.A., had put it all into an early lesson – it hadn't been any more difficult to accept then than the giant at the top of the beanstalk, and at the age of ten she had discarded both relentlessly. By that time she was starting algebra.

'Surely your father hasn't . . .'

'Oh no.'

She put on her sun-helmet and went out into the blazing ten o'clock heat to find the cook – she looked more fragile than ever and more indomitable. When she had given her orders she went to the warehouse to inspect the alligator skins tacked out on a wall, then to the stables to see that the mules were in good shape. She carried her responsibilities carefully like crockery across the hot yard: there was no question she wasn't prepared to answer; the vultures rose languidly at her approach.

She returned to the house and her mother. She said, 'It's Thursday.'

'Is it, dear?'

'Hasn't father got the bananas down to the quay?'

'I'm sure I don't know, dear.'

She went briskly back into the yard and rang a bell. An Indian came. No, the bananas were still in the store; no orders had been given. 'Get them down,' she said, 'at once, quickly. The boat will be here soon.' She fetched her father's ledger and counted the bunches as they were carried out – a hundred bananas or more to a bunch which was worth a few pence. It took more than two hours to empty the store; somebody had got to do the work, and once before her father had forgotten the day. After half an hour she began to feel tired – she wasn't used to weariness so early in the day. She leant against

53

the wall and it scorched her shoulder-blades. She felt no resentment at all at being there, looking after things: the word 'play' had no meaning to her at all – the whole of life was adult. In one of Henry Beckley's early reading-books there had been a picture of a doll's tea-party: it was incomprehensible like a ceremony she hadn't learned: she couldn't see the point of pretending. Four hundred and fifty-six. Four hundred and fifty-seven. The sweat poured down the peons' bodies steadily like a shower-bath. An awful pain took her suddenly in the stomach – she missed a load and tried to catch up in her calculations: she felt the sense of responsibility for the first time like a load borne for too many years. Five hundred and twenty-five. It was a new pain (not worms this time), but it didn't scare her; it was as if her body had expected it, had grown up to it, as the mind grows up to the loss of tenderness. You couldn't call it childhood draining out of her: of childhood she had never really been conscious.

'Is that the last?' she said.

'Yes, señorita.'

'Are you sure?'

'Yes, señorita.'

But she had to see for herself. Never before had it occurred to her to do a job unwillingly – if she didn't do a thing nobody would – but today she wanted to lie down, to sleep: if all the bananas didn't get away it was her father's fault. She wondered whether she had fever, her feet felt so cold on the hot ground. Oh well, she thought, and went patiently into the barn, found the torch, and switched it on. Yes, the place seemed empty enough, but she never left a job half done. She advanced towards the back wall, holding the torch in front of her. An empty bottle rolled away – she dropped the light on it: Cerveza Moctezuma. Then the torch lit the back wall: low down near the ground somebody had scrawled in chalk – she came closer: a lot of little crosses leant in the circle of light. He must have lain down among the bananas and tried to relieve his fear by writing something, and this was all he could think of. The child stood in her woman's pain and looked at them: a horrible novelty enclosed her whole morning: it was as if today everything were memorable.

The Chief of Police was in the cantina playing billiards when the lieutenant found him. He had a handkerchief tied all round his face with some idea that it relieved the toothache. He was chalking his cue for a difficult shot as the lieutenant pushed through the swing door. On the shelves behind were nothing but gaseosa bottles and a yellow liquid called Sidral – warranted non-alcoholic. The lieutenant stood protestingly in the doorway. The situation was ignoble; he wanted to eliminate anything in the state at which a foreigner might have cause to sneer. He said, 'Can I speak to you?' The jefe winced at a sudden jab of pain and came with unusual alacrity towards the door; the lieutenant glanced at the score, marked in rings strung on a cord across the room – the jefe was losing. 'Back – moment,' the jefe said, and explained to the lieutenant, 'Don't want open mouth.' As they pushed the door somebody raised a cue and surreptitiously pushed back one of the jefe's rings.

They walked up the street side by side, the fat one and the lean. It was a Sunday and all the shops closed at noon – that was the only relic of the old time. No bells rang anywhere. The lieutenant said, 'Have you seen the Governor?'

'You can do anything,' the jefe said, 'anything.'

'He leaves it to us?'

'On conditions,' he winced.

'What are they?'

'He'll hold you – responsible – if – not caught before – rains.'

'As long as I'm not responsible for anything else . . .' the lieutenant said moodily.

'You asked for it. You got it.'

'I'm glad.' It seemed to the lieutenant that all the world he cared about now lay at his feet. They passed the new hall built for the Syndicate of Workers and Peasants: through the window they could see the big bold clever murals – of one priest caressing a woman in the confessional, another tippling on the sacramental wine. The lieutenant said, 'We will soon make

55

these unnecessary.' He looked at the pictures with the eye of a foreigner: they seemed to him barbarous.

'One day they'll forget there ever was a Church here.'

The jefe said nothing. The lieutenant knew he was thinking, what a fuss about nothing. He said sharply, 'Well, what are my orders?'

'Orders?'

'You are my chief.'

The jefe was silent. He studied the lieutenant unobtrusively with little astute eyes. Then he said, 'You know I trust you. Do what you think best.'

'Will you put that in writing?'

'Oh – not necessary. We know each other.'

All the way up the road they fenced warily for positions.

'Didn't the Governor give you anything in writing?' the lieutenant asked.

'No. He said we knew each other.'

It was the lieutenant who gave way because it was he who really cared. He was indifferent to his personal future. He said, 'I shall take hostages from every village.'

'Then he won't stay in the villages.'

'Do you imagine,' the lieutenant asked bitterly, 'that they don't know where he is? He has to keep some touch – or what good is he?'

'Just as you like,' the jefe said.

'And I shall shoot as often as it's necessary.'

The jefe said with facetious brightness, 'A little blood never hurt anyone. Where will you start?'

'His parish, I think, Concepción, and then – perhaps – his home.'

'Why there?'

'He may think he's safe there.' He brooded past the shuttered shops. 'It's worth a few deaths, but will *he*, do you think, support me if they make a fuss in Mexico City?'

'It isn't likely, is it?' the jefe said. 'But it's what –' he was stopped by a stab of pain.

'It's what I wanted,' the lieutenant said for him.

He made his way on alone towards the police station, and

56

the chief went back to billiards. There were few people about; it was too hot. If only, he thought, we had a proper photograph – he wanted to know the features of his enemy. A swarm of children had the plaza to themselves. They were playing some obscure and intricate game from bench to bench. An empty gaseosa bottle sailed through the air and smashed at the lieutenant's feet. His hand went to his holster and he turned; he caught a look of consternation on a boy's face.

'Did you throw that bottle?'

The heavy brown eyes stared sullenly back at him.

'What were you doing?'

'It was a bomb.'

'Were you throwing it at me?'

'No.'

'What then?'

'A gringo.'

The lieutenant smiled – an awkward movement of the lips. 'That's right, but you must aim better.' He kicked the broken bottle into the road and tried to think of words which would show these children that they were on the same side. He said, 'I suppose the gringo was one of those rich Yankees . . .' and surprised an expression of devotion in the boy's face; it called for something in return, and the lieutenant became aware in his own heart of a sad and unsatisfiable love. He said, 'Come here.' The child approached, while his companions stood in a scared semicircle and watched from a safe distance. 'What is your name?'

'Luis.'

'Well,' the lieutenant said, at a loss for words, 'you must learn to aim properly.'

The boy said passionately, 'I wish I could.' He had his eye on the holster.

'Would you like to see my gun?' the lieutenant asked. He pulled his heavy automatic from the holster and held it out: the children drew cautiously in. He said, 'This is the safety-catch. Lift it. So. Now it's ready to fire.'

'Is it loaded?' Luis asked.

'It's always loaded.'

57

*haplness w. / gun*

The tip of the boy's tongue appeared: he swallowed. Saliva came from the glands as if he smelt food. They all stood close in now. A daring child put out his hand and touched the holster. They ringed the lieutenant round: he was surrounded by an insecure happiness as he fitted the gun back on his hip.

'What is it called?' Luis asked.

'A Colt ·38.'

'How many bullets?'

'Six.'

'Have you killed somebody with it?'

'Not yet,' the lieutenant said.

They were breathless with interest. He stood with his hand on his holster and watched the brown intent patient eyes: it was for these he was fighting. He would eliminate from their childhood everything which had made him miserable, all that was poor, superstitious, and corrupt. They deserved nothing less than the truth – a vacant universe and a cooling world, the right to be happy in any way they chose. He was quite prepared to make a massacre for their sakes – first the Church and then the foreigner and then the politician – even his own chief would one day have to go. He wanted to begin the world again with them, in a desert.

'Oh,' Luis said, 'I wish . . . I wish . . .' as if his ambition were too vast for definition. The lieutenant put out his hand in a gesture of affection – a touch, he didn't know what to do with it. He pinched the boy's ear and saw him flinch away with the pain; they scattered from him like birds and he went on alone across the plaza to the police station, a little dapper figure of hate carrying his secret of love. On the wall of the office the gangster still stared stubbornly in profile towards the first communion party. Somebody had inked round the priest's head to detach him from the girls' and the women's faces: the unbearable grin peeked out of a halo. The lieutenant called furiously out into the patio, 'Is there nobody here?' Then he sat down at the desk while the gun-butts scraped the floor.

# PART TWO

## *Chapter 1*

THE mule suddenly sat down under the priest. It was not an unnatural thing to do, for they had been travelling through the forest for nearly twelve hours. They had been going west, but news of soldiers met them there and they had turned east; the Red Shirts were active in that direction, so they had tacked north, wading through the swamps, diving into the mahogany darkness. Now they were both tired out and the mule simply sat down. The priest scrambled off and began to laugh. He was feeling happy. It is one of the strange discoveries a man can make that life, however you lead it, contains moments of exhilaration; there are always comparisons which can be made with worse times: even in danger and misery the pendulum swings.

He came cautiously out of the belt of trees into a marshy clearing. The whole state was like that, river and swamp and forest. He knelt down in the late sunlight and bathed his face in a brown pool which reflected back at him like a piece of glazed pottery the round, stubbly and hollow features. They were so unexpected that he grinned at them – with the shy evasive untrustworthy smile of a man caught out. In the old days he often practised a gesture a long while in front of a glass so that he had come to know his own face as well as an actor does. It was a form of humility – his own natural face hadn't seemed the right one. It was a buffoon's face, good enough for mild jokes to women, but unsuitable at the altar-rail. He had tried to change it – and indeed, he thought, indeed I have succeeded, they'll never recognize me now, and the cause of his happiness came back to him like the taste of brandy, promising temporary relief from fear, loneliness, a lot of things. He was being driven by the presence of soldiers to the very place where he most wanted to be. He had avoided it for six years, but now it wasn't his fault – it was his duty

59

to go there – it couldn't count as sin. He went back to his mule and kicked it gently, 'Up, mule, up,' a small gaunt man in torn peasant's clothes going for the first time in many years, like any ordinary man, to his home.

In any case, even if he could have gone south and avoided the village, it was only one more surrender. The years behind him were littered with similar surrenders – feast days and fast days and days of abstinence had been the first to go: then he had ceased to trouble more than occasionally about his breviary – and finally he had left it behind altogether at the port in one of his periodic attempts at escape. Then the altar stone went – too dangerous to carry with him. He had no business to say Mass without it; he was probably liable to suspension, but penalties of the ecclesiastical kind began to seem unreal in a state where the only penalty was the civil one of death. The routine of his life like a dam was cracked and forgetfulness came dribbling through, wiping out this and that. Five years ago he had given way to despair – the unforgivable sin – and he was going back now to the scene of his despair with a curious lightening of the heart. For he had got over despair too. He was a bad priest, he knew it. They had a word for his kind – a whisky priest, but every failure dropped out of sight and mind: somewhere they accumulated in secret – the rubble of his failures. One day they would choke up, he supposed, altogether the source of grace. Until then he carried on, with spells of fear, weariness, with a shamefaced lightness of heart.

The mule splashed across the clearing and they entered the forest again. Now that he no longer despaired it didn't mean, of course, that he wasn't damned – it was simply that after a time the mystery became too great, a damned man putting God into the mouths of men: an odd sort of servant, that, for the devil. His mind was full of a simplified mythology: Michael dressed in armour slew a dragon, and the angels fell through space like comets with beautiful streaming hair because they were jealous, so one of the Fathers had said, of what God intended for men – the enormous privilege of life – this life.

There were signs of cultivation; stumps of trees and the ashes of fires where the ground was being cleared for a crop. He stopped beating the mule on; he felt a curious shyness . . . A woman came out of a hut and watched him lagging up the path on the tired mule. The tiny village, not more than two dozen huts round a dusty plaza, was made to pattern, but it was a pattern which lay close to his heart. He felt secure – he was confident of a welcome, confident that in this place there would be at least one person he could trust not to betray him to the police. When he was quite close the mule sat down again – this time he had to roll on the ground to escape. He picked himself up and the woman watched him as if he were an enemy. 'Ah, Maria,' he said, 'and how are you?'

'Well,' she exclaimed, 'it is you, father?'

He didn't look directly at her: his eyes were sly and cautious. He said, 'You didn't recognize me?'

'You've changed.' She looked him up and down with a kind of contempt. She said, 'When did you get those clothes, father?'

'A week ago.'

'What did you do with yours?'

'I gave them in exchange.'

'Why? They were good clothes.'

'They were very ragged – and conspicuous.'

'I'd have mended them and hidden them away. It's a waste. You look like a common man.'

He smiled, looking at the ground, while she chided him like a housekeeper: it was just as in the old days when there was a presbytery and meetings of the Children of Mary and all the guilds and gossip of a parish, except of course that . . . He said gently, not looking at her, with the same embarrassed smile, 'How's Brigitta?' His heart jumped at the name: a sin may have enormous consequences: it was six years since he had been – home.

'She's as well as the rest of us. What did you expect?'

He had his satisfaction, but it was connected with his crime; he had no business to feel pleasure at anything attached to

61

that past. He said mechanically, 'That's good,' while his heart beat with its secret love. He said, 'I'm very tired. The police were about near Zapata . . .'

'Why didn't you make for Monte Cristo?'

He looked quickly up with anxiety. It wasn't the welcome that he had expected; a small knot of people had gathered between the huts and watched him from a safe distance – there was a little decaying bandstand and a single stall for gaseosas – people had brought their chairs out for the evening. Nobody came forward to kiss his hand and ask his blessing. It was as if he had descended by means of his sin into the human struggle to learn other things besides despair and love, that a man can be unwelcome even in his own home. He said, 'The Red Shirts were there.'

'Well, father,' the woman said, 'we can't turn you away. You'd better come along.' He followed her meekly, tripping once in the long peon's trousers, with the happiness wiped off his face and the smile somehow left behind like the survivor of a wreck. There were seven or eight men, two women, half a dozen children: he came among them like a beggar. He couldn't help remembering the last time . . . the excitement, the gourds of spirit brought out of holes in the ground . . . his guilt had still been fresh, yet how he had been welcomed. It was as if he had returned to them in their vicious prison as one of themselves – an émigré who comes back to his native place enriched.

'This is the father,' the woman said. Perhaps it was only that they hadn't recognized him, he thought, and waited for their greetings. They came forward one by one and kissed his hand and then stood back and watched him. He said, 'I am glad to see you . . .' he was going to say 'my children', but then it seemed to him that only the childless man has the right to call strangers his children. The real children were coming up now to kiss his hand, one by one, under the pressure of their parents. They were too young to remember the old days when the priests dressed in black and wore Roman collars and had soft superior patronizing hands; he could see they were mystified at the show of respect to a peasant like

62

their parents. He didn't look at them directly, but he was watching them closely all the same. Two were girls – a thin washed-out child – of five, six, seven? he couldn't tell, and one who had been sharpened by hunger into an appearance of devilry and malice beyond her age. A young woman stared out of the child's eyes. He watched them disperse again, saying nothing: they were strangers.

One of the men said, 'Will you be here long, father?'

He said, 'I thought, perhaps . . . I could rest . . . a few days.'

One of the other men said, 'Couldn't you go a bit farther north, father, to Pueblito?'

'We've been travelling for twelve hours, the mule and I.'

The woman suddenly spoke for him, angrily, 'Of course he'll stay here tonight. It's the least we can do.'

He said, 'I'll say Mass for you in the morning,' as if he were offering them a bribe, but it might almost have been stolen money from their expressions of shyness and unwillingness.

Somebody said, 'If you don't mind, father, very early . . . in the night perhaps.'

'What is the matter with you all?' he asked. 'Why should you be afraid?'

'Haven't you heard . . . ?'

'Heard?'

'They are taking hostages now – from all the villages where they think you've been. And if people don't tell . . . somebody is shot . . . and then they take another hostage. It happened in Concepción.'

'Concepción?' One of his lids began to twitch up and down, up and down. He said, 'Who?' They looked at him stupidly. He said furiously, 'Who did they murder?'

'Pedro Montez.'

He gave a little yapping cry like a dog's – the absurd shorthand of grief. The old-young child laughed. He said, 'Why don't they catch me? The fools. Why don't they catch *me*?' The little girl laughed again; he stared at her sightlessly, as if he could hear the sound but couldn't see the face. Happiness was dead again before it had had time to breathe; he was like

63

a woman with a stillborn child – bury it quickly and forget and begin again. Perhaps the next would live.

'You see, father,' one of the men said, 'why . . .'

He felt as a guilty man does before his judges. He said 'Would you rather that I was like . . . like Padre José in the capital . . . you have heard of him . . .?'

They said unconvincingly, 'Of course not that, father.'

He said, 'What am I saying now? It's not what you want or what I want.' He continued sharply, with authority, 'I will sleep now . . . You can wake me an hour before dawn . . . half an hour to hear your confessions . . . then Mass, and I will be gone.'

But where? There wouldn't be a village in the state to which he wouldn't be an unwelcome danger now.

The woman said, 'This way, father.'

He followed her into a small room where all the furniture had been made out of packing-cases – a chair, a bed of boards tacked together and covered with a straw mat, a crate on which a cloth had been laid and on the cloth an oil-lamp. He said, 'I don't want to turn anybody out of here.'

'It's mine.'

He looked at her doubtfully. 'Where will you sleep?' He was afraid of claims. He watched her covertly: was this all there was in marriage, this evasion and suspicion and lack of ease? When people confessed to him in terms of passion, was this all they meant – the hard bed and the busy woman and the not talking about the past?

'When you are gone.'

The light flattened out behind the forest and the long shadows of the trees pointed towards the door. He lay down upon the bed, and the woman busied herself somewhere out of sight: he could hear her scratching at the earth floor. He couldn't sleep. Had it become his duty then to run away? He had tried to escape several times, but he had always been prevented . . . now they wanted him to go. Nobody would stop him, saying a woman was ill or a man dying. He was a sickness now.

'Maria,' he said. 'Maria, what are you doing?'

'I have saved a little brandy for you.'

He thought: if I go, I shall meet other priests: I shall go to confession: I shall feel contrition and be forgiven: eternal life will begin for me all over again. The Church taught that it was every man's first duty to save his own soul. The simple ideas of hell and heaven moved in his brain; life without books, without contact with educated men, had peeled away from his memory everything but the simplest outline of the mystery.

'There,' the woman said. She carried a small medicine bottle filled with spirit.

If he left them, they would be safe, and they would be free from his example. He was the only priest the children could remember: it was from him they would take their ideas of the faith. But it was from him too they took God – in their mouths. When he was gone it would be as if God in all this space between the sea and the mountains ceased to exist. Wasn't it his duty to stay, even if they despised him, even if they were murdered for his sake? even if they were corrupted by his example? He was shaken with the enormity of the problem. He lay with his hands over his eyes: nowhere, in all the wide flat marshy land, was there a single person he could consult. He raised the brandy to his mouth.

He said shyly, 'And Brigitta . . . is she . . . well?'

'You saw her just now.'

'No.' He couldn't believe that he hadn't recognized her. It was making light of his mortal sin: you couldn't do a thing like that and then not even recognize . . .

'Yes, she was there.' Maria went to the door and called, 'Brigitta, Brigitta,' and the priest turned on his side and watched her come in out of the outside landscape of terror and lust – that small malicious child who had laughed at him.

'Go and speak to the father,' Maria said. 'Go on.'

He made an attempt to hide the brandy bottle, but there was nowhere . . . he tried to minimize it in his hands, watching her, feeling the shock of human love.

'She knows her catechism,' Maria said, 'but she won't say it . . .'

The child stood there, watching him with acuteness and contempt. They had spent no love in her conception: just fear and despair and half a bottle of brandy and the sense of loneliness had driven him to an act which horrified him – and this scared shame-faced overpowering love was the result. He said, 'Why not? Why won't you say it?' taking quick secret glances, never meeting her gaze, feeling his heart pound in his breast unevenly, like an old donkey engine, with the baulked desire to save her from – everything.

'Why should I?'

'God wishes it.'

'How do you know?'

He was aware of an immense load of responsibility: it was indistinguishable from love. This, he thought, must be what all parents feel: ordinary men go through life like this crossing their fingers, praying against pain, afraid. . . . This is what we escape at no cost at all, sacrificing an unimportant motion of the body. For years, of course, he had been responsible for souls, but that was different . . . a lighter thing. You could trust God to make allowances, but you couldn't trust small-pox, starvation, men . . . He said, 'My dear,' tightening his grip upon the brandy bottle . . . He had baptized her at his last visit: she had been like a rag doll with a wrinkled aged face – it had seemed unlikely that she would live long . . . He had felt nothing but a regret; it was difficult even to feel shame where no one blamed him. He was the only priest most of them had ever known – they took their standard of the priest-hood from him. Even the women.

'Are you the gringo?'

'What gringo?'

The woman said, 'The silly little creature. It's because the police have been looking for a man.' It seemed odd to hear of any other man they wanted but himself.

'What has he done?'

'He's a Yankee. He murdered some people in the north.'

'Why should he be here?'

'They think he's making for Quintana Roo – the chiceli plantations.' It was where many criminals in Mexico ended

66

up: you could work on a plantation and earn good money and nobody interfered.

'Are you the gringo?' the child repeated.

'Do I look like a murderer?'

'I don't know.'

If he left the state, he would be leaving her too, abandoned. He said humbly to the woman, 'Couldn't I stay a few days here?'

'It's too dangerous, father.'

He caught the look in the child's eyes which frightened him – it was again as if a grown woman was there before her time, making her plans, aware of far too much. It was like seeing his own mortal sin look back at him, without contrition. He tried to find some contact with the child and not the woman; he said, 'My dear, tell me what games you play . . .' The child sniggered. He turned his face quickly away and stared up at the roof, where a spider moved. He remembered a proverb – it came out of the recesses of his own childhood: his father had used it – 'The best smell is bread, the best savour salt, the best love that of children.' It had been a happy childhood, except that he had been afraid of too many things, and had hated poverty like a crime; he had believed that when he was a priest he would be rich and proud – that was called having a vocation. He thought of the immeasurable distance a man travels – from the first whipping-top to this bed, on which he lay clasping the brandy. And to God it was only a moment. The child's snigger and the first mortal sin lay together more closely than two blinks of the eye. He put out his hand as if he could drag her back by force from – something; but he was powerless. The man or the woman waiting to complete her corruption might not yet have been born. How could he guard her against the non-existent?

She started out of his reach and put her tongue out at him. The woman said, 'You little devil you,' and raised her hand.

'No,' the priest said. 'No.' He scrambled into a sitting position. 'Don't you dare . . .'

'I'm her mother.'

'We haven't any right.' He said to the child, 'If only I had

67

some cards I could show you a trick or two. You could teach your friends . . .' He had never known how to talk to children except from the pulpit. She stared back at him with insolence. He asked, 'Do you know how to send messages with taps – long, short, long . . . ?'

'What on earth, father!' the woman exclaimed.

'It's a game children play. I know.' He said to the child, 'Have you any friends?'

The child suddenly laughed again knowingly. The seven-year-old body was like a dwarf's: it disguised an ugly maturity.

'Get out of here,' the woman said. 'Get out before I teach you . . .'

She made a last impudent malicious gesture and was gone – perhaps for ever as far as he was concerned. You do not always say good-bye to those you love beside a deathbed, in an atmosphere of leisure and incense. He said, 'I wonder what *we* can teach . . .' He thought of his own death and her life going on; it might be his hell to watch her rejoining him gradually through the debasing years, sharing his weakness like tuberculosis. . . . He lay back on the bed and turned his head away from the draining light; he appeared to be sleeping, but he was wide awake. The woman busied herself with small jobs, and as the sun went down the mosquitoes came out, flashing through the air to their mark unerringly, like sailors' knives.

'Shall I put up a net, father?'

'No. It doesn't matter.' He had had more fevers in the last ten years than he could count: he had ceased to bother: they came and went and made no difference – they were part of his environment.

Presently she left the hut and he could hear her voice gossiping outside. He was astonished and a bit relieved by her resilience. Once for five minutes seven years ago they had been lovers – if you could give that name to a relationship in which she had never used his baptismal name: to her it was just an incident, a scratch which heals completely in the healthy flesh: she was even proud of having been the priest's woman. He alone carried a wound, as though a whole world had died.

It was dark: no sign as yet of the dawn. Perhaps two dozen people sat on the earth floor of the largest hut while he preached to them. He couldn't see them with any distinctness. The candles on the packing-case smoked steadily upwards – the door was shut and there was no current of air. He was talking about heaven, standing between them and the candles in the ragged peon trousers and the torn shirt. They grunted and moved restlessly. He knew they were longing for the Mass to be over: they had woken him very early, because there were rumours of police . . .

He said, 'One of the Fathers has told us that joy always depends on pain. Pain is part of joy. We are hungry and then think how we enjoy our food at last. We are thirsty . . .' He stopped suddenly, with his eyes glancing away into the shadows, expecting the cruel laugh that did not come. He said, 'We deny ourselves so that we can enjoy. You have heard of rich men in the north who eat salted foods, so that they can be thirsty – for what they call the cocktail. Before the marriage, too, there is the long betrothal . . .' Again he stopped. He felt his own unworthiness like a weight at the back of the tongue. There was a smell of hot wax from where a candle drooped in the nocturnal heat; people shifted on the hard floor in the shadows. The smell of unwashed human beings warred with the wax. He cried out stubbornly in a voice of authority, 'That is why I tell you that heaven is here: this is a part of heaven just as pain is a part of pleasure.' He said, 'Pray that you will suffer more and more and more. Never get tired of suffering. The police watching you, the soldiers gathering taxes, the beating you always get from the jefe because you are too poor to pay, smallpox and fever, hunger . . . that is all part of heaven – the preparation. Perhaps without them, who can tell, you wouldn't enjoy heaven so much. Heaven would not be complete. And heaven. What is heaven?' Literary phrases from what seemed now to be another life altogether – the strict quiet life of the seminary – became confused on his tongue: the names of precious stones: Jerusalem the Golden. But these people had never seen gold.

He went rather stumbling on, 'Heaven is where there is no

jefe, no unjust laws, no taxes, no soldiers and no hunger. Your children do not die in heaven.' The door of the hut opened and a man slipped in. There was whispering out of the range of the candlelight. 'You will never be afraid there – or unsafe. There are no Red Shirts. Nobody grows old. The crops never fail. Oh, it is easy to say all the things that there will *not* be in heaven: what is there is God. That is more difficult. Our words are made to describe what we know with our senses. We say "light", but we are thinking only of the sun, "love" . . .' It was not easy to concentrate: the police were not far away. The man had probably brought news. 'That means perhaps a child . . .' The door opened again: he could see another day drawn across like a grey slate outside. A voice whispered urgently to him, 'Father.'

'Yes?'

'The police are on the way. They are only a mile off, coming through the forest.'

This was what he was used to: the words not striking home, the hurried close, the expectation of pain coming between him and his faith. He said stubbornly, 'Above all remember this – heaven is here.' Were they on horseback or on foot? If they were on foot, he had twenty minutes left to finish Mass and hide. 'Here now, at this minute, your fear and my fear are part of heaven, where there will be no fear any more for ever.' He turned his back on them and began very quickly to recite the Credo. There was a time when he had approached the Canon of the Mass with actual physical dread – the first time he had consumed the body and blood of God in a state of mortal sin. But then life bred its excuses – it hadn't after a while seemed to matter very much, whether he was damned or not, so long as these others . . .

He kissed the top of the packing-case and turned to bless. In the inadequate light he could just see two men kneeling with their arms stretched out in the shape of a cross – they would keep that position until the consecration was over, one more mortification squeezed out of their harsh and painful lives. He felt humbled by the pain ordinary men bore voluntarily; his pain was forced on him. 'Oh Lord, I have loved the beauty of thy house . . .' The candles smoked and the people shifted on their knees – an absurd happiness bobbed up in him again before anxiety returned: it was as if he had been permitted to look in from the outside at the population of heaven. Heaven must contain just such scared and dutiful and hunger-lined faces. For a matter of seconds he felt an immense satisfaction that he could talk of suffering to them now without hypocrisy – it is hard for the sleek and well-fed priest to praise poverty. He began the prayer for the living: the long list of the Apostles and Martyrs fell like footsteps – Cornelii, Cypriani, Laurentii, Chrysogoni – soon the police would reach the clearing where his mule had sat down under him and he had washed in the pool. The Latin words ran into each other on his hasty tongue: he could feel impatience all round him. He began the Consecration of the Host (he had finished the wafers long ago – it was a piece of bread from Maria's oven); impatience abruptly died away: everything in time became a routine but this – 'Who the day before he suffered took Bread into his holy and venerable hands . . .' Whoever moved outside on the forest path, there was no movement here – '*Hoc est enim Corpus Meum.*' He could hear the sigh of breaths released: God was here in the body for the first time in six years. When he raised the Host he could imagine the faces lifted like famished dogs. He began the Consecration of the Wine – in a chipped cup. That was one more surrender – for two years he had carried a chalice around with him; once it would have cost him his life, if the police officer who opened his case had not been a Catholic. It may very well have cost the officer his life, if anybody had discovered the evasion – he didn't know; you went round making God knew what martyrs – in Concepción or elsewhere – when you yourself were without grace enough to die.

The Consecration was in silence: no bell rang. He knelt by the packing-case exhausted, without a prayer. Somebody opened the door: a voice whispered urgently, 'They're here.' They couldn't have come on foot then, he thought vaguely. Somewhere in the absolute stillness of the dawn – it couldn't have been more than a quarter of a mile away – a horse whinnied.

He got to his feet – Maria stood at his elbow. She said, 'The cloth, father, give me the cloth.' He put the Host hurriedly into his mouth and drank the wine: one had to avoid profanation: the cloth was whipped away from the packing-case. She nipped the candles, so that the wick should not leave a smell ... The room was already cleared, only the owner hung by the entrance waiting to kiss his hand. Through the door the world was faintly visible, and a cock in the village crowed.

Maria said, 'Come to the hut quickly.'

'I'd better go.' He was without a plan. 'Not be found here.'

'They are all round the village.'

Was this the end at last, he wondered? Somewhere fear waited to spring at him, he knew, but he wasn't afraid yet. He followed the woman, scurrying across the village to her hut, repeating an act of contrition mechanically as he went. He wondered when the fear would start. He had been afraid when the policeman opened his case – but that was years ago. He had been afraid hiding in the shed among the bananas, hearing the child argue with the police officer – that was only a few weeks away. Fear would undoubtedly begin again soon. There was no sign of the police – only the grey morning, and the chickens and turkeys astir, flopping down from the trees in which they had roosted during the night. Again the cock crew. If they were so careful, they must know beyond the shadow of doubt that he was here. It *was* the end.

Maria plucked at him. 'Get in. Quick. On to the bed.' Presumably she had an idea – women were appallingly practical: they built new plans at once out of the ruins of the old. But what was the good? She said, 'Let me smell your breath. O God, anyone can tell ... wine ... what would we be doing with wine?' She was gone again, inside, making a lot of bother in the peace and quiet of the dawn. Suddenly, out of the forest, a hundred yards away, an officer rode. In the absolute stillness you could hear the creaking of his revolver-holster as he turned and waved.

All round the little clearing the police appeared – they must have marched very quickly, for only the officer had a horse.

72

Rifles at the trail, they approached the small group of huts – an exaggerated and rather absurd show of force. One man had a puttee trailing behind him – it had probably caught on something in the forest. He tripped on it and fell with a great clatter of cartridge-belt on gunstock: the lieutenant on the horse looked round and then turned his bitter and angry face upon the silent huts.

The woman was pulling at him from inside the hut. She said, 'Bite this. Quick. There's no time . . .' He turned his back on the advancing police and came into the dusk of the room. She had a small raw onion in her hand. 'Bite it,' she said. He bit it and began to weep. 'Is that better?' she said. He could hear the pad, pad of the cautious horse hoofs advancing between the huts.

'It's horrible,' he said with a giggle.

'Give it to me.' She made it disappear somewhere into her clothes: it was a trick all women seemed to know. He asked, 'Where's my case?'

'Never mind your case. Get on to the bed.'

But before he could move a horse blocked the doorway. They could see a leg in riding-boots piped with scarlet: brass fittings gleamed: a hand in a glove rested on the high pommel. Maria put a hand upon his arm – it was as near as she had ever come to a movement of affection: affection was taboo between them. A voice cried, 'Come on out, all of you.' The horse stamped and a little pillar of dust went up. 'Come on out, I said.' Somewhere a shot was fired. The priest left the hut.

The dawn had really broken: light feathers of colour were blown up the sky: a man still held his gun pointed upwards: a little balloon of grey smoke hung at the muzzle. Was this how the agony would start?

Out of all the huts the villagers were reluctantly emerging – the children first: they were inquisitive and unfrightened. The men and women had the air already of people condemned by authority – authority was never wrong. None of them looked at the priest. They stared at the ground and waited. Only the children watched the horse as if it were the most important thing there.

73

The lieutenant said, 'Search the huts.' Time passed very slowly; even the smoke of the shot seemed to remain in the air for an unnatural period. Some pigs came grunting out of a hut, and a turkey-cock paced with evil dignity into the centre of the circle, puffing out its dusty feathers and tossing the long pink membrane from its beak. A soldier came up to the lieutenant and saluted sketchily. He said, 'They're all here.'

'You've found nothing suspicious?'

'No.'

'Then look again.'

Once more time stopped like a broken clock. The lieutenant drew out a cigarette-case, hesitated and put it back again. Again the policeman approached and reported, 'Nothing.'

The lieutenant barked out, 'Attention. All of you. Listen to me.' The outer ring of police closed in, pushing the villagers together into a small group in front of the lieutenant: only the children were left free. The priest saw his own child standing close to the lieutenant's horse; she could just reach above his boot: she put up her hand and touched the leather. The lieutenant said, 'I am looking for two men – one is a gringo, a yankee, a murderer. I can see very well he is not here. There is a reward of five hundred pesos for his capture. Keep your eyes open.' He paused and ran his eye over them. The priest felt his gaze come to rest; he looked down like the others at the ground.

'The other,' the lieutenant said, 'is a priest.' He raised his voice: 'You know what that means – a traitor to the republic. Anyone who shelters him is a traitor too.' Their immobility seemed to anger him. He said, 'You're fools if you still believe what the priests tell you. All they want is your money. What has God ever done for you? Have you got enough to eat? Have your children got enough to eat? Instead of food they talk to you about heaven. Oh, everything will be fine after you are dead, they say. I tell you – everything will be fine when *they* are dead, and you must help.' The child had her hand on his boot. He looked down at her with dark affection. He said with conviction, 'This child is worth more than the

74

Pope in Rome. The police leant on their guns; one of them yawned; the turkey-cock went hissing back towards the hut. The lieutenant said, 'If you've seen this priest speak up. There's a reward of seven hundred pesos . . .' Nobody spoke.

The lieutenant yanked his horse's head round towards them. He said, 'We know he's in this district. Perhaps you don't know what happened to a man in Concepción. One of the women began to weep. He said, 'Come up – one after the other – and let me have your names. No, not the women, the men.'

They filed sullenly up and he questioned them, 'What's your name? What do you do? Married? Which is your wife? Have you heard of this priest?' Only one man now stood between the priest and the horse's head. He recited an act of contrition silently with only half a mind – '. . . my sins, because they have crucified my loving Saviour . . . but above all because they have offended . . .' He was alone in front of the lieutenant – 'I hereby resolve never more to offend Thee . . .' It was a formal act, because a man had to be prepared: it was like making your will and might be as valueless.

'Your name?'

The name of the man in Concepción came back to him. He said, 'Montez.'

'Have you ever seen the priest?'

'No.'

'What do you do?'

'I have a little land.'

'Are you married?'

'Yes.'

'Which is your wife?'

Maria suddenly broke out, 'I'm his wife. Why do you want to ask so many questions? Do you think *he* looks like a priest?'

The lieutenant was examining something on the pommel of his saddle: it seemed to be an old photograph. 'Let me see your hands,' he said.

The priest held them up: they were as hard as a labourer's. Suddenly the lieutenant leant down from the saddle and sniffed at his breath. There was complete silence among the villagers – a dangerous silence, because it seemed to convey to the lieutenant a fear ... He stared back at the hollow stubbled face, looked back at the photograph. 'All right,' he said, 'next,' and then as the priest stepped aside, 'Wait.' He put his hand down to Brigitta's head and gently tugged at her black stiff hair. He said, 'Look up. You know everyone in this village, don't you?'

'Yes,' she said.

'Who's that man, then? What's his name?'

'I don't know,' the child said. The lieutenant caught his breath. 'You don't know his name?' he said. 'Is he a stranger?'

Maria cried, 'Why, the child doesn't know her own name. Ask her who her father is.'

'Who's your father?'

The child stared up at the lieutenant and then turned her knowing eyes upon the priest ... 'Sorry and beg pardon for all my sins,' he was repeating to himself with his fingers crossed for luck. The child said, 'That's him. There.'

'All right,' the lieutenant said, 'Next.' The interrogations went on: name? work? married? while the sun came up above the forest. The priest stood with his hands clasped in front of him: again death had been postponed. He felt an enormous temptation to throw himself in front of the lieutenant and declare himself – 'I am the one you want.' Would they shoot him out of hand? A delusive promise of peace tempted him. Far up in the sky a vulture watched; they must appear from that height as two groups of carnivorous animals who might at any time break into conflict, and it waited there, a tiny black spot, for carrion. Death was not the end of pain – to believe in peace was a kind of heresy.

The last man gave his evidence.

The lieutenant said, 'Is no one willing to help?'

They stood silent beside the decayed bandstand. He said, 'You heard what happened at Concepción. I took a hostage there ... and when I found that this priest had been in the neighbourhood I put the man against the nearest tree. I found out because there's always someone who changes his mind –

76

perhaps because somebody in Concepción loved the man's wife and wanted him out of the way. It's not my business to look into reasons. I only know we found wine later in Concepción ... Perhaps there's somebody in this village who wants your piece of land – or your cow. It's much safer to speak now. Because I'm going to take a hostage from here too.' He paused. Then he said, 'There's no need even to speak, if he's here among you. Just look at him. No one will know then that it was you who gave him away. He won't know himself if you're afraid of his curses. Now ... This is your last chance.'

The priest looked at the ground – he wasn't going to make it difficult for the man who gave him away.

'Right,' the lieutenant said, 'then I shall choose my man. You've brought it on yourselves.'

He sat on his horse watching them – one of the policemen had leant his gun against the bandstand and was doing up a puttee. The villagers still stared at the ground; everyone was afraid to catch his eye. He broke out suddenly, 'Why won't you trust me? I don't want any of you to die. In my eyes – can't you understand – you are worth far more than he is. I want to give you' – he made a gesture with his hands which was valueless, because no one saw him – 'everything.' He said in a dull voice, 'You. You there. I'll take you.'

A woman screamed. 'That's my boy. That's Miguel. You can't take my boy.'

He said dully, 'Every man here is somebody's husband or somebody's son. I know that.'

The priest stood silently with his hands clasped; his knuckles whitened as he gripped ... He could feel all round him the beginning of hate. Because he was no one's husband or son. He said, 'Lieutenant ...'

'What do you want?'

'I'm getting too old to be much good in the fields. Take me.'

A rout of pigs came rushing round the corner of a hut, taking no notice of anybody. The soldier finished his puttee and stood up. The sunlight coming up above the forest winked on the bottles of the gaseosa stall.

77

The lieutenant said, 'I'm choosing a hostage, not offering free board and lodging to the lazy. If you are no good in the fields, you are no good as a hostage.' He gave an order. 'Tie the man's hands and bring him along.'

It took no time at all for the police to be gone – they took with them two or three chickens, a turkey and the man called Miguel. The priest said aloud, 'I did my best.' He went on, 'It's *your* job – to give me up. What do you expect me to do? It's my job not to be caught.'

One of the men said, 'That's all right, father. Only will you be careful . . . to see that you don't leave any wine behind . . . like you did at Concepción?'

Another said, 'It's no good staying, father. They'll get you in the end. They won't forget your face again. Better go north, to the mountains. Over the border.'

'It's a fine state over the border,' a woman said. 'They've still got churches there. Nobody can go in them, of course – but they are there. Why, I've heard that there are priests too in the towns. A cousin of mine went over the mountains to Las Casas once and heard Mass – in a house, with a proper altar, and the priest all dressed up like in the old days. You'd be happy there, father.'

The priest followed Maria to the hut. The bottle of brandy lay on the table; he touched it with his fingers – there wasn't much left. He said, 'My case, Maria? Where's my case?'

'It's too dangerous to carry that around any more,' Maria said.

'How else can I take the wine?'

'There isn't any wine.'

'What do you mean?'

She said, 'I'm not going to bring trouble on you and everyone else. I've broken the bottle. Even if it brings a curse . . .'

He said gently and sadly, 'You mustn't be superstitious. That was simply – wine. There's nothing sacred in wine. Only it's hard to get hold of here. That's why I kept a store of it in Concepción. But they've found that.'

'Now perhaps you'll go – go away altogether. You're no good any more to anyone,' she said fiercely. 'Don't you understand, father? We don't want you any more.'

'Oh yes,' he said. 'I understand. But it's not what you want – or I want . . .'

She said savagely, 'I know about things. I went to school. I'm not like these others – ignorant. I know you're a bad priest. That time we were together – that wasn't all you've done. I've heard things, I can tell you. Do you think God wants you to stay and die – a whisky priest like you?' He stood patiently in front of her, as he had stood in front of the lieutenant, listening. He hadn't known she was capable of all this thought. She said, 'Suppose you die. You'll be a martyr, won't you? What kind of a martyr do you think you'll be? It's enough to make people mock.'

That had never occurred to him – that anybody would consider him a martyr. He said, 'It's difficult. Very difficult. I'll think about it. I wouldn't want the Church to be mocked . . .'

'Think about it over the border then . . .'

'Well . . .'

She said, 'When you-know-what happened, I was proud. I thought the good days would come back. It's not everyone who's a priest's woman. And the child . . . I thought you could do a lot for her. But you might as well be a thief for all the good . . .'

He said vaguely, 'There've been a lot of good thieves.'

'For God's sake take this brandy and go.'

'There was one thing,' he said. 'In my case . . . there was something . . .'

'Go and find it yourself on the rubbish-tip then. I won't touch it again.'

'And the child,' he said, 'you're a good woman, Maria. I mean – you'll try and bring her up well . . . as a Christian.'

'She'll never be good for anything, you can see that.'

'She can't be very bad – at her age,' he implored her.

'She'll go on the way she's begun.'

He said, 'The next Mass I say will be for her.'

She wasn't even listening. She said, 'She's bad through and through.' He was aware of faith dying out between the bed and the door – the Mass would soon mean no more to anyone than a black cat crossing the path. He was risking all their

79

lives for the sake of spilt salt or a crossed finger. He began,
'My mule . . .'

'They are giving it maize now.'

She added, 'You'd better go north. There's no chance to
the south any more.'

'I thought perhaps Carmen . . .'

'They'll be watching there.'

'Oh, well . . .' He said sadly, 'Perhaps one day . . . when
things are better . . .' He sketched a cross and blessed her,
but she stood impatiently before him, willing him to be gone
for ever.

'Well, good-bye, Maria.'

'Good-bye.'

He walked across the plaza with his shoulders hunched; he
felt that there wasn't a soul in the place who wasn't watching
him with satisfaction – the trouble-maker who for obscure
and superstitious reasons they preferred not to betray to the
police. He felt envious of the unknown gringo whom they
wouldn't hesitate to trap – he at any rate had no burden of
gratitude to carry round with him.

Down a slope churned up with the hoofs of mules and
ragged with tree-roots there was the river – not more than
two feet deep, littered with empty cans and broken bottles.
A notice, which hung on a tree, read, 'It is forbidden to deposit
rubbish . . .' Underneath all the refuse of the village was collected and slid gradually down into the river. When the rains
came it would be washed away. He put his foot among the
old tins and the rotting vegetables and reached for his case.
He sighed: it had been quite a good case: one more relic of
the quiet past . . . Soon it would be difficult to remember that
life had ever been any different. The lock had been torn off:
he felt inside the silk lining . . .

The papers were there; reluctantly he let the case fall – a
whole important and respected youth dropped among the
cans – he had been given it by his parishioners in Concepción
on the fifth anniversary of his ordination . . . Somebody
moved behind a tree. He lifted his feet out of the rubbish –
flies burred round his ankles. With the papers hidden in his

fist he came round the trunk to see who was spying. . . .
The child sat on a root, kicking her heels against the bark.
Her eyes were shut tight fast. He said, 'My dear, what
is the matter with you . . .?' They came open quickly
then – red-rimmed and angry, with an expression of absurd
pride.

She said, 'You . . . you . . .'

'Me?'

'You are the matter.'

He moved towards her with infinite caution, as if she were
an animal who distrusted him. He felt weak with longing. He
said, 'My dear, why me . . .?'

She said furiously, 'They laugh at me.'

'Because of me?'

She said, 'Everyone else has a father . . . who works.'

'I work too.'

'You're a priest, aren't you?'

'Yes.'

'Pedro says you aren't a man. You aren't any good for
women.' She said, 'I don't know what he means.'

'I don't suppose he knows himself.'

'Oh, yes he does,' she said. 'He's ten. And I want to know.
You're going away, aren't you?'

'Yes.'

He was appalled again by her maturity, as she whipped up
a smile from a large and varied stock. She said, 'Tell me –'
enticingly. She sat there on the trunk of the tree by the rubbish-
tip with an effect of abandonment. The world was in her heart
already, like the small spot of decay in a fruit. She was without protection – she had no grace, no charm to plead for her;
his heart was shaken by the conviction of loss. He said, 'My
dear, be careful . . .'

'What of? Why are you going away?'

He came a little nearer; he thought – a man may kiss his
own daughter, but she started away from him. 'Don't you
touch me,' she screeched at him in her ancient voice and
giggled. Every child was born with some kind of knowledge
of love, he thought; they took it with the milk at the breast:

81

but on parents and friends depended the kind of love they knew – the saving or the damning kind. Lust too was a kind of love. He saw her fixed in her life like a fly in amber – Maria's hand raised to strike: Pedro talking prematurely in the dusk: and the police beating the forest – violence everywhere. He prayed silently, 'O God, give me any kind of death – without contrition, in a state of sin – only save this child.'

He was a man who was supposed to save souls. It had seemed quite simple once, preaching at Benediction, organizing the guilds, having coffee with elderly ladies behind barred windows, blessing new houses with a little incense, wearing black gloves ... It was as easy as saving money: now it was a mystery. He was aware of his own desperate inadequacy.

He went down on his knees and pulled her to him, while she giggled and struggled to be free: 'I love you. I am your father and I love you. Try to understand that.' He held her tightly by the wrist and suddenly she stayed still, looking up at him. He said, 'I would give my life, that's nothing, my soul ... my dear, my dear, try to understand that you are – so important.' That was the difference, he had always known, between his faith and theirs, the political leaders of the people who cared only for things like the state, the republic: this child was more important than a whole continent. He said, 'You must take care of yourself because you are so – necessary. The president up in the capital goes guarded by men with guns – but my child, you have all the angels of heaven –' She stared back at him out of dark and unconscious eyes; he had a sense that he had come too late. He said, 'Good-bye, my dear,' and clumsily kissed her – a silly infatuated ageing man, who as soon as he released her and started padding back to the plaza could feel behind his hunched shoulders the whole vile world coming round the child to ruin her. His mule was there, saddled, by the gaseosa stall. A man said, 'Better go north, father,' and stood waving his hand. One mustn't have human affections – or rather one must love every soul as if it were one's own child. The passion to protect must extend itself over a world – but he felt it tethered and aching like

82

a hobbled animal to the tree trunk. He turned his mule south.

He was travelling in the actual track of the police. So long as he went slowly and didn't overtake any stragglers it seemed a fairly safe route. What he wanted now was wine. Without it he was useless; he might as well escape north into the mountains and the safe state beyond, where the worst that could happen to him was a fine and a few days in prison because he couldn't pay. But he wasn't ready yet for the final surrender – every small surrender had to be paid for in a further endurance, and now he felt the need of somehow ransoming his child. He would stay another month, another year ... Jogging up and down on the mule he tried to bribe God with promises of firmness. . . . The mule suddenly dug in its hoofs and stopped dead: a tiny green snake raised itself on the path and then hissed away into the grass like a match-flame. The mule went on.

When he came near a village he would stop the mule and advance as close as he could on foot – the police might have stopped there. Then he would ride quickly through, speaking to nobody beyond a '*Buenos días*', and again on the forest path he would pick up the track of the lieutenant's horse. He had no clear idea now about anything; he only wanted to put as great a distance as possible between him and the village where he had spent the night. In one hand he still carried the crumpled ball of paper. Somebody had tied a bunch of about fifty bananas to his saddle, beside the machete and the small bag which contained his store of candles, and every now and then he ate one – ripe, brown, and sodden, tasting of soap. It left a smear like a moustache over his mouth.

After six hours' travelling he came to La Candelaria, which lay, a long mean tin-roofed village, beside one of the tributaries of the Grijalva River. He came cautiously out into the dusty street – it was early afternoon. The vultures sat on the roofs with their small heads hidden from the sun, and a few men lay in hammocks in the narrow shade the houses cast.

The mule plodded forward very slowly through the heavy day. The priest leant forward on his pommel.

The mule came to a stop of its own accord beside a hammock. A man lay in it, bunched diagonally, with one leg trailing to keep the hammock moving, up and down, up and down, making a tiny current of air. The priest said, '*Buenas tardes.*' The man opened his eyes and watched him.

'How far is it to Carmen?'

'Three leagues.'

'Can I get a canoe across the river?'

'Yes.'

'Where?'

The man waved a languid hand – as much as to say anywhere but here. He had only two teeth left, canines which stuck yellowly out at either end of his mouth like the teeth you find enclosed in clay which have belonged to long-extinct animals.

'What were the police doing here?' the priest asked, and a cloud of flies came down, settling on the mule's neck; he poked at them with a stick and they rose heavily, leaving a small trickle of blood, and dropped again on the tough grey skin. The mule seemed to feel nothing, standing in the sun with his head drooping.

'Looking for someone,' the man said.

'I've heard,' the priest said, 'that there's a reward out – for a gringo.'

The man swung his hammock back and forth. He said, 'It's better to be alive and poor than rich and dead.'

'Can I overtake them if I go towards Carmen?'

'They aren't going to Carmen.'

'No?'

'They are making for the city.'

The priest rode on. Twenty yards farther he stopped again beside a gaseosa stall and asked the boy in charge, 'Can I get a boat across the river?'

'There isn't a boat.'

'No boat?'

'Somebody stole it.'

'Give me a sidral.' He drank down the yellow bubbly chemical liquid: it left him thirstier than before. He said, 'How do I get across?'

'Why do you want to get across?'

'I'm making for Carmen. How did the police get over?'

'They swam.'

'*Mula, Mula,*' the priest said, urging the mule on, past the inevitable bandstand and a statue in florid taste of a woman in a toga waving a wreath. Part of the pedestal had been broken off and lay in the middle of the road – the mule went round it. The priest looked back; far down the street the mestizo was sitting upright in the hammock watching him. The mule turned off down a steep path to the river, and again the priest looked back – the half-caste was still in the hammock, but he had both feet upon the ground. An habitual uneasiness made the priest beat at the mule – '*Mula, Mula,*' but the mule took its time, sliding down the bank towards the river.

By the riverside it refused to enter the water. The priest split the end of his stick with his teeth and jabbed a sharp point into the mule's flank. It waded reluctantly in, and the water rose to the stirrups and then to the knees; the mule began to swim, splayed out flat with only the eyes and nostrils visible, like an alligator. Somebody shouted from the bank.

The priest looked round. At the river's edge the mestizo stood and called, not very loudly: his voice didn't carry. It was as if he had a secret purpose which nobody but the priest must hear. He waved his arm, summoning the priest back, but the mule lurched out of the water and up the bank beyond and the priest paid no attention – uneasiness was lodged in his brain. He urged the mule forward through the green half-light of a banana grove, not looking behind. All these years there had been two places to which he could always return and rest safely in hiding – one had been Concepción, his old parish, and that was closed to him now: the other was Carmen, where he had been born and where his parents were buried. He had imagined there might be a third, but he would never go back now. .... He turned the mule's head towards

Carmen, and the forest took them again. At this rate they would arrive in the dark, which was what he wanted. The mule unbeaten went with extreme langour, head drooping, smelling a little of blood. The priest, leaning forward on the high pommel, fell asleep. He dreamed that a small girl in stiff white muslin was reciting her Catechism – somewhere in the background, there was a bishop and a group of Children of Mary, elderly women with grey hard pious faces wearing pale blue ribbons. The bishop said, 'Excellent . . . Excellent,' and clapped his hands, plop, plop. A man in a morning coat said, 'There's a deficit of five hundred pesos on the new organ. We propose to hold a special musical performance, when it is hoped . . .' He remembered with appalling suddenness that he oughtn't to be there at all . . . he was in the wrong parish . . . he should be holding a retreat at Concepción. The man Montez appeared behind the child in white muslin, gesticulating, reminding him . . . Something had happened to Montez, he had a dry wound on his forehead. He felt with dreadful certainty a threat to the child. He said, 'My dear, my dear,' and woke to the slow rolling stride of the mule and the sound of footsteps.

He turned. It was the mestizo, padding behind him, dripping water: he must have swum the river. His two teeth stuck out over his lower lip, and he grinned ingratiatingly. 'What do you want?' the priest asked sharply.

'You didn't tell me you were going to Carmen.'

'Why should I?'

'You see, I want to go to Carmen, too. It's better to travel in company.' He was wearing a shirt, a pair of white trousers, and gym shoes through which one big toe showed – plump and yellow like something which lives underground. He scratched himself under the armpits and came chummily up to the priest's stirrup. He said, 'You are not offended, señor?'

'Why do you call me señor?'

'Anyone can tell you're a man of education.'

'The forest is free to all,' the priest said.

'Do you know Carmen well?' the man asked.

'Not well. I have a few friends.'

'You're going on business, I suppose?'

The priest said nothing. He could feel the man's hand on his foot, a light and deprecating touch. The man said, 'There's a *finca* off the road two leagues from here. It would be as well to stay the night.'

'I am in a hurry,' the priest said.

'But what good would it be reaching Carmen at one, two in the morning? We could sleep at the *finca* and be there before the sun was high.'

'I do what suits me.'

'Of course, señor, of course.' The man was silent for a little while, and then said, 'It isn't wise travelling at night if the señor hasn't got a gun. It's different for a man like me ...'

'I am a poor man,' the priest said. 'You can see for yourself. I am not worth robbing.'

'And then there's the gringo – they say he's a wild kind of a man, a real *pistolero*. He comes up to you and says in his own language – Stop: what is the way to – well, some place, and you do not understand what he is saying and perhaps you make a movement and he shoots you dead. But perhaps you know Americano, señor?'

'Of course I don't. How should I? I am a poor man. But I don't listen to every fairy-tale.'

'Do you come from far?'

The priest thought a moment: 'Concepción.' He could do no more harm there.

The man for the time being seemed satisfied. He walked along by the mule, a hand on the stirrup. Every now and then he spat. When the priest looked down he could see the big toe moving like a grub along the ground – he was probably harmless. It was the general condition of life that made for suspicion. The dusk fell and then almost at once the dark. The mule moved yet more slowly. Noise broke out all round them; it was like a theatre when the curtain falls and behind in the wings and passages hubbub begins. Things you couldn't put a name to – jaguars perhaps – cried in the undergrowth, monkeys moved in the upper boughs, and the mosquitoes hummed all round like sewing machines. 'It's thirsty walking,' the man said. 'Have you by any chance, señor, got a little drink . . . ?'

'No.'

'If you want to reach Carmen before three, you will have to beat the mule. Shall I take the stick . . . ?'

'No, no, let the brute take its time. It doesn't matter to me . . .' he said drowsily.

'You talk like a priest.'

He came quickly awake, but under the tall dark trees he could see nothing. He said, 'What nonsense you talk.'

'I am a very good Christian,' the man said, stroking the priest's foot.

'I dare say. I wish I were.'

'Ah, you ought to be able to tell which people you can trust.' He spat in a comradely way.

'I have nothing to trust anyone with,' the priest said. 'Except these trousers – they are very torn. And this mule – it isn't a good mule; you can see for yourself.'

There was silence for a while, and then, as if he had been considering the last statement, the half-caste went on, 'It wouldn't be a bad mule if you treated it right. Nobody can teach me anything about mules. I can see for myself it's tired out.'

The priest looked down at the grey swinging stupid head. 'Do you think so?'

'How far did you travel yesterday?'

'Perhaps twelve leagues.'

'Even a mule needs rest.'

The priest took his bare feet from out of the deep leather stirrups and scrambled to the ground. The mule for less than a minute took a longer stride and then dropped to a yet slower pace. The twigs and roots of the forest path cut the priest's feet – after five minutes he was bleeding. He tried in vain not to limp. The half-caste exclaimed, 'How delicate your feet are. You should wear shoes.'

Stubbornly he reasserted, 'I am a poor man.'

'You will never get to Carmen at this rate. Be sensible, man. If you don't want to go as far off the road as the *finca*,

I know a little hut less than half a league from here. We can sleep a few hours and still reach Carmen at daybreak.' There was a rustle in the grass beside the path – the priest thought of snakes and his unprotected feet. The mosquitoes jabbed at his wrists; they were like little surgical syringes filled with poison and aimed at the bloodstream. Sometimes a firefly held its lighted globe close to the half-caste's face, turning it on and off like a torch. He said accusingly, 'You don't trust me. Just because I am a man who likes to do a good turn to strangers, because I try to be a Christian, you don't trust me.' He seemed to be working himself into a little artificial rage. He said, 'If I wanted to rob you, couldn't I have done it already? You're an old man.'

'Not so very old,' the priest said mildly. His conscience began automatically to work: it was like a slot machine into which any coin could be fitted, even a cheater's blank disk. The words proud, lustful, envious, cowardly, ungrateful – they all worked the right springs – he was all these things. The half-caste said, 'Here I have spent many hours guiding you to Carmen – I don't want any reward because I am a good Christian. I have probably lost money by it at home – never mind that . . .'

'I thought you said you had business in Carmen?' the priest said gently.

'When did I say that?' It was true – he couldn't remember . . . perhaps he was unjust too . . . 'Why should I say a thing which isn't true? No, I give up a whole day to helping you, and you pay no attention when your guide is tired . . .'

'I didn't need a guide,' he protested mildly.

'You say that when the road is plain, but if it wasn't for me, you'd have taken the wrong path a long time ago. You said yourselı you didn't know Carmen well. That was why I came.'

'But of course,' the priest said, 'if you are tired, we will rest.' He felt guilty at his own lack of trust, but all the same, it remained like a growth only a knife could rid him of.

After half an hour they came to the hut. Made of mud and twigs, it had been set up in a minute clearing by a small farmer whom the forest must have driven out, edging in on him, an unstayable natural force which he couldn't defeat with his machete and his small fires. There were still signs in the blackened ground of an attempt to clear the brushwood for some meagre and inadequate crop. The man said, 'I will see to the mule. You go in and lie down and rest.'

'But it is you who are tired.'

'Me tired?' the half-caste said. 'What makes you say that? I am never tired.'

With a heavy heart the priest took off his saddlebag, pushed at the door and went in to complete darkness. He struck a light – there was no furniture; only a raised dais of hard earth and a straw mat too torn to have been worth removing. He lit a candle and stuck it in its own wax on the dais: then sat down and waited: the man was a long time. In one fist he still carried the ball of paper salvaged from his case – a man must retain some sentimental relics if he is to live at all. The argument of danger only applies to those who live in relative safety. He wondered whether the mestizo had stolen his mule, and reproached himself for the necessary suspicion. Then the door opened and the man came in – the two yellow canine teeth, the finger-nails scratching in the armpit. He sat down on the earth, with his back against the door, and said, 'Go to sleep. You are tired. I'll wake you when we need to start.'

'I'm not very sleepy.'

'Blow out the candle. You'll sleep better.'

'I don't like darkness,' the priest said. He was afraid.

'Won't you say a prayer, father, before we sleep?'

'Why do you call me that?' he asked sharply, peering across the shadowy floor to where the half-caste sat against the door.

'Oh, I guessed, of course. But you needn't be afraid of me. I'm a good Christian.'

'You're wrong.'

'I could easily find out, couldn't I?' the half-caste said. 'I'd just have to say – father, hear my confession. You couldn't refuse a man in mortal sin.'

The priest said nothing, waiting for the demand to come: the hand which held the papers twitched. 'Oh, you needn't fear me,' the mestizo went carefully on. 'I wouldn't betray you. I'm a Christian. I just thought a prayer ... would be good ...'

'You don't need to be a priest to know a prayer.' He began, '*Pater noster qui es in coelis ...*' while the mosquitoes came droning towards the candle-flame. He was determined not to sleep – the man had some plan. His conscience ceased to accuse him of uncharity. He knew. He was in the presence of Judas.

He leant his head back against the wall and half closed his eyes – he remembered Holy Week in the old days when a stuffed Judas was hanged from the belfry and boys made a clatter with tins and rattles as he swung out over the door. Old staid members of the congregation had sometimes raised objections: it was blasphemous, they said, to make this ьuy out of Our Lord's betrayer; but he had said nothing and let the practice continue – it seemed to him a good thing that the world's traitor should be made a figure of fun. It was too easy otherwise to idealize him as a man who fought with God – a Prometheus, a noble victim in a hopeless war.

'Are you awake?' a voice whispered from the door. The priest suddenly giggled, as if this man, too, were absurd with stuffed straw legs and a painted face and an old straw hat who would presently be burnt in the plaza while people made political speeches and the fireworks went off.

'Can't you sleep?'

'I was dreaming,' the priest whispered. He opened his eyes and saw the man by the door was shivering – the two sharp teeth jumped up and down on the lower lip. 'Are you ill?'

'A little fever,' the man said. 'Have you any medicine?'

'No.'

The door creaked as the man's back shook. He said, 'It was getting wet in the river ...' He slid farther down upon the floor and closed his eyes – mosquitoes with singed wings crawled over the earth bed. The priest thought: I mustn't sleep, it's dangerous, I must watch him. He opened his fist and smoothed out the paper. There were faint pencil lines visible – single words, the beginnings and ends of sentences, figures. Now that his case was gone, it was the only evidence left that life had ever been different: he carried it with him as a charm, because if life had been like that once, it might be so again. The candle-flame in the hot marshy lowland air burned to a smoky point vibrating. ... The priest held the paper close to it and read the words Altar Society, Guild of the Blessed Sacrament, Children of Mary, and then looked up again and across the dark hut saw the yellow malarial eyes of the mestizo watching him. Christ would not have found Judas sleeping in the garden: Judas could watch more than one hour.

'What's that paper . . . father?' he said enticingly, shivering against the door.

'Don't call me father. It is a list of seeds I have to buy in Carmen.'

'Can you write?'

'I can read.'

He looked at the paper again and a little mild impious joke stared up at him in faded pencil – something about 'of one substance'. He had been referring to his corpulency and the good dinner he had just eaten: the parishioners had not much relished his humour.

It had been a dinner given at Concepción in honour of the tenth anniversary of his ordination. He sat in the middle of the table with – who was it on his right hand? There were twelve dishes – he had said something about the Apostles, too, which was not thought to be in the best of taste. He was quite young and he had been moved by a gentle devilry, surrounded by all the pious and middle-aged and respectable people of Concepción, wearing their guild ribbons and badges. He had drunk just a little too much; in those days he wasn't used to liquor. It came back to him now suddenly who was on his right hand – it was Montez, the father of the man they had shot.

Montez had talked at some length. He had reported the progress of the Altar Society in the last year – they had a balance in hand of twenty-two pesos. He had noted it down for comment – there it was, A.S. 22. Montez had been very anxious to start a branch of the Society of St Vincent de Paul, and some woman had complained that bad books were being sold in Concepción, fetched in from the capital by mule: her child had got hold of one called *A Husband for a Night*. In his speech he said he would write to the Governor on the subject.

The moment he had said that the local photographer had set off his flare, and so he could remember himself at that instant, just as if he had been a stranger looking in from the outside – attracted by the noise – on some happy and festal and strange occasion: noticing with envy, and perhaps a little amusement, the fat youngish priest who stood with one plump hand splayed authoritatively out while the tongue played pleasantly with the word 'Governor'. Mouths were open all round fishily, and the faces glowed magnesium-white, with the lines and individuality wiped out.

That moment of authority had jerked him back to seriousness – he had ceased to unbend and everybody was happier. He said, 'The balance of twenty-two pesos in the accounts of the Altar Society – though quite revolutionary for Concepción – is not the only cause for congratulation in the last year. The Children of Mary have increased their membership by nine – and the Guild of the Blessed Sacrament last autumn made our annual retreat more than usually successful. But we mustn't rest on our laurels, and I confess I have got plans you may find a little startling. You already think me a man, I know, of inordinate ambitions – well, I want Concepción to have a better school – and that means a better presbytery too, of course. We are a big parish and the priest has a position to keep up. I'm not thinking of myself but of the Church. And we shall not stop there – though it will take a good many years, I'm afraid, even in a place the size of Concepción, to raise the money for that.' As he talked a whole serene life lay ahead – he *had* ambition: he saw no reason why one day he might not find himself in the state capital, attached to the cathedral, leaving another man to pay off the debts in Concepción. An energetic priest was always known by his debts. He went on, waving a plump and eloquent hand, 'Of course, many dangers here in Mexico threaten our dear Church. In this state we are unusually lucky – men have lost their lives in the north and we must be prepared' – he refreshed his dry mouth with a draught of wine – 'for the worst. Watch and pray,' he went vaguely on, 'watch and pray. The devil like a raging lion –' The Children of Mary stared up at him with their mouths a little open, the pale blue ribbons slanting across their dark best blouses.

He talked for a long while, enjoying the sound of his own voice: he had discouraged Montez on the subject of the St Vincent de Paul Society, because you had to be careful not to encourage a layman too far, and he had told a charming story about a child's deathbed – she was dying of consumption very firm in her faith at the age of eleven. She asked who it was standing at the end of her bed, and they had said, 'That's Father So-and-so,' and she had said, 'No, no. I know Father So-and-so. I mean the one with the golden crown.' One of the Guild of the Blessed Sacrament had wept. Everybody was very happy. It was a true story too, though he couldn't quite remember where he had heard it. Perhaps he had read it in a book once. Somebody refilled his glass. He took a long breath and said, 'My children . . .'

. . . and as the mestizo stirred and grunted by the door he opened his eyes and the old life peeled away like a label: he was lying in torn peon trousers in a dark unventilated hut with a price upon his head. The whole world had changed – no church anywhere: no brother priest, except Padre José, the outcast, in the capital. He lay listening to the heavy breathing of the half-caste and wondered why he had not gone the same road as Padre José and conformed to the laws. I was too ambitious, he thought, that was it. Perhaps Padre José was the better man – he was so humble that he was ready to accept any amount of mockery; at the best of times he had never considered himself worthy of the priesthood. There had been a conference once of the parochial clergy in the capital, in the happy days of the old governor, and he could remember Padre José slinking in at the tail of every meeting, curled up

94

half out of sight in a back row, never opening his mouth. It was not, like some more intellectual priests, that he was over-scrupulous: he had been simply filled with an overwhelming sense of God. At the Elevation of the Host you could see his hands trembling – he was not like St Thomas who needed to put his hands into the wounds in order to believe: the wounds bled anew for him over every altar. Once Padre José had said to him in a burst of confidence, 'Every time ... I have such fear.' His father had been a peon.

But it was different in his case – he had ambition. He was no more an intellectual than Padre José, but his father was a storekeeper, and he knew the value of a balance of twenty-two pesos and how to manage mortgages. He wasn't content to remain all his life the priest of a not very large parish. His ambitions came back to him now as something faintly comic, and he gave a little gulp of astonished laughter in the candle-light. The half-caste opened his eyes and said, 'Are you still not asleep?'

'Sleep yourself,' the priest said, wiping a little sweat off his face with his sleeve.

'I am so cold.'

'Just a fever. Would you like this shirt? It isn't much, but it might help.'

'No, no. I don't want anything of yours. You don't trust me.'

No, if he had been humble like Padre José, he might be living in the capital now with Maria on a pension. This was pride, devilish pride, lying here offering his shirt to the man who wanted to betray him. Even his attempts at escape had been half-hearted because of his pride – the sin by which the angels fell. When he was the only priest left in the state his pride had been all the greater; he thought himself the devil of a fellow carrying God around at the risk of his life; one day there would be a reward. .... He prayed in the half-light: 'O God, forgive me – I am a proud, lustful, greedy man. I have loved authority too much. These people are martyrs – protecting me with their own lives. They deserve a martyr to care for them – not a man like me, who loves all the wrong things. Perhaps I had better escape – if I tell people how it is

95

over here, perhaps they will send a good man with a fire of love . . .' As usual his self-confession dwindled away into the practical problem – what am I to do?

Over by the door the mestizo was uneasily asleep.

How little his pride had to feed on – he had celebrated only four Masses this year, and he had heard perhaps a hundred confessions. It seemed to him that the dunce of any seminary could have done as well . . . or better. He raised himself very carefully and began to move on his naked toes across the floor. He must get to Carmen and away again quickly before this man . . . the mouth was open, showing the pale hard toothless gums. In his sleep he was grunting and struggling; then he collapsed upon the floor and lay still.

There was a sense of abandonment, as if he had given up every struggle from now on and lay there a victim of some power. . . . The priest had only to step over his legs and push the door – it opened outwards.

He put one leg over the body and a hand gripped his ankle. The mestizo stared up at him. 'Where are you going?'

'I want to relieve myself,' the priest said.

The hand still held his ankle. 'Why can't you do it here?' the man whined at him. 'What's preventing you, father? You are a father, aren't you?'

'I have a child,' the priest said, 'if that's what you mean.'

'You know what I mean. You understand about God, don't you?' The hot hand clung. 'Perhaps you've got him there – in a pocket. You carry him around, don't you, in case there's anybody sick. . . . Well, I'm sick. Why don't you give him to me? or do you think he wouldn't have anything to do with me . . . if he knew?'

'You're feverish.'

But the man wouldn't stop. The priest was reminded of an oil-gusher which some prospectors had once struck near Concepción – it wasn't a good enough field apparently to justify further operations, but there it had stood for forty-eight hours against the sky, a black fountain spouting out of the marshy useless soil and flowing away to waste – fifty thousand gallons an hour. It was like the religious sense in man, cracking

96

suddenly upwards, a black pillar of fumes and impurity, running to waste. 'Shall I tell you what I've done? – It's your business to listen. I've taken money from women to do you know what, and I've given money to boys . . .'

'I don't want to hear.'

'It's your business.'

'You're mistaken.'

'Oh no, I'm not. You can't deceive me. Listen. I've given money to boys – you know what I mean. And I've eaten meat on Fridays.' The awful jumble of the gross, the trivial, and the grotesque shot up between the two yellow fangs, and the hand on the priest's ankle shook and shook with the fever. 'I've told lies, I haven't fasted in Lent for I don't know how many years. Once I had two women – I'll tell you what I did . . .' He had an immense self-importance; he was unable to picture a world of which he was only a typical part – a world of treachery, violence, and lust in which his shame was altogether insignificant. How often the priest had heard the same confession – Man was so limited he hadn't even the ingenuity to invent a new vice: the animals knew as much. It was for this world that Christ had died; the more evil you saw and heard about you, the greater glory lay around the death. It was too easy to die for what was good or beautiful, for home or children or a civilization – it needed a God to die for the half-hearted and the corrupt. He said, 'Why do you tell me all this?'

The man lay exhausted, saying nothing; he was beginning to sweat, his hand loosed its hold on the priest's ankle. He pushed the door open and went outside – the darkness was complete. How to find the mule? He stood listening – something howled not very far away. He was frightened. Back in the hut the candle burned – there was an odd bubbling sound: the man was weeping. Again he was reminded of oil land, the little black pools and the bubbles blowing slowly up and breaking and beginning again.

The priest struck a match and walked straight forward – one, two, three paces into a tree. A match in that immense darkness was of no more value than a firefly. He whispered,

'*Mula, mula,*' afraid to call out in case the half-caste heard him; besides, it was unlikely that the stupid beast would make any reply. He hated it – the lurching mandarin head, the munching greedy mouth, the smell of blood and ordure. He struck another match and set off again, and again after a few paces he met a tree. Inside the hut the gaseous sound of grief went on. He had got to get to Carmen and away before that man found a means of communicating with the police. He began again, quartering the clearing – one, two, three, four – and then a tree. Something moved under his foot, and he thought of scorpions. One, two, three, and suddenly the grotesque cry of the mule came out of the dark; it was hungry, or perhaps it smelt some animal.

It was tethered a few yards behind the hut – the candle-flame swerved out of sight. His matches were running low, but after two more attempts he found the mule. The half-caste had stripped it and hidden the saddle. He couldn't waste time looking any more. He mounted, and only then realized how impossible it was to make it move without even a piece of rope round the neck; he tried twisting its ears, but they had no more sensitivity than door-handles: it stood planted there like an equestrian statue. He struck a match and held the flame against its side – it struck up suddenly with its back hooves and he dropped the match; then it was still again, with drooping sullen head and great antediluvian haunches. A voice said accusingly, 'You are leaving me here to die.'

'Nonsense,' the priest said. 'I am in a hurry. You will be all right in the morning, but I can't wait.'

There was a scuffle in the darkness and then a hand gripped his naked foot. 'Don't leave me alone,' the voice said. 'I appeal to you – as a Christian.'

'You won't come to any harm here.'

'How do you know with the gringo somewhere about?'

'I don't know anything about the gringo. I've met nobody who has seen him. Besides, he's only a man – like one of us.'

'I won't be left alone. I have an instinct . . .'

'Very well,' the priest said wearily, 'find the saddle.'

When they had saddled the mule they set off again, the

98

mestizo holding the stirrup. They were silent – sometimes the half-caste stumbled, and the grey false dawn began; a small coal of cruel satisfaction glowed at the back of the priest's mind – this was Judas sick and unsteady and scared in the dark. He had only to beat the mule on to leave him stranded in the forest once he dug in the point of his stick and forced it forward at a weary trot, and he could feel the pull, pull of the half-caste's arm on the stirrup holding him back. There was a groan – it sounded like 'Mother of God', and he let the mule slacken its pace. He prayed silently, 'God forgive me.' Christ had died for this man too: how could he pretend with his pride and lust and cowardice to be any more worthy of that death than the half-caste? This man intended to betray him for money which he needed, and he had betrayed God for what? Not even for real lust. He said, 'Are you sick?' and there was no reply. He dismounted and said, 'Get up. I'll walk for a while.'

'I'm all right,' the man said in a tone of hatred.

'Better get up.'

'You think you're very fine,' the man said. 'Helping your enemies. That's Christian, isn't it?'

'Are you my enemy?'

'That's what you think. You think I want seven hundred pesos – that's the reward. You think a poor man like me can't afford not to tell the police...'

'You're feverish.'

The man said in a sick voice of cunning, 'You're right, of course.'

'Better mount.' The man nearly fell: he had to shoulder him up. He leant hopelessly down from the mule with his mouth almost on a level with the priest's, breathing bad air into the other's face. He said, 'A poor man has no choice, father. Now if I was a rich man – only a little rich – I should be good.'

The priest suddenly – for no reason – thought of the Children of Mary eating pastries. He giggled and said, 'I doubt it.' If that were goodness...

'What was that you said, father? You don't trust me,' he went ambling on, 'because I'm poor, and because you don't

99

trust me – ' he collapsed over the pommel of the saddle, breathing heavily and shivering. The priest held him on with one hand and they proceeded slowly towards Carmen. It was no good; he couldn't stay there now. It would be unwise even to enter the village, for if it became known, somebody would lose his life – they would take a hostage. Somewhere a long way off a cock crew. The mist came up knee-high out of a spongy ground, and he thought of the flashlight going off in the bare church hall among the trestle tables. What hour did the cocks crow? One of the oddest things about the world these days was that there were no clocks – you could go a year without hearing one strike. They went with the churches, and you were left with the grey slow dawns and the precipitate nights as the only measurements of time.

Slowly, slumped over the pommel, the half-caste became visible, the yellow canines jutting out of the open mouth; really, the priest thought, he deserved his reward – seven hundred pesos wasn't so much, but he could probably live on it – in that dusty hopeless village – for a whole year. He giggled again; he could never take the complications of destiny quite seriously, and it was just possible, he thought, that a year without anxiety might save this man's soul. You only had to turn up the underside of any situation and out came scuttling these small absurd contradictory situations. He had given way to despair – and out of that had emerged a human soul and love – not the best love, but love all the same. The mestizo said suddenly, 'It's fate. I was told once by a fortune-teller... a reward...'

He held the half-caste firmly in the saddle and walked on. His feet were bleeding, but they would soon harden. An odd stillness dropped over the forest, and welled up in the mist from the ground. The night had been noisy, but now all was quiet. It was like an armistice with the guns silent on either side: you could imagine the whole world listening to what they had never heard before – peace.

A voice said 'You *are* the priest, aren't you?'

'Yes.' It was as if they had climbed out of their opposing trenches and met to fraternize among the wires in No Man's

100

Land. He remembered stories of the European war – how during the last years men had sometimes met on an impulse between the lines.

'Yes,' he said again, and the mule plodded on. Sometimes, instructing children in the old days, he had been asked by some black lozenge-eyed Indian child, 'What is God like?' and he would answer facilely with references to the father and the mother, or perhaps more ambitiously he would include brother and sister and try to give some idea of all loves and relationships combined in an immense and yet personal passion. . . . But at the centre of his own faith there always stood the convincing mystery – that we were made in God's image. God was the parent, but He was also the policeman, the criminal, the priest, the maniac, and the judge. Something resembling God dangled from the gibbet or went into odd attitudes before the bullets in a prison yard or contorted itself like a camel in the attitude of sex. He would sit in the confessional and hear the complicated dirty ingenuities which God's image had thought out, and God's image shook now, up and down on the mule's back, with the yellow teeth sticking out over the lower lip, and God's image did its despairing act of rebellion with Maria in the hut among the rats. He said, 'Do you feel better now? Not so cold, eh? Or so hot?' and pressed his hand with a kind of driven tenderness upon the shoulders of God's image.

The man didn't answer, as the mule's backbone slid him first to one side, then the other.

'It isn't more than two leagues now,' the priest said encouragingly – he had to make up his mind. He carried around with him a clearer picture of Carmen than any other village or town in the state: the long slope of grass which led up from the river to the cemetery on a tiny hill where his parents were buried. The wall of the burial-ground had fallen in: one or two crosses had been smashed by enthusiasts: an angel had lost one of its stone wings, and what gravestones were left undamaged leant at an acute angle in the long marshy grass. One image of the Mother of God had lost ears and arms and stood like a pagan Venus over the grave of some rich forgotten timber merchant. It was odd -- this fury to deface, because, of course, you could never deface enough. If God had been like a toad, you could have rid the globe of toads, but when God was like yourself, it was no good being content with stone figures – you had to kill yourself among the graves.

He said, 'Are you strong enough now to hold on?' He took away his hand. The path divided – one way led to Carmen, the other west. He pushed the mule on, down the Carmen path, flogging at its haunches. He said, 'You'll be there in two hours,' and stood watching the mule go on towards his home with the informer humped over the pommel.

The half-caste tried to sit upright. 'Where are you going?'

'You'll be my witness,' the priest said. 'I haven't been in Carmen. But if you mention me, they'll give you food.'

'Why . . . why . . .' The half-caste tried to wrench round the mule's head, but he hadn't enough strength: it just went on. The priest called out, 'Remember. I haven't been in Carmen.' But where else now could he go? The conviction came to him that there was only one place in the whole state where there was no danger of an innocent man being taken as a hostage – but he couldn't go there in these clothes. . . . The half-caste held hard on to the pommel and swivelled his yellow eyes beseechingly, 'You wouldn't leave me here – alone.' But it was more than the half-caste he was leaving behind on the forest track: the mule stood sideways like a barrier, nodding a stupid head, between him and the place where he had been born. He felt like a man without a passport who is turned away from every harbour.

The half-caste was calling after him, 'Call yourself a Christian.' He had somehow managed to get himself upright. He began to shout abuse – a meaningless series of indecent words which petered out in the forest like the weak blows of a hammer. He whispered, 'If I see you again, you can't blame *me* . . .' Of course, he had every reason to be angry: he had lost seven hundred pesos. He shrieked hopelessly, 'I don't forget a face.'

## Chapter 2

THE young men and women walked round and round the plaza in the hot electric night, the men one way, the girls another, never speaking to each other. In the northern sky the lightning flapped. It was like a religious ceremony which had lost all meaning, but at which they still wore their best clothes. Sometimes a group of older women would join in the procession with a little more excitement and laughter, as if they retained some memory of how things used to go before all the books were lost. A man with a gun on his hip watched from the Treasury steps, and a small withered soldier sat by the prison door with a gun between his knees and the shadows of the palms pointed at him like a zareba of sabres. Lights were burning in a dentist's window, shining on the swivel chair and the red plush cushions and the glass for rinsing on its little stand and the child's chest-of-drawers full of fittings. Behind the wire-netted windows of the private houses grandmothers swung back and forth in rocking-chairs, among the family photographs – nothing to do, nothing to say, with too many clothes on, sweating a little. This was the capital city of a state.

The man in the shabby drill suit watched it all from a bench. A squad of armed police went by to their quarters walking out of step, carrying their rifles anyhow. The plaza was lit at each corner by clusters of three globes joined by ugly trailing overhead wires, and a beggar worked his way from seat to seat without success.

He sat down next to the man in drill and started a long explanation. There was something confidential, and at the same time threatening, in his manner. On every side the streets ran down towards the river and the port and the marshy plain. He said that he had a wife and so many children, and that during the last few week they had eaten so little – he broke off and fingered the cloth of the other's drill suit. 'And how much,' he said, 'did this cost?'

'You'd be surprised how little.'

103

Suddenly as a clock struck nine-thirty all the lights went out. The beggar said, 'It's enough to make a man desperate.' He looked this way and that as the parade drifted away down hill. The man in drill got up, and the other got up too, tagging after him towards the edge of the plaza: his flat bare feet went slap, slap on the pavement. He said, 'A few pesos wouldn't make any difference to you...'

'Ah, if you knew what a difference they would make.'

The beggar was put out. He said, 'A man like me sometimes feels that he would do anything for a few pesos.' Now that the lights were out all over town, they stood intimately in the shadow. He said, 'Can you blame me?'

'No, no. It would be the last thing I would do.'

Everything he said seemed to feed the beggar's irritation. 'Sometimes,' the beggar said, 'I feel as if I could kill...'

'That, of course, would be very wrong.'

'Would it be wrong if I got a man by the throat...?'

'Well, a starving man has got the right to save himself, certainly.'

The beggar watched with rage, while the other talked on as if he were considering a point of academic interest. 'In my case, of course, it would hardly be worth the risk. I possess exactly fifteen pesos seventy-five centavos in the world. I haven't eaten myself for forty-eight hours.'

'Mother of God,' the beggar said, 'you're as hard as a stone. Haven't you a heart?'

The man in the drill suit suddenly giggled. The other said, 'You're lying. Why haven't you eaten – if you've got fifteen pesos?'

'You see, I want to spend them on drink.'

'What sort of drink?'

'The kind of drink a stranger doesn't know how to get in a place like this.'

'You mean spirits?'

'Yes – and wine.'

The beggar came very close. His leg touched the leg of the other man, he put a hand upon the other's sleeve. They might have been great friends or even brothers standing intimately

104

together in the dark. Even the lights in the houses were going out now, and the taxis, which during the day waited half-way down the hill for fares that never seemed to come, were already dispersing – a tail-lamp winked and went out past the police barracks. The beggar said, 'Man, this is your lucky day. How much would you pay me...?'

'For some drink?'

'For an introduction to someone who could let you have a little brandy – real fine Vera Cruz brandy.'

'With a throat like mine,' the man in drill explained, 'it's wine I really want.'

'Pulque or mescal – he's got everything.'

'Wine?'

'Quince wine.'

'I'd give everything I've got,' the other swore solemnly and exactly, ' – except the centavos, that's to say – for some real genuine grape wine.' Somewhere down the hill by the river a drum was beating, one-two, one-two, and the sound of marching feet kept a rough time: the soldiers – or the police – were going home to bed.

'How much?' the beggar repeated impatiently.

'Well, I would give you the fifteen pesos and you would get the wine for me for what you cared to spend.'

'You come with me.'

They began to go down the hill. At the corner where one street ran up past the chemist's shop towards the barracks and another ran down to the hotel, the quay, the warehouse of the United Banana Company, the man in drill stopped. The police were marching up, rifles slung at ease. 'Wait a moment.' Among them walked a half-caste with two fang-like teeth jutting out over his lip. The man in drill standing in the shadow watched him go by: once the mestizo turned his head and their eyes met. Then the police went by, up into the plaza. 'Let's go. Quickly.'

The beggar said, 'They won't interfere with us. They're after bigger game.'

'What was that man doing with them, do you think?'

'Who knows? A hostage perhaps.'

'If he had been a hostage, they would have tied his hands, wouldn't they?'

'How do I know?' He had the grudging independence you find in countries where it is the right of a poor man to beg. He said, 'Do you want the spirits or don't you?'

'I want wine.'

'I can't say he'll have this or that. You must take what comes.'

He led the way down towards the river. He said, 'I don't even know if he's in town.' The beetles were flocking out and covering the pavements; they popped under the feet like puff-balls, and a sour green smell came up from the river. The white bust of a general glimmered in a tiny public garden, all hot paving and dust, and an electric dynamo throbbed on the ground floor of the only hotel. Wide wooden stairs crawling with beetles ran up to the first floor. 'I've done my best,' the beggar said, 'a man can't do more.'

On the first floor a man dressed in formal dark trousers and a white skin-tight vest came out of a bedroom with a towel over his shoulder. He had a little grey aristocratic beard and he wore braces as well as a belt. Somewhere in the distance a pipe gurgled, and the beetles detonated against a bare globe. The beggar was talking earnestly, and once as he talked the light went off altogether and then flickered unsatisfactorily on again. The head of the stairs was littered with wicker rocking-chairs, and on a big slate were chalked the names of the guests – three only for twenty rooms.

The beggar turned back to his companion. 'The gentleman,' he said, 'is not in. The manager says so. Shall we wait for him?'

'Time to me is of no account.'

They went into a big bare bedroom with a tiled floor. The little black iron bedstead was like something somebody has left behind by accident when moving out. They sat down on it side by side and waited, and the beetles came popping in through the gaps in the mosquito wire. 'He is a very important man,' the beggar said. 'He is the cousin of the Governor – he can get anything for you, anything at all. But, of course, you must be introduced by someone he trusts.'

106

'And he trusts you?'

'I worked for him once.' He added frankly, 'He has to trust me.'

'Does the Governor know?'

'Of course not. The Governor is a hard man.'

Every now and then the water-pipes swallowed noisily.

'And why should he trust me?'

'Oh, anyone can tell a drinker. You'll want to come back for more. It's good stuff he sells. Better give me the fifteen pesos.' He counted them carefully twice. He said, 'I'll get you a bottle of the best Vera Cruz brandy. You see if I don't.' The light went off, and they sat in the dark; the bed creaked as one of them shifted.

'I don't want brandy,' a voice said. 'At least – not very much.'

'What do you want then?'

'I told you – wine.'

'Wine's expensive.'

'Never mind that. Wine or nothing.'

'Quince wine?'

'No, no. French wine.'

'Sometimes he has Californian wine.'

'That would do.'

'Of course himself – he gets it for nothing. From the Customs.'

The dynamo began throbbing again below and the light came dimly on. The door opened and the manager beckoned the beggar; a long conversation began. The man in the drill suit leant back on the bed. His chin was cut in several places where he had been shaving too closely; his face was hollow and ill – it gave the impression that he had once been plump and round-faced but had caved in. He had the appearance of a business man who had fallen on hard times.

The beggar came back. He said, 'The gentleman's busy, but he'll be back soon. The manager sent a boy to look for him.'

'Where is he?'

'He can't be interrupted. He's playing billiards with the

107

Chief of Police.' He came back to the bed, squashing two beetles under his naked feet. He said, 'This is a fine hotel. Where do you stay? You're a stranger, aren't you?'

'Oh, I'm just passing through.'

'This gentleman is very influential. It would be a good thing to offer him a drink. After all, you won't want to take it all away with you. You may as well drink here as anywhere else.'

'I should like to keep a little – to take home.'

'It's all one. I say that home is where there is a chair and a glass.'

'All the same — ' Then the light went out again, and on the horizon the lightning bellied out. The sound of thunder came through the mosquito-net from very far away like the noise you hear from the other end of a town when the Sunday bull-fight is on.

The beggar said confidentially, 'What's your trade?'

'Oh, I pick up what I can – where I can.'

They sat in silence together listening to the sound of feet on the wooden stairs. The door opened, but they could see nothing. A voice swore resignedly and asked, 'Who's there?' Then a match was struck and showed a large blue jaw and went out. The dynamo churned away and the light went on again. The stranger said wearily, 'Oh, it's you.'

'It's me.'

He was a small man with a too large pasty face and he was dressed in a tight grey suit. A revolver bulged under his waistcoat. He said, 'I've got nothing for you. Nothing.'

The beggar padded across the room and began to talk earnestly in a very low voice: once he gently squeezed the other's polished shoe with his bare toes. The man sighed and blew out his cheeks and watched the bed closely as if he feared they had designs on it. He said sharply to the one in the drill suit, 'So you want some Vera Cruz brandy, do you? It's against the law.'

'Not brandy. I don't want brandy.'

'Isn't beer good enough for you?'

He came fussily and authoritatively into the middle of the

108

room, his shoes squeaking on the tiles – the Governor's cousin. 'I could have you arrested,' he threatened.

The man in the drill suit cringed formally. He said, 'Of course, your Excellency...'

'Do you think I've got nothing better to do than slake the thirst of every beggar who chooses...?'

'I would never have troubled you if this man had not...'

The Governor's cousin spat on the tiles.

'But if your Excellency would rather I went away...'

He said sharply, 'I'm not a hard man. I always try to oblige my fellows ... when it's in my power and does no harm. I have a position, you understand. These drinks come to me quite legally.'

'Of course.'

'And I have to charge what they cost me.'

'Of course.'

'Otherwise I'd be a ruined man.' He walked delicately to the bed as if his shoes were cramping him and began to unmake it. 'Are you a talker?' he asked over his shoulder.

'I know how to keep a secret.'

'I don't mind you telling the right people.' There was a large rent in the mattress; he pulled out a handful of straw and put his fingers in again. The man in drill gazed out with false indifference at the public gardens, the dark mud-banks and the masts of sailing ships; the lightning flapped behind them, and the thunder came nearer.

'There,' said the Governor's cousin, 'I can spare you that. It's good stuff.'

'It wasn't really brandy I wanted.'

'You must take what comes.'

'Then I think I'd rather have my fifteen pesos back.'

The Governor's cousin exclaimed sharply, '*Fifteen* pesos.' The beggar began rapidly to explain that the gentleman wanted to buy a little wine as well as brandy: they began to argue fiercely by the bed in low voices about prices. The Governor's cousin said, 'Wine's very difficult to get. I can let you have two bottles of brandy.'

'One of brandy and one of...'

'It's the best Vera Cruz brandy.'

'But I am a wine drinker . . . you don't know how I long for wine . . .'

'Wine costs me a great deal of money. How much more can you pay?'

'I have only seventy-five centavos left in the world.'

'I could let you have a bottle of tequila.'

'No, no.'

'Another fifty centavos then. . . . It will be a large bottle.' He began to scrabble in the mattress again, pulling out straw. The beggar winked at the man in drill and made the motions of drawing a cork and filling a glass.

'There,' the Governor's cousin said, 'take it or leave it.'

'Oh, I will take it.'

The Governor's cousin suddenly lost his surliness. He rubbed his hands and said, 'A stuffy night. The rains are going to be early this year, I think.'

'Perhaps your Excellency would honour me by taking a glass of brandy to toast our business.'

'Well, well . . . perhaps . . .' The beggar opened the door and called briskly for glasses.

'It's a long time,' the Governor's cousin said, 'since I had a glass of wine. Perhaps it would be more suitable for a toast.'

'Of course,' the man in drill said, 'as your Excellency chooses.' He watched the cork drawn with a look of painful anxiety. He said, 'If you will excuse me, I think I will have brandy,' and smiled raggedly, with an effort, watching the wine level fall.

They toasted each other, all three sitting on the bed – the beggar drank brandy. The Governor's cousin said, 'I'm proud of this wine. It's good wine. The best Californian.' The beggar winked and motioned and the man in drill said, 'One more glass, your Excellency – or can I recommend this brandy?'

'It's good brandy – but I think another glass of wine.' They refilled their glasses. The man in drill said, 'I'm going to take some of that wine back – to my mother. She loves a glass.'

110

'She couldn't do better,' the Governor's cousin said emptying his own. He said, 'So you have a mother?'

'Haven't we all?'

'Ah, you're lucky. Mine's dead. His hand strayed towards the bottle, grasped it. 'Sometimes I miss her. I called her "my little friend".' He tilted the bottle. 'With your permission?'

'Of course, your Excellency,' the other said hopelessly, taking a long draught of brandy. The beggar said, 'I too have a mother.'

'Who cares?' the Governor's cousin said sharply. He leant back and the bed creaked. He said, 'I have often thought a mother is a better friend than a father. Her influence is towards peace, goodness, charity. . . . Always on the anniversary of her death I go to her grave with flowers.'

The man in drill caught a hiccup politely. He said, 'Ah, if I could too . . .'

'But you said your mother was alive?'

'I thought you were speaking of your grandmother.'

'How could I? I can't remember my grandmother.'

'Nor can I.'

'I can,' the beggar said.

The Governor's cousin said, 'You talk too much.'

'Perhaps I could send him to have this wine wrapped up. . . . For your Excellency's sake I mustn't be seen . . .'

'Wait, wait. There's no hurry. You are very welcome here. Anything in this room is at your disposal. Have a glass of wine.'

'I think brandy . . .'

'Then with your permission . . .' He tilted the bottle: a little of it splashed over on to the sheets. 'What were we talking about?'

'Our grandmothers.'

'I don't think it can have been that. I can't even remember mine. The earliest thing I can remember . . .'

The door opened. The manager said, 'The Chief of Police is coming up the stairs.'

'Excellent. Show him in.'

'Are you sure?'

'Of course. He's a good fellow.' He said to the others. 'But at billiards you can't trust him.'

A large stout man in a singlet, white trousers and a revolver-holster appeared in the doorway. The Governor's cousin said, 'Come in. Come in. How is your toothache? We were talking about our grandmothers.' He said sharply to the beggar, 'Make room for the jefe.'

The jefe stood in the doorway, watching them with dim embarrassment. He said, 'Well, well...'

'We're having a little private party. Will you join us? It would be an honour.'

The jefe's face suddenly lit up at the sight of the wine. 'Of course – a little beer never comes amiss.'

'That's right. Give the jefe a glass of beer.' The beggar filled his own glass with wine and held it out. The jefe took his place upon the bed and drained the glass: then he took the bottle himself. He said, 'It's good beer. Very good beer. Is this the only bottle?' The man in drill watched him with frigid anxiety.

'I'm afraid the only bottle.'

'*Salud!*'

'And what,' the Governor's cousin said, 'were we talking about?'

'About the first thing you could remember,' the beggar said.

'The first thing I can remember,' the jefe began, with deliberation, '– but this gentleman is not drinking.'

'I will have a little brandy.'

'*Salud!*'

'*Salud!*'

'The first thing I can remember with any distinctness is my first communion. Ah, the thrill of the soul, my parents round me...'

'How many parents then have you got?'

'Two, of course.'

'They could not have been around you – you would have needed at least four – ha, ha.'

'*Salud!*'

'*Salud!*'

'No, but as I was saying – life has such irony. It was my painful duty to watch the priest who gave me that communion shot – an old man. I am not ashamed to say that I wept. The comfort is that he is probably a saint and that he prays for us. It is not everyone who earns a saint's prayers.'

'An unusual way...'

'But then life is mysterious.'

'*Salud!*'

The man in drill said, 'A glass of brandy, jefe?'

'There is so little in this bottle that I may as well...'

'I was very anxious to take a little back for my mother.'

'Oh, a drop like this. It would be an insult to take it. Just the dregs.' He turned it up over his glass and chuckled, 'If you can talk of beer having dregs.' Then he stopped with the bottle held over the glass and said with astonishment, 'Why, man, you're crying.' All three watched the man in drill with their mouths a little open. He said, 'It always takes me like this – brandy. Forgive me, gentlemen. I get drunk very easily and then I see...'

'See what?'

'Oh, I don't know, all the hope of the world draining away.'

'Man, you're a poet.'

The beggar said, 'A poet is the soul of his country.'

Lightning filled the windows like a white sheet, and thunder crashed suddenly overhead. The one globe flickered and faded up near the ceiling. 'This is bad news for my men,' the jefe said, stamping on a beetle which had crawled too near.

'Why bad news?'

'The rains coming so early. You see they are on a hunt.'

'The gringo...?'

'He doesn't really matter, but the Governor's found there's still a priest, and you know what he feels about that. If it was me, I'd let the poor devil alone. He'd starve or die of fever or give up. He can't be doing any good – or any harm. Why, nobody even noticed he was about till a few months ago.'

'You'll have to hurry.'

'Oh, he hasn't any real chance. Unless he gets over the

113

border. We've got a man who knows him. Spoke to him, spent a night with him. Let's talk of something else. Who wants to be a policeman?'

'Where do you think he is?'

'You'd be surprised.'

'Why?'

'He's here – in this town, I mean. That's deduction. You see since we started taking hostages from the villages, there's really nowhere else ... They turn him away, they won't have him. So we've set this man I told you about loose like a dog – he'll run into him one day or another – and then ...'

The man in drill said, 'Have you had to shoot many hostages?'

'Not yet. Three or four perhaps. Well, here goes the last of the beer. *Salud!*' He put the glass regretfully down. 'Perhaps now I could have just a drop of your – sidral, shall we say?'

'Yes. Of course.'

'Have I met you before? Your face somehow ...'

'I don't think I've had the honour.'

'That's another mystery,' the jefe said, stretching out a long fat limb and gently pushing the beggar towards the bed-knobs, 'how you think you've seen people – and places – before. Was it in a dream or in a past life? I once heard a doctor say it was something to do with the focusing of the eyes. But he was a Yankee. A materialist.'

'I remember once ...' the Governor's cousin said. The lightning shot down over the harbour and the thunder beat on the roof; this was the atmosphere of a whole state – the storm outside and the talk just going on – words like 'mystery' and 'soul' and 'the source of life' came in over and over again, as they sat on the bed talking, with nothing to do and nothing to believe and nowhere better to go.

The man in drill said, 'I think perhaps I had better be moving on.'

'Where to?'

'Oh ... friends,' he said vaguely, sketching widely with his hands a whole world of fictitious friendships.

'You'd better take your drink with you,' the Governor's cousin said. He admitted, 'After all you paid for it.'

'Thank you, Excellency.' He picked up the brandy bottle. Perhaps there were three fingers left. The bottle of wine, of course, was quite empty.

'Hide it, man, hide it,' the Governor's cousin said sharply.

'Oh, of course, Excellency, I will be careful.'

'You don't have to call him Excellency,' the jefe said. He gave a bellow of laughter and thrust the beggar right off the bed on to the floor.

'No, no, that is . . .' He sidled cautiously out, with a smudge of tears under his red sore eyes and from the hall heard the conversation begin again – 'mystery', 'soul' – going interminably on to no end.

The beetles had disappeared; the rain had apparently washed them away: it came perpendicularly down, with a sort of measured intensity, as if it were driving nails into a coffin lid. But the air was no clearer: sweat and rain hung together on the clothes. The priest stood for a few seconds in the doorway of the hotel, the dynamo thudding behind him, then he darted a few yards into another doorway and hesitated, staring over past the bust of the general to the tethered sailing boats and one old barge with a tin funnel. He had nowhere to go. Rain hadn't entered into his calculations: he had believed that it would be possible just to hang on somehow, sleeping on benches or by the river.

A couple of soldiers arguing furiously came down the street towards the quay – they just let the rain fall on them, as if it didn't matter, as if things were so bad anyway you couldn't notice. . . . The priest pushed the wooden door against which he stood, a cantina door coming down only to the knees, and went in out of the rain: stacks of gaseosa bottles and a single billiard table with the score strung on rings, three or four men – somebody had laid his holster on the bar. The priest moved too quickly and jolted the elbow of a man who was making a shot. He turned furiously: 'Mother of God!' He was a Red Shirt. Was there no safety anywhere, even for a moment?

115

The priest apologized humbly, edging back towards the door but, again he was too quick – his pocket caught against the wall and the brandy bottle chinked. Three of four faces looked at him with malicious amusement: he was a stranger and they were going to have fun. 'What's that you've got in your pocket?' the Red Shirt asked. He was a youth not out of his teens, with gold teeth and a jesting conceited mouth.

'Lemonade,' the priest said.

'What do you want to carry lemonade with you for?'

'I take it at night – with my quinine.'

The Red Shirt swaggered up and poked the pocket with the butt of his cue. 'Lemonade, eh?'

'Yes, lemonade.'

'Let's have a look at the lemonade.' He turned proudly to the others and said, 'I can scent a smuggler at ten paces.' He thrust his hand into the priest's pocket and hauled at the brandy bottle. 'There,' he said. 'Didn't I tell you – ' The priest flung himself against the swing door and burst out into the rain. A voice shouted, 'Catch him.' They were having the time of their lives.

He was off up the street towards the plaza, turned left and right again – it was lucky the streets were dark and the moon obscured. As long as he kept away from lighted windows he was almost invisible – he could hear them calling to each other. They were not giving up: it was better than billiards: somewhere a whistle blew – the police were joining in.

This was the town to which it had been his ambition to be promoted, leaving the right kind of debts behind at Concepción: he thought of the cathedral and Montez and a Monsignor he once knew, as he doubled this way and that. Something buried very deep, the will to escape, cast a momentary and appalling humour over the whole situation – he giggled and panted and giggled again. He could hear them hallooing and whistling in the dark, and the rain came down; it drove and jumped upon the cement floor of the useless frontón which had once been the cathedral (it was too hot to play pelota and a few iron swings stood like gallows at its edge). He worked his way downhill again: he had an idea.

The shouts came nearer, and then up from the river a new lot of men approached; these were pursuing the hunt methodically – he could tell it by their slow pace, the police, the official hunters. He was between the two – the amateurs and the professionals. But he knew the door – he pushed it open, came quickly through into the patio and closed it behind him.

He stood in the dark and panted, hearing the steps come nearer up the street, while the rain drove down. Then he realized that somebody was watching him from the window, a small dark withered face, like one of the preserved heads tourists buy. He came up to the grill and said, 'Padre José?'

'Over there.' A second face appeared behind the other's shoulder, lit uncertainly by a candle-flame, then a third face: faces sprouted like vegetables. He could feel them watching him as he splashed back across the patio and banged on a door.

He didn't for a second or two recognize Padre José in the absurd billowing nightshirt, holding a lamp. The last time he had seen him was at the conference, sitting in the back row, biting his nails, afraid to be noticed. It hadn't been necessary: none of the busy cathedral clergy even knew what he was called. It was odd to think that now he had won a kind of fame superior to theirs. He said 'José' gently, winking up at him from the splashing dark.

'Who are you?'

'Don't you remember me? Of course, it's years now . . . don't you remember the conference at the cathedral . . . ?'

'O God,' Padre José said.

'They are looking for me. I thought perhaps just for tonight you could perhaps . . .'

'Go away,' Padre José said, 'go away.'

'They don't know who I am. They think I'm a smuggler – but up at the police station they'll know.'

'Don't talk so loud. My wife . . .'

'Just show me some corner,' he whispered. He was beginning to feel fear again. Perhaps the effect of the brandy was wearing off (it was impossible in this hot damp climate to stay drunk for long: alcohol came out again under the armpits: it dripped from the forehead), or perhaps it was only that

117

the desire of life which moves in cycles was returning – any sort of life.

In the lamplight Padre José's face wore an expression of hatred. He said, 'Why come to me? Why should you think ... ? I'll call the police if you don't go. You know what sort of a man I am.'

He pleaded gently. 'You're a good man, José. I've always known that.'

'I'll shout if you don't go.'

He tried to remember some cause of hatred. There were voices in the street – arguments, a knocking – were they searching the houses? He said, 'If I ever offended you, José, forgive me. I was conceited, proud, overbearing – a bad priest. I always knew in my heart you were the better man.'

'Go,' José screeched at him, 'go. I don't want martyrs here. I don't belong any more. Leave me alone. I'm all right as I am.' He tried to gather up his venom into spittle and shot it feebly at the other's face: it didn't even reach, but fell impotently through the air. He said, 'Go and die quickly. That's your job,' and slammed the door to. The door of the patio came suddenly open and the police were there. He caught a glimpse of Padre José peering through a window and then an enormous shape in a white nightshirt engulfed him and drew him away – whisked him off, like a guardian spirit, from the disastrous human struggle. A voice said, 'That's him.' It was the young Red Shirt. He let his fist open and dropped by Padre José's wall a little ball of paper: it was like the final surrender of a whole past.

He knew it was the beginning of the end – after all these years. He began to say silently an act of contrition, while they picked the brandy bottle out of his pocket, but he couldn't give his mind to it. That was the fallacy of the death-bed repentance – penitence was the fruit of long training and discipline: fear wasn't enough. He tried to think of his child with shame, but he could only think of her with a kind of famished love – what would become of her? And the sin itself was so old that like an ancient picture the deformity had faded and left a kind of grace. The Red Shirt smashed the bottle on the stone paving and the smell of spirit rose all round them – not very strongly: there hadn't been much left.

Then they took him away. Now that they had caught him they treated him in a friendly way, poking fun at his attempt to escape, except the Red Shirt whose shot he had spoiled. He couldn't find any answer to their jokes: self-preservation lay across his brain like a horrifying obsession. When would they discover who he really was? When would he meet the half-caste, or the lieutenant who had interrogated him already? They moved in a bunch slowly up the hill to the plaza. A rifle-butt grounded outside the station as they came in. A small lamp fumed against the dirty white-washed wall; in the court-yard hammocks swung, bunched around sleeping bodies like the nets in which poultry are tied. 'You can sit down,' one of the men said, and pushed him in a comradely way towards a bench. Everything now seemed irrevocable; the sentry passed back and forth outside the door, and in the courtyard among the hammocks the ceaseless murmur of sleep went on.

Somebody had spoken to him: he gaped helplessly up. 'What?' There seemed to be an argument in progress between the police and the Red Shirt as to whether somebody should be disturbed. 'But it's his duty,' the Red Shirt kept on repeat-ing: he had rabbity front teeth. He said, 'I'll report it to the Governor.'

A policeman said, 'You plead guilty, don't you?'

'Yes,' the priest said.

'There. What more do you want? It's a fine of five pesos. Why disturb anybody?'

'And who gets the five pesos, eh?'

'That's none of your business.'

The priest said suddenly, 'No one gets them.'

'No one?'

'I have only twenty-five centavos in the world.'

The door of an inner room opened and the lieutenant came out. He said. 'What in God's name is all the noise . . . ?' The police came raggedly and unwillingly to attention.

'I've caught a man carrying spirits,' the Red Shirt said.

The priest sat with his eyes on the ground . . . 'because it

119

has crucified . . . crucified . . . crucified . . .' contrition stuck hopelessly over the formal words. He felt no emotion but fear.

'Well,' the lieutenant said, 'what is it to do with you? We catch dozens.'

'Shall we bring him in?' one of the men asked.

The lieutenant took a look at the bowed servile figure on the bench. 'Get up,' he said. The priest rose. Now, he thought, now . . . he raised his eyes. The lieutenant looked away, out of the door where the sentry slouched to and fro. His dark pinched face looked rattled, harassed. . . .

'He has no money,' one of the policemen said.

'Mother of God,' the lieutenant said, 'can I never teach you . . . ?' He took two steps towards the sentry and turned, 'Search him. If he has no money, put him in a cell. Give him some work. . . .' He went outside and suddenly raising his open hand he struck the sentry on the ear. He said, 'You're asleep. March as if you have some pride . . . pride,' he repeated again, while the small acetylene lamp fumed up the white-washed wall and the smell of urine came up out of the yard and the men lay in their hammocks netted and secured.

'Shall we take his name?' a sergeant asked.

'Yes, of course,' the lieutenant said, not looking at him, walking briskly and nervously back past the lamp into the courtyard; he stood there unsheltered, looking round while the rain fell on his dapper uniform. He looked like a man with something on his mind: it was as if he were under the influence of some secret passion which had broken up the routine of his life. Back he came. He couldn't keep still.

The sergeant pushed the priest ahead into the inner room. A bright commercial calendar hung on the flaking whitewash – a dark-skinned mestizo girl in a bathing-dress advertised some gaseous water; somebody had pencilled in a neat pedagogic hand a facile and over-confident statement about man having nothing to lose but his chains.

'Name?' the sergeant said. Before he could check himself he had replied, 'Montez.'

'Home?'

He named a random village: he was absorbed in his own

120

portrait. There he sat among the white-starched dresses of the first communicants. Somebody had put a ring round his face to pick it out. There was another picture on the wall too — the gringo from San Antonio, Texas, wanted for murder and bank robbery.

'I suppose,' the sergeant said cautiously, 'that you bought the drink from a stranger...'

'Yes.'

'Whom you can't identify?'

'No.'

'That's the way,' the sergeant said approvingly: it was obvious he didn't want to start anything. He took the priest quite confidingly by the arm and led him out and across the courtyard; he carried a large key like the ones used in morality plays or fairy stories as a symbol. A few men moved in the hammocks — a large unshaven jaw hung over the side like something left unsold on a butcher's counter: a big torn ear: a naked black-haired thigh. He wondered when the mestizo's face would appear, elated with recognition.

The sergeant unlocked a small grated door and let out with his boot at something straddled across the entrance. He said, 'They are all good fellows, all good fellows here,' kicking his way in. A heavy smell lay on the air and somebody in the absolute darkness wept.

The priest lingered on the threshold trying to see. He said, 'I am so dry. Could I have water?' the stench poured up his nostrils and he retched.

'In the morning,' the sergeant said, 'you've drunk enough now,' and laying a large considerate hand upon the priest's back, he pushed him in, then slammed the door to. He trod on a hand, an arm, and pressing his face against the grill, protested, 'There's no room. I can't see. Who are these people?' Outside among the hammocks the sergeant began to laugh. 'Hombre,' he said, 'hombre, have you never been in jail before?'

## Chapter 3

A VOICE near his foot said, 'Got a cigarette?'

He drew quickly back and trod on an arm. A voice said imperatively, 'Water, quick,' as if whoever it was thought he could take a stranger unawares, and make him fork out.

'Got a cigarette?'

'No.' He said weakly, 'I have nothing at all,' and imagined he could feel enmity fuming up all round him. He moved again. Somebody said, 'Look out for the bucket.' That was where the stench came from. He stood perfectly still and waited for his sight to return. Outside the rain began to stop: it dropped haphazardly and the thunder moved away. You could count forty now between the lightning flash and the roll. Halfway to the sea, or halfway to the mountains. He felt around with his foot, trying to find enough space to sit down but there seemed to be no room at all. When the lightning went on he could see the hammocks at the edge of the courtyard.

'Got something to eat?' a voice asked, and when he didn't answer, 'Got something to eat?'

'No.'

'Got any money?' another voice said.

'No.'

Suddenly, from about five feet away, there came a tiny scream – a woman's. A tired voice said, 'Can't you be quiet?' Among the furtive movements came again the muffled painless cries. He realized that pleasure was going on even in this crowded darkness. Again he put out his foot and began to edge his way inch by inch away from the grill. Behind the human voices another noise went permanently on: it was like a small machine, an electric belt set at a certain tempo. It filled any silences that there were louder than human breath. It was the mosquitoes.

He had moved perhaps six feet from the grill, and his eyes began to distinguish heads – perhaps the sky was clearing: they hung around him like gourds. A voice said, 'Who are

122

you?' He made no reply, feeling panic, edging in. Suddenly he found himself against the back wall: the stone was wet against his hand – the cell could not have been more than twelve feet deep. He found he could just sit down if he kept his feet drawn up under him. An old man lay slumped against his shoulder; he told his age from the featherweight lightness of the bones, the feeble uneven flutter of the breath. He was either somebody close to birth or death – and he could hardly be a child in this place. The old man said suddenly, 'Is that you, Catarina?' and his breath went out in a long patient sigh, as if he had been waiting a long while and could afford to wait a lot longer.

The priest said, 'No. Not Catarina.' When he spoke everybody came suddenly silent, listening, as if what he said had importance: then the voices and movements began again. But the sound of his own voice, the sense of communication with a neighbour, calmed him.

'You wouldn't be,' the old man said. 'I didn't really think you were. She'll never come.'

'Is she your wife?'

'What's that you're saying? I haven't got a wife.'

'Catarina?'

'She's my daughter.' Everybody was listening except the two invisible people who were concerned only in their cramped pleasure.

'Perhaps they won't allow her here.'

'She'll never try,' the old hopeless voice pronounced with absolute conviction. The priest's feet began to ache, drawn up under his haunches. He said, 'If she loves you . . .' Somewhere across the huddle of dark shapes the woman cried again – that finished cry of protest and abandonment and pleasure.

'It's the priests who've done it,' the old man said.

'The priests?'

'The priests.'

'Why the priests?'

'The priests.'

A low voice near his knees said, 'The old man's crazy. What's the use of asking him questions?'

123

'Is that you, Catarina?' He added, 'I don't really believe it, you know. It's just a question.'

'Now *I've* got something to complain about,' the voice went on. 'A man's got to defend his honour. You'll admit that, won't you?'

'I don't know anything about honour.'

'I was in the cantina and the man I'm telling you about came up to me and said, "Your mother's a whore." Well, I couldn't do anything about it: he'd got his gun on him. All I could do was wait. He drank too much beer – I knew he would – and when he was staggering I followed him out. I had a bottle and I smashed it against a wall. You see, I hadn't got my gun. His family's got influence with the jefe or I'd never be here.'

'It's a terrible thing to kill a man.'

'You talk like a priest.'

'It was the priests who did it,' the old man said. 'You're right there.'

'What does he mean?'

'What does it matter what an old man like that means? I'd like to tell you about something else...'

A woman's voice said, 'They took the child away from him.'

'Why?'

'It was a bastard. They acted quite correctly.'

At the word 'bastard' his heart moved painfully, as when a man in love hears a stranger name a flower which is also the name of his woman. 'Bastard!' the word filled him with miserable happiness. It brought his own child nearer: he could see her under the tree by the rubbish-dump, unguarded. He repeated 'Bastard?' as he might have repeated her name – with tenderness disguised as indifference.

'They said he was no fit father. But, of course, when the priests fled, she had to go with him. Where else could she go?' It was like a happy ending until she said, 'Of course she hated him. They'd taught her about things.' He could imagine the small set mouth of an educated woman. What was she doing here?

'Why is he in prison?'

'He had a crucifix.'

The stench from the pail got worse all the time; the night stood round them like a wall, without ventilation, and he could hear somebody making water, drumming on the tin sides. He said, 'They had no business...'

'They were doing what was right, of course. It was a mortal sin.'

'No right to make her hate him.'

'They knew what's right.'

He said, 'They were bad priests to do a thing like that. The sin was over. It was their duty to teach – well, love.'

'You don't know what's right. The priests know.'

He said after a moment's hesitation, very distinctly, 'I am a priest.'

It was like the end: there was no need to hope any longer. The ten years' hunt was over at last. There was silence all round him. This place was very like the world: overcrowded with lust and crime and unhappy love, it stank to heaven; but he realized that after all it was possible to find peace there, when you knew for certain that the time was short.

'A priest?' the woman said at last.

'Yes.'

'Do *they* know?'

'Not yet.'

He could feel a hand fumbling at his sleeve. A voice said, 'You shouldn't have told us. Father, there are all sorts here. Murderers...'

The voice which had described the crime to him said, 'You've no cause to abuse me. Because I kill a man it doesn't mean . . .' Whispering started everywhere. The voice said bitterly, 'I'm not an informer just because when a man says "Your mother was a whore..."'

The priest said, 'There's no need for anyone to inform on me. That would be a sin. When it's daylight they'll discover for themselves.'

'They'll shoot you, father,' the woman's voice said.

'Yes.'

'Are you afraid?'

'Yes. Of course.'

A new voice spoke, in the corner from which the sounds of pleasure had come. It said roughly and obstinately, 'A man isn't afraid of a thing like that.'

'No?' the priest asked.

'A bit of pain. What do you expect? It has to come.'

'All the same,' the priest said, 'I *am* afraid.'

'Toothache is worse.'

'We can't all be brave men.'

The voice said with contempt, 'You believers are all the same. Christianity makes you cowards.'

'Yes. Perhaps you are right. You see I am a bad priest and a bad man. To die in a state of mortal sin' – he gave an uneasy chuckle – 'it makes you think.'

'There. It's as I say. Believing in God makes cowards.' The voice was triumphant, as if it had proved something.

'So then?' the priest said.

'Better not to believe – and be a brave man.'

'I see – yes. And of course, if one believed the Governor did not exist or the jefe, if we could pretend that this prison was not a prison at all but a garden, how brave we could be then.'

'That's just foolishness.'

'But when we found that the prison was a prison, and the Governor up there in the square undoubtedly existed, well, it wouldn't much matter if we'd been brave for an hour or two.'

'Nobody could say that this prison was not a prison.'

'No? You don't think so? I can see you don't listen to the politicians.' His feet were giving him great pain: he had cramp in the soles, but he could bring no pressure on the muscles to relieve them. It was not yet midnight; the hours of darkness stretched ahead interminably.

The woman said suddenly, 'Think. We have a martyr here...'

The priest giggled: he couldn't stop himself. He said, 'I don't think martyrs are like this.' He became suddenly serious, remembering Maria's words – it wouldn't be a good thing to bring mockery on the Church. He said, 'Martyrs are holy men.

126

It is wrong to think that just because one dies ... no. I tell you I am in a state of mortal sin. I have done things I couldn't talk to you about. I could only whisper them in the confessional.' Everybody, when he spoke, listened attentively to him as if he were addressing them in church. He wondered where the inevitable Judas was sitting now, but he wasn't aware of Judas as he had been in the forest hut. He was moved by an irrational affection for the inhabitants of this prison. A phrase came to him: 'God so loved the world ...' He said, 'My children, you must never think the holy martyrs are like me. You have a name for me. Oh, I've heard you use it before now. I am a whisky priest. I am in here now because they found a bottle of brandy in my pocket.' He tried to move his feet from under him: the cramp had passed: now they were lifeless: all feeling gone. Oh well, let them stay. He wouldn't have to use them often again.

The old man was muttering and the priest's thoughts went back to Brigitta. The knowledge of the world lay in her like the dark explicable spot in an X-ray photograph; he longed – with a breathless feeling in the breast – to save her, but he knew the surgeon's decision – the ill was incurable.

The woman's voice said pleadingly, 'A little drink, father ... it's not so important.' He wondered why she was here – probably for having a holy picture in her house. She had the tiresome intense note of a pious woman. They were extraordinarily foolish over pictures. Why not burn them? One didn't need a picture ... He said sternly, 'Oh, I am not only a drunkard.' He had always been worried by the fate of pious women. As much as politicians, they fed on illusion. He was frightened for them: they came to death so often in a state of invincible complacency, full of uncharity. It was one's duty, if one could, to rob them of their sentimental notions of what was good ... He said in hard accents, 'I have a child.'

What a worthy woman she was! Her voice pleaded in the darkness; he couldn't catch what she said, but it was something about the Good Thief. He said, 'My child, the thief repented. I haven't repented.' He remembered her coming into the hut, the dark malicious knowing look with the sunlight at

127

her back. He said, 'I don't know how to repent.' That was true: he had lost the faculty. He couldn't say to himself that he wished his sin had never existed, because the sin seemed to him now so unimportant and he loved the fruit of it. He needed a confessor to draw his mind slowly down the drab passages which led to grief and repentance.

The woman was silent now: he wondered whether after all he had been too harsh with her. If it helped her faith to believe that he was a martyr . . . But he rejected the idea: one was pledged to truth. He shifted an inch or two on his hams and said, 'What time does it get light?'

'Four . . . five . . .' a man replied. 'How can we tell, father? We haven't clocks'.

'Have you been here long?'

'Three weeks.'

'Are you kept here all day?'

'Oh no. They let us out to clean the yard.'

He thought: that is when I shall be discovered – unless it's earlier, for surely one of these people will betray me first. A long train of thought began, which led him to announce after a while, 'They are offering a reward for me. Five hundred, six hundred pesos, I'm not sure.' Then he was silent again. He couldn't urge any man to inform against him – that would be tempting him to sin – but at the same time if there was an informer here, there was no reason why the wretched creature should be bilked of his reward. To commit so ugly a sin – it must count as murder – and to have no compensation in this world . . . He thought: it wouldn't be fair.

'Nobody here,' a voice said, 'wants their blood money.'

Again he was touched by an extraordinary affection. He was just one criminal among a herd of criminals . . . He had a sense of companionship which he had never experienced in the old days when pious people came kissing his black cotton glove.

The pious woman's voice leapt hysterically out at him, 'It is so stupid to tell them that. You don't know the sort of wretches who are here, father. Thieves, murderers . . .'

'Well,' an angry voice said, 'why are you here?'

128

'I had good books in my house,' she announced, with unbearable pride. He had done nothing to shake her complacency. He said, 'They are everywhere. It's no different here.'

'Good books?'

He giggled. 'No, no. Thieves, murderers . . . Oh, well, my child, if you had more experience you would know there are worse things to be.' The old man seemed to be uneasily asleep; his head lay sideways against the priest's shoulder, and he muttered angrily. God knows, it had never been easy to move in this place, but the difficulty seemed to increase as the night wore on and limbs stiffened. He couldn't twitch his shoulder now without waking the old man to another night of suffering. Well, he thought, it was my kind who robbed him: it's only fair to be made a little uncomfortable . . . He sat silent and rigid against the damp wall, with his dead feet under his haunches. The mosquitoes droned on; it was no good defending yourself by striking at the air: they pervaded the whole place like an element. Somebody as well as the old man had fallen asleep and was snoring, a curious note of satisfaction, as though he had eaten and drunk well at a good dinner and was now taking a snooze. . . . The priest tried to calculate the hour: how much time had passed since he had met the beggar in the plaza? It was probably not long after midnight: there would be hours more of this.

It was, of course, the end, but at the same time you had to be prepared for everything, even escape. If God intended him to escape He could snatch him away from in front of a firing-squad. But God was merciful. There was only one reason, surely, which would make Him refuse His peace – if there was any peace – that he could still be of use in saving a soul, his own or another's. But what good could he do now? They had him on the run; he dared not enter a village in case somebody else should pay with his life – perhaps a man who was in mortal sin and unrepentant. It was impossible to say what souls might not be lost simply because he was obstinate and proud and wouldn't admit defeat. He couldn't even say Mass any longer – he had no wine. It had gone down the dry gullet

129

of the Chief of Police. It was appallingly complicated. He was still afraid of death, he would be more afraid of death yet when the morning came, but it was beginning to attract him by its simplicity.

The pious woman was whispering to him. She must have somehow edged her way nearer. She was saying, 'Father, will you hear my confession?'

'My dear child, here! It's quite impossible. Where would be the secrecy?'

'It's been so long . . .'

'Say an Act of Contrition for your sins. You must trust God, my dear, to make allowances . . .'

'I wouldn't mind suffering . . .'

'Well, you are here.'

'That's nothing. In the morning my sister will have raised the money for my fine.'

Somewhere against the far wall pleasure began again; it was unmistakable: the movements, the breathlessness, and then the cry. The pious woman said aloud with fury, 'Why won't they stop it? The brutes, the animals!'

'What's the good of your saying an Act of Contrition now in this state of mind?'

'But the ugliness . . .'

'Don't believe that. It's dangerous. Because suddenly we discover that our sins have so much beauty.'

'Beauty,' she said with disgust. 'Here. In this cell. With strangers all round.'

'Such a lot of beauty. Saints talk about the beauty of suffering. Well, we are not saints, you and I. Suffering to us is just ugly. Stench and crowding and pain. *That* is beautiful in that corner – to them. It needs a lot of learning to see things with a saint's eye: a saint gets a subtle taste for beauty and can look down on poor ignorant palates like theirs. But we can't afford to.'

'It's mortal sin.'

'We don't know. It may be. But I'm a bad priest, you see. I know – from experience – how much beauty Satan carried down with him when he fell. Nobody ever said the fallen angels were the ugly ones. Oh no, they were just as quick and light and . . .'

Again the cry came, an expression of intolerable pleasure. The woman said, 'Stop them. It's a scandal.' He felt fingers on his knee, grasping, digging. He said, 'We're all fellow prisoners. I want drink at this moment more than anything, more than God. That's a sin too.'

'Now,' the woman said, 'I can see you're a bad priest. I wouldn't believe it before. I do now. You sympathize with these animals. If your bishop heard you . . .'

'Ah, he's a very long way off.' He thought of the old man now in Mexico City, living in one of those ugly comfortable pious houses, full of images and holy pictures, saying Mass on Sundays at one of the cathedral altars.

'When I get out of here, I shall write . . .'

He couldn't help laughing: she had no sense of how life had changed. He said, 'If he gets the letter he'll be interested to hear I'm alive.' But again he became serious. It was more difficult to feel pity for her than for the half-caste who a week ago had tagged him through the forest, but her case might be worse. The other had so much excuse – poverty and fever and innumerable humiliations. He said, 'Try not to be angry. Pray for me instead.'

'The sooner you are dead the better.'

He couldn't see her in the darkness, but there were plenty of faces he could remember from the old days which fitted the voice. When you visualized a man or woman carefully, you could always begin to feel pity – that was a quality God's image carried with it. When you saw the lines at the corners of the eyes, the shape of the mouth, how the hair grew, it was impossible to hate. Hate was just a failure of imagination. He began to feel an overwhelming responsibility for this pious woman. 'You and Father José,' she said. 'It's people like you who make people mock – at real religion.' She had, after all, as many excuses as the half-caste. He saw the kind of salon in which she spent her days, with the rocking-chair and the photographs, meeting no one. He said gently, 'You are not married, are you?'

'Why do you want to know?'

'And you never had a vocation?'

'They wouldn't believe it,' she said bitterly.

He thought: poor woman, she's had nothing, nothing at all. If only one could find the right word . . . He leant hopelessly back, moving carefully so as not to waken the old man. But the right words never came to him. He was more out of touch with her kind than he had ever been; he would have known what to say to her in the old days, feeling no pity at all, speaking with half a mind a platitude or two. Now he felt useless. He was a criminal and ought only to talk to criminals; he had done wrong again, trying to break down her complacency. He might just as well have let her go on thinking him a martyr.

His eyes closed and immediately he began to dream. He was being pursued; he stood outside a door banging on it, begging for admission, but nobody answered – there was a word, a password, which would save him, but he had forgotten it. He tried desperately at random – cheese and child, California, excellency, milk, Vera Cruz. His feet had gone to sleep and he knelt outside the door. Then he knew why he wanted to get in: he wasn't being pursued after all: that was a mistake. His child lay beside him bleeding to death and this was a doctor's house. He banged on the door and shouted, 'Even if I can't think of the right word, haven't you a heart?' The child was dying and looked up at him with middle-aged complacent wisdom. She said, 'You animal,' and he woke again crying. He couldn't have slept for more than a few seconds because the woman was still talking about the vocation the nuns had refused to recognize. He said, 'That made you suffer, didn't it? To suffer like that – perhaps it was better than being a nun and happy,' and immediately after he had spoken he thought: a silly remark, what does it mean? Why can't I find something to say to her which she could remember?

He didn't sleep again: he was striking yet another bargain with God. This time, if he escaped from the prison, he would escape altogether. He would go north, over the border. His escape was so improbable that, if it happened, it couldn't be anything else but a sign – an indication that he was doing more harm by his example than good by his occasional confessions. The old man moved against his shoulder and the night just stayed around them. The darkness was always the same and there were no clocks – there was nothing to indicate time passing. The only punctuation of the night was the sound of urination.

Suddenly, he realized that he could see a face, and then another; he had begun to forget that it would ever be another day, just as one forgets that one will ever die. It comes suddenly on one in a screeching brake or a whistle in the air, the knowledge that time moves and comes to an end. All the voices slowly became faces – there were no surprises. The confessional teaches you to recognize the shape of a voice – the loose lip of the weak chin and the false candour of the too straightforward eyes. He saw the pious woman a few feet away, uneasily dreaming with her prim mouth open, showing strong teeth like tombs: the old man: the boaster in the corner, and his woman asleep untidily across his knees. Now that the day was at last here, he was the only one awake, except for a small Indian boy who sat cross-legged near the door with an expression of interested happiness, as if he had never known such friendly company. Over the courtyard the whitewash became visible upon the opposite wall. He began formally to pay his farewell to the world: he couldn't put any heart in it. His corruption was less evident to his senses than his death. One bullet, he thought, is almost certain to go directly through the heart – a squad must contain one accurate marksman. Life would go out in a 'fraction of a second' (that was the phrase), but all night he had been realizing that time depends on clocks and the passage of light. There were no clocks and the light wouldn't change. Nobody really knew how long a second of pain could be. It might last a whole purgatory – or for ever. For some reason he thought of a man he had once shrived who was on the point of death with cancer – his relatives had had to bandage their faces, the smell of the rotting interior was so appalling. He wasn't a saint. Nothing in life was as ugly as death.

A voice in the yard called 'Montez.' He sat on upon his dead feet; he thought automatically: This suit isn't good for much more. It was smeared and fouled by the cell floor and his fellow prisoners. He had obtained it at great risk in a store down by the river, pretending to be a small farmer with ideas above his station. Then he remembered he wouldn't need it much longer – it came with an odd shock, like locking the door of one's house for the last time. The voice repeated impatiently, 'Montez.'

He remembered that that, for the moment, was his name. He looked up from his ruined suit and saw the sergeant unlocking the cell door. 'Here, Montez.' He let the old man's head fall gently back against the sweating wall and tried to stand up, but his feet crumpled like pastry. 'Do you want to sleep all night?' the sergeant complained testily: something had irritated him: he wasn't as friendly as he had been the night before. He let out a kick at a sleeping man and beat on the cell door, 'Come on. Wake up all of you. Out into the yard.' Only the Indian boy obeyed, sliding unobtrusively out with his look of alien happiness. The sergeant complained, 'The dirty hounds. Do they want us to wash them? You, Montez.' Life began to return painfully to his feet. He managed to reach the door.

The yard had come sluggishly to life. A queue of men were bathing their faces at a single tap; a man in a vest and pants sat on the ground hugging a rifle. 'Get out into the yard and wash,' the sergeant yelled at them, but when the priest stepped out he snapped at him, 'Not you, Montez.'

'Not me?'

'We've got other plans for you,' the sergeant said.

The priest stood waiting while his fellow prisoners filed out into the yard. One by one they went past him; he looked at their feet and not their faces, standing like a temptation at the door. Nobody said a word: a woman's feet went draggingly by in black worn low-heeled shoes. He was shaken by the sense of his own uselessness. He whispered without looking up, 'Pray for me.'

'What's that you said, Montez?'

134

He couldn't think of a lie; he felt as if ten years had exhausted his whole stock of deceit.

'What's that you said?'

The shoes had stopped moving. The woman's voice said, 'He was begging.' She added mercilessly, 'He ought to have more sense. I've nothing for him.' Then she went on, flat-footed into the yard.

'Did you sleep well, Montez?' the sergeant badgered him.

'Not very well.'

'What do you expect?' the sergeant said. 'It'll teach you to like brandy too well, won't it?'

'Yes.' He wondered how much longer all these preliminaries would take.

'Well, if you spend all your money on brandy, you've got to do a bit of work in return for a night's lodging. Fetch the pails out of the cells and mind you don't spill them – this place stinks enough as it is.'

'Where do I take them to?'

The sergeant pointed to the door of the *excusados* beyond the tap. 'Report to me when you've finished that,' he said, and went bellowing orders back into the yard.

The priest bent down and took the pail. It was full and very heavy: he went bowed with the weight across the yard. Sweat got into his eyes. He wiped them free and saw one behind the other in the washing queue faces he knew – the hostages. There was Miguel, whom he had seen taken away; he remembered the mother screaming out and the lieutenant's tired anger and the sun coming up. They saw him at the same time; he put down the heavy pail and looked at them. Not to recognize them would have been like a hint, a claim, a demand to them to go on suffering and let him escape. Miguel had been beaten up: there was a sore under his eye – flies buzzed round it as they buzz round a mule's raw flank. Then the queue moved on; they looked on the ground and passed him; strangers took their place. He prayed silently: Oh God, send them someone more worthwhile to suffer for. It seemed to him a damnable mockery that they should sacrifice themselves for a whisky priest with a bastard child. The soldier sat in his

135

pants with the gun between his knees paring his nails and biting off the loose skin. In an odd way he felt abandoned because they had shown no sign of recognition.

The *excusados* was a cesspool with two planks across it on which a man could stand. He emptied the pail and went back across the yard to the row of cells. There were six: one by one he took the pails: once he had to stop and retch: splash, splash, to and fro across the yard. He came to the last cell. It wasn't empty; a man lay back against the wall; the early sun just reached his feet. Flies buzzed around a mound of vomit on the floor. The eyes opened and watched the priest stooping over the pail: two fangs protruded. . . .

The priest moved quickly and splashed the floor. The half-caste said in that too-familiar nagging tone, 'Wait a moment. You can't do that in here.' He explained proudly, 'I'm not a prisoner. I'm a guest.' The priest made a motion of apology (he was afraid to speak) and moved again. 'Wait a moment,' the half-caste commanded him again. 'Come here.'

The priest stood stubbornly, half-turned away, near the door.

'Come here,' the half-caste said. 'You're a prisoner, aren't you? – and I'm a guest – of the Governor. Do you want me to shout for a policeman? Then do as you're told: come here.'

It seemed as if God were deciding . . . finally. He came, pail in hand, stood beside the large flat naked foot, and the half-caste looked up at him from the shadow of the wall, asking him sharply and anxiously, 'What are you doing here?'

'Cleaning up.'

'You know what I mean.'

'I was caught with a bottle of brandy,' the priest said, trying to roughen his voice.

'I know you,' the half-caste said. 'I couldn't believe my eyes, but when you speak . . .'

'I don't think . . .'

'That priest's voice,' the half-caste said with disgust. He was like a dog of a different breed: he couldn't help his hackles rising. The big toe moved plumply and inimically.

The priest put down the pail. He argued hopelessly, 'You're drunk.'

'Beer, beer,' the half-caste said, 'nothing but beer. They promised me the best of everything, but you can't trust them. Don't I know the jefe's got his own brandy locked away?'

'I must empty the pail.'

'If you move, I'll shout. I've got so many things to think about,' the half-caste complained bitterly. The priest waited: there was nothing else to do; he was at the man's mercy – a silly phrase, for those malarial eyes had never known what mercy was. He was saved at any rate from the indignity of pleading.

'You see,' the mestizo carefully explained, 'I'm comfortable here.' His yellow toes curled luxuriously beside the vomit. 'Good food, beer, company, and this roof doesn't leak. You don't have to tell me what'll happen after – they'll kick me out like a dog, like a dog.' He became shrill and indignant. 'What have they got you here for? That's what I want to know. It looks crooked to me. It's my job, isn't it, to find you. Who's going to have the reward if they've got you already? The jefe, I shouldn't wonder, or that bastard sergeant.' He brooded unhappily. 'You can't trust a soul these days.'

'And there's a Red Shirt,' the priest said.

'A Red Shirt?'

'He really caught me.'

'Mother of God,' the mestizo said, 'and they all have the ear of the Governor.' He looked up beseechingly. He said, 'You're an educated man. Advise me.'

'It would be murder,' the priest said, 'a mortal sin.'

'I don't mean that. I mean about the reward. You see as long as they don't *know*, well, I'm comfortable here. A man deserves a few weeks' holiday. And you can't escape far, can you? It would be better, wouldn't it, to catch you out of here. In the town somewhere. I mean nobody else could claim . . .' He said furiously, 'A poor man has so much to think about.'

'I dare say,' the priest said, 'they'd give you *something* even here.'

137

'Something,' the mestizo said, levering himself up against the wall, 'why shouldn't I have it all?'

'What's going on in here?' the sergeant asked. He stood in the doorway, in the sunlight, looking in.

The priest said slowly, 'He wanted me to clear up his vomit. I said you hadn't told me . . .'

'Oh, he's a guest,' the sergeant said. 'He's got to be treated right. You do as he says.'

The mestizo smirked. He said, 'And another bottle of beer, sergeant?'

'Not yet,' the sergeant said. 'You've got to look round the town first.'

The priest picked up the pail and went back across the yard, leaving them arguing. He felt as if a gun were levelled at his back. He went into the *excusados* and emptied the pail, then came out again into the sun – the gun was levelled at his breast. The two men stood in the cell door talking. He walked across the yard: they watched him come. The sergeant said to the mestizo, 'You say you're bilious and can't see properly this morning. You clean up your own vomit then. If you don't do *your* job . . .' Behind the sergeant's back the mestizo gave him a cunning and unreassuring wink. Now that the immediate fear was over, he felt only regret. God had decided. He had to go on with life, go on making decisions, acting on his own advice, making plans . . .

It took him another half-hour to finish cleaning the cells, throwing a bucket of water over each floor; he watched the pious woman go off through the archway to where her sister waited with the fine; they were both tied up in black shawls like things bought in the market, things hard and dry and second-hand. Then he reported again to the sergeant, who inspected the cells and criticized his work and ordered him to throw more water down, and then suddenly got tired of the whole business and told him he could go to the jefe for permission to leave. So he waited another hour on the bench outside the jefe's door, watching the sentry move lackadaisically to and fro in the hot sun.

And when at last a policeman led him in, it wasn't the jefe

138

who sat at the desk but the lieutenant. The priest stood not far from his own portrait on the wall and waited. Once he glanced quickly and nervously up at the old crumpled newspaper cutting and thought, It's not very like me now. What an unbearable creature he must have been in those days – and yet in those days he had been comparatively innocent. That was another mystery: it sometimes seemed to him that venial sins – impatience, an unimportant lie, pride, a neglected opportunity – cut you off from grace more completely than the worst sins of all. Then, in his innocence, he had felt no love for anyone; now in his corruption he had learnt . . .

'Well,' the lieutenant asked, 'has he cleaned up the cells?' He didn't take his eyes from his papers. He went on, 'Tell the sergeant I want two dozen men with properly cleaned rifles – within two minutes.' He looked abstractedly up at the priest and said, 'Well, what are you waiting for?'

'For permission, Excellency, to go away.'

'I am not an excellency. Learn to call things by their right names.' He said sharply, 'Have you been here before?'

'Never.'

'Your name is Montez. I seem to come across too many people of that name in these days. Relations of yours?' He sat watching him closely, as if memory were beginning to work.

The priest said hurriedly, 'My cousin was shot at Concepción.'

'That was not my fault.'

'I only meant – we were much alike. Our fathers were twins. Not half an hour between them. I thought your Excellency seemed to think . . .'

'As I remember him, he was quite different. A tall thin man . . . narrow shoulders . . .'

The priest said hurriedly, 'Perhaps only to the family eye . . .'

'But then I only saw him once.' It was almost as if the lieutenant had something on his conscience, as he sat with his dark Indian-blooded hands restless on the pages, brooding.

139

... He asked, 'Where are you going?'

'God knows.'

'You are all alike, you people. You never learn the truth – that God knows nothing.' Some tiny scrap of life like a grain of smut went racing across the page in front of him; he pressed his finger down on it and said, 'You had no money for your fine?' and watched another smut edge out between the leaves, scurrying for refuge: in this heat there was no end to life.

'No.'

'How will you live?'

'Some work perhaps . . .'

'You are getting too old for work.' He put his hand suddenly in his pocket and pulled out a five-peso piece. 'There,' he said. 'Get out of here, and don't let me see your face again. Mind that.'

The priest held the coin in his fist – the price of a Mass. He said with astonishment, 'You're a good man.'

## Chapter 4

It was still very early in the morning when he crossed the river and came dripping up the other bank. He wouldn't have expected anybody to be about. The bungalow, the tin-roofed shed, the flagstaff: he had an idea that all Englishmen lowered their flag at sunset and sang 'God Save the King'. He came carefully round the corner of the shed and the door gave to his pressure. He was inside in the dark where he had been before: how many weeks ago? He had no idea. He only remembered that then the rains were a long way off: now they were beginning to break. In another week only an aeroplane would be able to cross the mountains.

He felt around him with his foot; he was so hungry that even a few bananas would be better than nothing – he had had no food for two days – but there were none here, none at all. He must have arrived on a day when the crop had gone downriver. He stood just inside the door trying to remember what the child had told him – the Morse code, her window: across

140

the dead-white dusty yard the mosquito wire caught the sun. He was reminded suddenly of an empty larder. He began to listen anxiously. There wasn't a sound anywhere; the day here hadn't yet begun with that first sleepy slap of a shoe on a cement floor, the claws of a dog scratching as it stretched, the knock-knock of a hand on a door. There was just nothing, nothing at all.

What was the time? How many hours of light had there been? It was impossible to tell. Suppose, after all, it was not very early – it might be six, seven.... He realized how much he had counted on this child. She was the only person who could help him without endangering herself. Unless he got over the mountains in the next few days he was trapped – he might as well hand himself over to the police, because how could he live through the rains with nobody daring to give him food or shelter? It would have been better, quicker, if he had been recognized in the police station a week ago: so much less trouble. Then he heard a sound; it was like hope coming tentatively back: a scratching and a whining. This was what one meant by dawn – the noise of life. He waited for it – hungrily – in the doorway.

And it came: a mongrel bitch dragging herself across the yard, an ugly creature with bent ears, trailing a wounded or a broken leg, whimpering. There was something wrong with her back. She came very slowly. He could see her ribs like an exhibit in a natural history museum. It was obvious that she hadn't had food for days: she had been abandoned.

Unlike him, she retained a kind of hope. Hope is an instinct only the reasoning human mind can kill. An animal never knows despair. Watching her wounded progress he had a sense that this had happened daily – perhaps for weeks; he was watching one of the well-rehearsed effects of the new day, like bird-song in happier regions. She dragged herself up to the veranda door and began to scratch with one paw, lying oddly spreadeagled. Her nose was down to a crack: she seemed to be breathing in the unused air of empty rooms; then she whined impatiently, and once her tail beat as if she heard something move inside. At last she began to howl.

141

The priest could bear it no longer. He knew now what it meant: he might as well let his eyes see. He came out into the yard and the animal turned awkwardly – the parody of a watchdog – and began to bark at him. It wasn't anybody she wanted: she wanted what she was used to: she wanted the old world back.

He looked in through the window – perhaps this was the child's room. Everything had been removed from it except the useless or the broken. There was a cardboard box full of torn paper and a small chair which had lost a leg. There was a large nail in the whitewashed wall where a mirror perhaps had been hung or a picture. There was a broken shoe-horn.

The bitch was dragging itself along the veranda growling: instinct is like a sense of duty – one can confuse it with loyalty very easily. He avoided the animal simply by stepping out into the sun; it couldn't turn quickly enough to follow him. He pushed at the door and it opened – nobody had bothered to lock up. An ancient alligator's skin which had been badly cut and inefficiently dried hung on the wall. There was a snuffle behind him and he turned; the bitch had two paws over the threshold, but now that he was established in the house, she didn't mind him. He was there, in possession, the master, and there were all kinds of smells to occupy her mind. She pushed herself across the floor, making a wet noise.

The priest opened a door on the left – perhaps it had been the bedroom. In a corner lay a pile of old medicine bottles. There were medicines for headaches, stomach-aches, medicines to be taken after meals and before meals. Somebody must have been very ill to need so many? There was a hair-slide, broken, and a ball of hair-combings – very fair hair turning dusty white. He thought with relief: It was her mother, only her mother.

He tried another room which faced, through the mosquito wire, the slow and empty river. This had been the living-room, for they had left behind the table, a folding card-table of plywood bought for a few shillings which hadn't been worth taking with them wherever they'd gone. Had the mother been dying, he wondered? They had cleared the crop perhaps,

142

and gone to the capital where there was a hospital. He left that room and entered another: this was the one he had seen from the outside – the child's. He turned over the contents of the wastepaper box with sad curiosity. He felt as if he were clearing up after a death, deciding what would be too painful to keep.

He read, 'The immediate cause of the American War of Independence was what is called the Boston Tea Party.' It seemed to be part of an essay written in large firm letters, carefully. 'But the real issue' (the word was spelt wrongly, crossed out and re-written) 'was whether it was right to tax people who were not represented in Parliament.' It must have been a rough copy – there were so many corrections. He picked out another scrap at random – it was about people called Whigs and Tories – the words were incomprehensible to him. Something like a duster flopped down off the roof into the yard: it was a vulture. He read on, 'If five men took three days to mow a meadow of four acres five roods, how much would two men mow in one day?' There was a neat line ruled under the question, and then the calculations began – a hopeless muddle of figures which didn't work out. There was a hint of heat and irritation in the crumpled paper tossed aside. He could see her very clearly, dispensing with that question decisively: the neat accurately moulded face with the two pinched pigtails. He remembered her readiness to swear eternal enmity against anyone who hurt him, and he remembered his own child enticing him by the rubbish-dump.

He shut the door carefully behind him as if he were preventing an escape. He could hear the bitch – somewhere – growling, and followed her into what had once been the kitchen. She lay in a deathly attitude over a bone with her old teeth bared. An Indian's face hung outside the mosquito wire like something hooked up to dry – dark, withered, and unappetizing. He had his eyes on the bone as if he coveted it. He looked up as the priest came across the kitchen and immediately was gone as if he had never been there, leaving the house just as abandoned. The priest, too, looked at the bone.

There was a lot of meat on it still. A small cloud of flies hung above it a few inches from the bitch's mouth, and the bitch kept her eye fixed, now that the Indian was gone, on the priest. They were all in competition. The priest advanced a step or two and stamped twice. 'Go,' he said, 'go,' flapping his hands, but the mongrel wouldn't move, flattened above the bone, with all the resistance left in the broken body concentrated in the yellow eyes, burring between her teeth. It was like hate on a deathbed. The priest came cautiously forward; he wasn't yet used to the idea that the animal couldn't spring. One associates a dog with action, but this creature, like any crippled human being, could only think. You could see the thoughts – hunger and hope and hatred – stuck on the eyeball.

The priest put out his hand towards the bone and the flies buzzed upwards. The animal became silent, watching. 'There, there,' the priest said cajolingly; he made little enticing movements in the air and the animal stared back. Then the priest turned and moved away as if he were abandoning the bone; he droned gently to himself a phrase from the Mass, elaborately paying no attention. Then he switched quickly round again. It hadn't worked. The bitch watched him, screwing round her neck to follow his ingenious movements.

For a moment he became furious – that a mongrel bitch with a broken back should steal the only food. He swore at it – popular expressions picked up beside bandstands: he would have been surprised in other circumstances that they came so readily to his tongue. Then suddenly he laughed: this was human dignity disputing with a bitch over a bone. When he laughed the animal's ears went back, twitching at the tips, apprehensive. But he felt no pity – her life had no importance beside that of a human being. He looked round for something to throw, but the room had been cleared of nearly everything except the bone. Perhaps, who knows? it might have been left deliberately for this mongrel; he could imagine the child remembering, before she left with the sick mother and the stupid father: he had the impression that it was always she who had to think. He could find for his purpose nothing better than a broken wire rack which had been used for vegetables.

He advanced again towards the bitch and struck her lightly on the head. She snapped at the wire with her old broken teeth and wouldn't move. He beat at her again more fiercely and she caught the wire – he had to rasp it away. He struck again and again before he realized that she couldn't, except with great exertion, move at all: she was unable to escape his blows or leave the bone. She just had to endure, her eyes yellow and scared and malevolent shining back at him between the blows.

So then he changed his method; he used the vegetable rack as a kind of muzzle, holding back the teeth with it, while he bent and captured the bone. One paw tugged at it and gave way; he lowered the wire and jumped back – the animal tried without success to follow him, then lapsed upon the floor. The priest had won: he had his bone. The bitch no longer tried to growl.

The priest tore off some raw meat with his teeth and began to chew: no food had ever tasted so good, and now that for the moment he was happy he began to feel a little pity. He thought: I will eat just so much and she can have the rest. He marked mentally a point upon the bone and tore off another piece. The nausea he had felt for hours now began to die away and leave an honest hunger; he ate on and the bitch watched him. Now that the fight was over she seemed to bear no malice; her tail began to beat the floor, hopefully, questioningly. The priest reached the point he had marked, but now it seemed to him that his previous hunger had been imaginary: this was hunger, what he felt now. A man's need was greater than a dog's: he would leave that knuckle of meat at the joint. But when the moment came he ate that too – after all, the dog had teeth: it would eat the bone itself. He dropped it and left the kitchen.

He made one more progress through the empty rooms. A broken shoe-horn: medicine bottles: an essay on the American War of Independence – there was nothing to tell him why they had gone away. He came out on to the veranda and saw through a gap in the planks that a book had fallen to the ground and lay between the rough pillars of brick which

145

raised the house out of the track of ants. It was months since he had seen a book. It was almost like a promise, mildewing there under the piles, of better things to come – life going on in private houses with wireless sets and bookshelves and beds made ready for the night and a cloth laid for food. He knelt down on the ground and reached for it. He suddenly realized that when once the long struggle was over and he had crossed the mountains and the state line, life might, after all, be enjoyed again.

It was an English book, but from his years in an American seminary he retained enough English to read it, with a little difficulty. Even if he had been unable to understand a word, it would still have been a book. It was called *Jewels Five Words Long: A Treasury of English Verse*, and on the fly-leaf was pasted a printed certificate – Awarded to ... and then the name of Coral Fellows filled up in ink ... for proficiency in English Composition, Third Grade. There was an obscure coat of arms, which seemed to include a griffon and oak leaf, a Latin motto, '*Virtus Laudata Crescit*,' and a signature from a rubber stamp, Henry Beckley, B.A., Principal of Private Tutorials, Ltd.

The priest sat down on the veranda steps. There was silence everywhere – no life around the abandoned banana station except the vulture which hadn't yet given up hope. The Indian might never have existed at all. After a meal, the priest thought with sad amusement, a little reading, and opened the book at random. Coral – so that was the child's name. He thought of the shops in Vera Cruz full of it – the hard brittle jewellery which was thought for some reason so suitable for young girls after their first communion.

> 'I come,' he read, 'from haunts of coot and hern,
> I make a sudden sally,
> And sparkle out among the fern,
> To bicker down a valley.'

It was a very obscure poem, full of words which were like Esperanto. He thought: So this is English poetry: how odd. The little poetry he knew dealt mainly with agony, remorse,

146

and hope. These verses ended on a philosophical note – 'For men may come and men may go, But I go on for ever.' The triteness and untruth of 'for ever' shocked him a little: a poem like this ought not to be in a child's hands. The vulture came picking its way across the yard, a dusty and desolate figure; every now and then it lifted sluggishly from the earth and flapped down twenty yards on. The priest read:

> '"Come back! Come back!" he cried in grief
> Across the stormy water:
> "And I'll forgive your Highland chief –
> My daughter, O my daughter."'

That sounded to him more impressive – though hardly perhaps, any more than the other, stuff for children. He felt in the foreign words the ring of genuine passion and repeated to himself on his hot and lonely perch the last line – 'My daughter, O my daughter.' The words seemed to contain all that he felt himself of repentance, longing and unhappy love.

It was an odd thing that ever since that hot and crowded night in the cell he had passed into a region of abandonment – almost as if he had died there with the old man's head on his shoulder and now wandered in a kind of limbo, because he wasn't good or bad enough. . . . Life didn't exist any more: it wasn't merely a matter of the banana station. Now as the storm broke and he scurried for shelter he knew quite well what he would find – nothing.

The huts leapt up in the lightning and stood there shaking, then disappeared again in the rumbling darkness. The rain hadn't come yet: it was sweeping up from Campeche Bay in great sheets, covering the whole state in its methodical advance. Between the thunder-breaks he could imagine that he heard it – a gigantic rustle moving across towards the mountains which were now so close to him – a matter of twenty miles.

He reached the first hut; the door was open, and as the lightning quivered he saw as he expected nobody at all. Just a pile of maize and the indistinct grey movement of – perhaps –

a rat. He dashed for the next hut, but it was the same as ever (the maize and nothing else), just as if all human life were receding before him, as if Somebody had determined that from now on he was to be left alone – altogether alone. As he stood there the rain reached the clearing; it came out of the forest like thick white smoke and moved on. It was as if an enemy were laying a gas-cloud across a whole territory, carefully, to see that nobody escaped. The rain spread and stayed just long enough, as though the enemy had his stop-watch out and knew to a second the limit of the lungs' endurance. The roof held the rain out for a while and then let it through – the twigs bent under the weight of water and shot apart; it came through in half a dozen places, pouring down in black funnels; then the downpour stopped and the roof dripped and the rain moved on, with the lightning quivering on its flanks like a protective barrage. In a few minutes it would reach the mountains: a few more storms like this and they would be impassable.

He had been walking all day and he was very tired; he found a dry spot and sat down. When the lightning struck he could see the clearing. All around was the gentle noise of the dripping water. It was nearly like peace, but not quite. For peace you needed human company – his aloneness was like a threat of things to come. Suddenly he remembered – for no apparent reason – a day of rain at the American seminary, the glass windows of the library steamed over with the central heating, the tall shelves of sedate books, and a young man – a stranger from Tuscon – drawing his initials on the pane with his finger – that was peace. He looked at it from the outside: he couldn't believe that he would ever again get in. He had made his own world, and this was it – the empty broken huts, the storm going by, and fear again – fear because he was not alone after all.

Somebody was moving outside, cautiously. The footsteps would come a little way and then stop. He waited apathetically, and the roof dripped behind him. He thought of the mestizo padding around the city, seeking a really cast-iron occasion for his betrayal. A face peered round the hut door at him and quickly withdrew – an old woman's face, but you could never tell with Indians – she mightn't have been more than twenty. He got up and went outside. She scampered back from before him in her heavy sack-like skirt, her black plaits swinging heavily. Apparently his loneliness was only to be broken by these evasive faces, creatures who looked as if they had come out of the Stone Age, who withdrew again quickly.

He was stirred by a sort of sullen anger – this one should not withdraw. He pursued her across the clearing, splashing in the pools, but she had a start and no sense of shame and she got into the forest before him. It was useless looking for her there, and he returned towards the nearest hut. It wasn't the hut which he had been sheltering in before, but it was just as empty. What had happened to these people? He knew well enough that these more or less savage encampments were temporary only; the Indians would cultivate a small patch of ground and when they had exhausted the soil for the time being, they would simply move away. They knew nothing about the rotation of crops, but when they moved they would take their maize with them. This was more like flight, from force or disease. He had heard of such flights in the case of sickness, and the horrible thing, of course, was that they carried the sickness with them wherever they moved; sometimes they became panicky like flies against a pane, but discreetly, letting nobody know, muting their hubbub. He turned moodily again to stare out at the clearing, and there was the Indian woman creeping back towards the hut where she had sheltered. He called out to her sharply and again she fled, shambling, towards the forest. Her clumsy progress reminded him of a bird feigning a broken wing. . . . He made no movement to follow her, and before she reached the trees she stopped and watched him; he began to move slowly back towards the other hut. Once he turned: she was following him at a distance, keeping her eyes on him. Again he was reminded of something animal or bird-like, full of anxiety. He walked on, aiming directly at the hut. Far away beyond it the lightning stabbed down, but you could hardly hear the thunder; the sky was clearing overhead and the moon came out. Suddenly he heard an odd artificial cry, and turning he saw the woman making back towards the forest; then she stumbled, flung up her arms and fell to the ground, like the bird offering herself.

He felt quite certain now that something valuable was in the hut, perhaps hidden among the maize, and he paid her no attention, going in. Now that the lightning had moved on, he couldn't see – he felt across the floor until he reached the pile of maize. Outside the padding footsteps came nearer. He began to feel all over it – perhaps food was hidden there – and the dry crackle of the leaves was added to the drip of water and the cautious footsteps, like the faint noises of people busy about their private businesses. Then he put his hand on a face.

He couldn't be frightened any more by a thing like that – it was something human he had his fingers on. They moved down the body; it was a child's which lay completely quiet under his hand. In the doorway the moonlight showed the woman's face indistinctly. She was probably convulsed with anxiety, but you couldn't tell. He thought – I must get this into the open where I can see . . .

It was a male child – perhaps three years old: a withered bullet head with a mop of black hair: unconscious, but not dead: he could feel the faintest movement in the breast. He thought of disease again until he took out his hand and found that the child was wet with blood, not sweat. Horror and disgust touched him – violence everywhere: was there no end to violence? He said to the woman sharply, 'What happened?' It was as if man in all this state had been left to man.

The woman knelt two or three feet away, watching his hands. She knew a little Spanish, because she replied, '*Americano*.' The child wore a kind of brown one-piece smock. He lifted it up to the neck: the child had been shot in three places. Life was going out of him all the time: there was nothing – really – to be done, but one had to try. . . . He said 'Water' to the woman, 'Water,' but she didn't seem to understand, squatting there, watching him. It was a mistake one easily made, to think that just because the eyes expressed nothing there was no grief. When he touched the child he could see her move on her haunches – she was ready to attack him with her teeth if the child so much as moaned.

He began to speak slowly and gently (he couldn't tell how much she understood): 'We must have water. To wash him. You needn't be afraid of me. I will do him no harm.' He took off his shirt and began to tear it into strips – it was hopelessly insanitary, but what else was there to do? except pray, of course, but one didn't pray for life, this life. He repeated again, 'Water.' The woman seemed to understand – she gazed hopelessly round at where the rain stood in pools – that was all there was. Well, he thought, the earth's as clean as any vessel would have been. He soaked a piece of his shirt and leant over the child; he could hear the woman slide closer along the ground – a menacing approach. He tried to reassure her again, 'You needn't be afraid of me. I am a priest.'

The word 'priest' she understood; she leant forward and grabbed at the hand which held the wet scrap of shirt and kissed it. At that moment, while her lips were on his hand, the child's face wrinkled, the eyes opened and glared at them, the tiny body shook with a kind of fury of pain; they watched the eyeballs roll up and suddenly become fixed, like marbles in a solitaire-board, yellow and ugly with death. The woman let go his hand and scrambled to a pool of water, cupping her fingers for it. The priest said, 'We don't need that any more,' standing up with his hands full of wet shirt. The woman opened her fingers and let the water fall. She said 'Father' imploringly, and he wearily went down on his knees and began to pray.

He could feel no meaning any longer in prayers like these. The Host was different: to lay that between a dying man's lips was to lay God. That was a fact – something you could touch, but this was no more than a pious aspiration. Why should anyone listen to *his* prayers? Sin was a constriction which prevented their escape; he could feel his prayers weigh him down like undigested food.

When he had finished he lifted up the body and carried it back into the hut; it seemed a waste of time to have taken it

151

out, like a chair you carry out into the garden and back again because the grass is wet. The woman followed him meekly; she didn't seem to want to touch the body, just watched him put it back in the dark upon the maize. He sat down on the ground and said slowly, 'It will have to be buried.'

She understood that, nodding.

He said, 'Where is your husband? Will he help you?'

She began to talk rapidly. It might have been Camacho she was speaking: he couldn't understand more than an occasional Spanish word here and there. The word *'Americano'* occurred again, and he remembered the wanted man whose portrait had shared the wall with his. He asked her, 'Did *he* do this?' She shook her head. What had happened? he wondered. Had the man taken shelter here and had the soldiers fired into the huts? It was not unlikely. He suddenly had his attention caught. She had said the name of the banana station – but there had been no dying person there: no sign of violence, unless silence and desertion were signs. He had assumed the mother had been taken ill, but it might be something worse – and he imagined that stupid Captain Fellows taking down his gun, presenting himself clumsily armed to a man whose chief talent it was to draw quickly or to shoot directly from the pocket. That poor child ... what responsibilities she had perhaps been forced to undertake.

He shook the thought away and said, 'Have you a spade?' She didn't understand that, and he had to go through the motions of digging. Another roll of thunder came between them. A second storm was coming up, as if the enemy had discovered that the first barrage after all had left a few survivors – this would flatten them. Again he could hear the enormous breathing of the rain miles away. He realized the woman had spoken the one word 'church'. Her Spanish consisted of isolated words. He wondered what she meant by that. Then the rain reached them. It came down like a wall between him and escape, fell altogether in a heap and built itself up around them. All the light went out except when the lightning flashed.

The roof couldn't keep out *this* rain. It came dripping

152

through everywhere: the dry maize leaves where the dead child lay crackled like burning wood. He shivered with cold; he was probably on the edge of fever – he must get away before he was incapable of moving at all. The woman (he couldn't see her now) said '*Iglesia*' again imploringly. It occurred to him that she wanted the child buried near a church or perhaps only taken to an altar, so that he might be touched by the feet of a Christ. It was a fantastic notion.

He took advantage of a long quivering stroke of blue light to describe with his hands his sense of the impossibility. 'The soldiers,' he said, and she replied immediately, '*Americano*.' That word always came up, like one with many meanings which depends on the accent whether it is to be taken as an explanation, a warning or a threat. Perhaps she meant that the soldiers were all occupied in the chase, but even so, this rain was ruining everything. It was still twenty miles to the border, and the mountain paths after the storm were probably impassable – and a church – he hadn't the faintest idea of where there would be a church. He hadn't so much as seen such a thing for years now; it was difficult to believe that they still existed only a few days' journey off. When the lightning went on again he saw the woman watching him with stony patience.


For the last thirty hours they had only had sugar to eat – large brown lumps of it the size of a baby's skull; they had seen no one, and they had exchanged no words at all. What was the use when almost the only words they had in common were '*Iglesia*' and '*Americano*'? The woman followed at his heels with the dead child strapped on her back. She never seemed to tire. A day and a night brought them out of the marshes to the foothills; they slept fifty feet up above the slow green river, under a projecting piece of rock where the soil was dry – everywhere else was deep mud. The woman sat with her knees drawn up, and her head down. She showed no emotion, but she put the child's body behind her as if it

153

needed protection from marauders like other possessions. They had travelled by the sun until the black wooded bar of mountain told them where to go. They might have been the only survivors of a world which was dying out; they carried the visible marks of the dying with them.

Sometimes he wondered whether he was safe, but when there are no visible boundaries between one state and another – no passport examination or customs house – danger just seems to go on, travelling with you, lifting its heavy feet in the same way as you do. There seemed to be so little progress: the path would rise steeply, perhaps five hundred feet, and fall again, clogged with mud. Once it took an enormous hairpin bend, so that after three hours they had returned to a point opposite their starting-place, less than a hundred yards away.

At sunset on the second day they came out on to a wide plateau covered with short grass. A grove of crosses stood up blackly against the sky, leaning at different angles – some as high as twenty feet, some not much more than eight. They were like trees that had been left to seed. The priest stopped and stared at them. They were the first Christian symbols he had seen for more than five years publicly exposed – if you could call this empty plateau in the mountains a public place. No priest could have been concerned in the strange rough group; it was the work of Indians and had nothing in common with the tidy vestments of the Mass and the elaborately worked out symbols of the liturgy. It was like a short cut to the dark and magical heart of the faith – to the night when the graves opened and the dead walked. There was a movement behind him and he turned.

The woman had gone down on her knees and was shuffling slowly across the cruel ground towards the group of crosses; the dead baby rocked on her back. When she reached the tallest cross she unhooked the child and held the face against the wood and afterwards the loins; then she crossed herself, not as ordinary Catholics do, but in a curious and complicated pattern which included the nose and ears. Did she expect a miracle? and if she did, why should it not be granted her, the

154

priest wondered? Faith, one was told, could move mountains, and here was faith – faith in the spittle that healed the blind man and the voice that raised the dead. The evening star was out: it hung low down over the edge of the plateau – it looked as if it was within reach – and a small hot wind stirred. The priest found himself watching the child for some movement. When none came, it was as if God had missed an opportunity. The woman sat down, and taking a lump of sugar from her bundle began to eat, and the child lay quietly at the foot of the cross. Why, after all, should we expect God to punish the innocent with more life?

'*Vamos*,' the priest said, but the woman scraped the sugar with her sharp front teeth, paying no attention. He looked up at the sky and saw the evening star blotted out by black clouds. '*Vamos*.' There was no shelter anywhere on this plateau.

The woman never stirred; the broken snub-nosed face between the black plaits was completely passive: it was as if she had fulfilled her duty and could now take up her everlasting rest. The priest suddenly shivered; the ache which had pressed like a stiff hat-rim across his forehead all day dug deeper in. He thought: I have to get to shelter – a man's first duty is to himself – even the Church taught that, in a way. The whole sky was blackening. The crosses stuck up like dry and ugly cacti. He made off to the edge of the plateau. Once, before the path led down, he looked back – the woman was still biting at the lump of sugar, and he remembered that it was all the food they had.

The way was very steep – so steep that he had to turn and go down backwards; on either side trees grew perpendicularly out of the grey rock, and five hundred feet below the path climbed up again. He began to sweat and he had an appalling thirst, and when the rain came it was at first a kind of relief. He stayed where he was, hunched back against a boulder. There was no shelter before he reached the bottom of the barranca, and it hardly seemed worth while to make that effort. He was shivering now more or less continuously, and the ache seemed no longer inside his head – it was something outside, almost

155

anything, a noise, a thought, a smell. The senses were jumbled up together. At one moment the ache was like a tiresome voice explaining to him that he had taken the wrong path. He remembered a map he had once seen of the two adjoining states. The state from which he was escaping was peppered with villages – in the hot marshy land people bred as readily as mosquitoes, but in the next state – in the north-west corner – there was hardly anything but blank white paper. You're on that blank paper now, the ache told him. But there's a path, he argued wearily. Oh, a path, the ache said, a path may take you fifty miles before it reaches anywhere at all: you know you won't last that distance. There's just white paper all around.

At another time the ache was a face. He became convinced that the American was watching him – he had a skin all over spots like a newspaper photograph. Apparently he had followed them because he wanted to kill the mother as well as the child: he was sentimental in that respect. It was necessary to do something. The rain was like a curtain behind which almost anything might happen. He thought: I shouldn't have left her alone like that. God forgive me. I have no sense of responsibility: what can you expect of a whisky priest? and he struggled to his feet and began to climb back towards the plateau. He was tormented by ideas; it wasn't only the woman: he was responsible for the American as well: the two faces – his own and the gunman's – were hanging together on the police station wall, as if they were brothers in a family portrait gallery. You didn't put temptation in a brother's way.

Shivering and sweating and soaked with rain he came up over the edge of the plateau. There was nobody there – a dead child was not someone, just a useless object abandoned at the foot of one of the crosses. The mother had gone home. She had done what she wanted to do. The surprise lifted him, as it were, out of his fever before it dropped him back again. A small lump of sugar – all that was left – lay by the child's mouth – in case a miracle should happen or for the spirit to eat? The priest bent down with an obscure sense of shame and took it: the dead child couldn't growl back at him like a

156

broken dog: but who was he to disbelieve in miracles? He hesitated, while the rain poured down; then he put the sugar in his mouth. If God chose to give back life, couldn't He give food as well?

Immediately he began to eat, the fever returned: the sugar stuck in his throat: he felt an appalling thirst. Crouching down he tried to lick some water from the uneven ground; he even sucked at his soaked trousers. The child lay under the streaming rain like a dark heap of cattle dung. The priest moved away again, back to the edge of the plateau and down the barranca side; it was loneliness he felt now – even the face had gone, he was moving alone across that blank white sheet, going deeper every moment into the abandoned land.

Somewhere, in some direction, there were towns, of course: go far enough and you reached the coast, the Pacific, the railway track to Guatemala; there were roads there and motor-cars. He hadn't seen a railway train for ten years. He could imagine the black line following the coast along the map, and he could see the fifty, hundred miles of unknown country. That was where he was: he had escaped too completely from men. Nature would kill him now.

All the same, he went on; there was no point in going back towards the deserted village, the banana station with its dying mongrel and its shoe-horn. There was nothing you could do except put one foot forward and then the other, scrambling down and then scrambling up; from the top of the barranca, when the rain passed on, there was nothing to see except a huge crumpled land, forest and mountain, with the grey wet veil moving over. He looked once and never looked again. It was too like watching despair.

It must have been hours later that he ceased to climb. It was evening and forest; monkeys crashed invisibly among the trees with an effect of clumsiness and recklessness, and what were probably snakes hissed away like match-flames through the grass. He wasn't afraid of them. They were a form of life, and he could feel life retreating from him all the time. It wasn't only people who were going, even the animals and the reptiles moved away; presently he would be left alone with nothing but his own breath. He began to recite to himself, 'O God, I have loved the beauty of Thy house,' and the smell of soaked and rotting leaves and the hot night and the darkness made him believe that he was in a mine shaft, going down into the earth to bury himself. Presently he would find his grave.

When a man came towards him carrying a gun he did nothing at all. The man approached cautiously; you didn't expect to find another person underground. He said, 'Who are you?' with his gun ready.

The priest gave his name to a stranger for the first time in ten years because he was tired and there seemed no object in going on living.

'A priest?' the man asked, with astonishment. 'Where have you come from?'

The fever lifted again: a little reality seeped back. He said, 'It is all right. I will not bring you any trouble. I am going on.' He screwed up all his remaining energy and walked on. A puzzled face penetrated his fever and receded: there were going to be no more hostages, he assured himself aloud. Footsteps followed him, he was like a dangerous man you see safely off an estate before you go home. He repeated aloud, 'It is all right. I am not staying here. I want nothing.'

'Father . . .' the voice said, humbly and anxiously.

'I will go right away.' He tried to run and came suddenly out of the forest on to a long slope of grass. There were lights and huts below, and up there at the edge of the forest a big whitewashed building – a barracks? were there soldiers? He said, 'If I have been seen I will give myself up. I assure you no one shall get into trouble because of me.'

'Father . . .' He was racked with his headache, he stumbled and put his hand against the wall for support. He felt immeasurably tired. He asked, 'The barracks?'

'Father,' the voice said, puzzled and worried, 'it is our church.'

'A church?' The priest ran his hands incredulously over the wall like a blind man trying to recognize a particular house, but he was too tired to feel anything at all. He heard the man with the gun babbling out of sight, 'Such an honour, father. The bell must be rung . . .' and he sat down suddenly on the rain-drenched grass, and leaning his head against the white wall, he fell asleep, with home behind his shoulder-blades.

His dream was full of a jangle of cheerful noise.

# PART THREE

## Chapter 1

THE middle-aged woman sat on the veranda darning socks; she wore pince-nez and she had kicked off her shoes for further comfort. Mr Lehr, her brother, read a New York magazine – it was three weeks old, but that didn't really matter: the whole scene was like peace.

'Just help yourself to water,' Miss Lehr said, 'when you want it.'

A huge earthenware jar stood in a cool corner with a ladle and a tumbler. 'Don't you have to boil the water?' the priest asked.

'Oh no, *our* water's fresh and clean,' Miss Lehr said primly, as if she couldn't answer for anybody else's.

'Best water in the state,' her brother said. The shiny magazine leaves crackled as they turned, covered with photographs of big clean-shaven mastiff jowls – Senators and Congressmen. Pasture stretched away beyond the garden fence, undulating gently towards the next mountain range, and a tulipan tree blossomed and faded daily at the gate.

'You certainly are looking better, father,' Miss Lehr said. They both spoke rather guttural English with slight American accents – Mr Lehr had left Germany when he was a boy to escape military service: he had a shrewd, lined and idealistic face. You needed to be shrewd in this country if you were going to retain any ideals at all and he was cunning in the defence of the good life.

'Oh,' Mr Lehr said, 'he only needed to rest up a few days.' He was quite incurious about this man whom his foreman had brought in on a mule in a state of collapse three days before. All he knew the priest had told him. That was another thing this country taught you – never ask questions or to look ahead.

'So I can go on,' the priest said.

'You don't have to hurry,' said Miss Lehr, turning over her brother's sock, looking for holes.

'It's so quiet here.'

'Oh,' Mr Lehr said, 'we've had our troubles.' He turned a page and said, 'That Senator – Hiram Long – they ought to control him. It doesn't do any good insulting other countries.'

'Haven't they tried to take your land?'

The idealistic face turned his way: it wore a look of innocent craft. 'Oh, I gave them as much as they asked for – five hundred acres of barren land. I saved a lot on taxes. I never could get anything to grow there.' He nodded towards the veranda posts. 'That was the last *real* trouble. See the bullet-holes. Villa's men.'

The priest got up again and drank more water. He wasn't very thirsty; he was satisfying a sense of luxury. He asked, 'How long will it take me to get to Las Casas?'

'You could do it in four days,' Mr Lehr said.

'Not in *his* condition,' Miss Lehr said. 'Six.'

'It will seem so strange,' the priest said. 'A city with churches, a university ...'

'Of course,' Mr Lehr said, 'my sister and I are Lutherans. We don't hold with your Church, father. Too much luxury, it seems to me, while the people starve.'

Miss Lehr said, 'Now, dear, it isn't the father's fault.'

'Luxury?' the priest asked. He stood by the earthenware jar, glass in hand, trying to collect his thoughts, staring out over the long peaceful glassy slopes. 'You mean ...' Perhaps Mr Lehr was right; he had lived very easily once and here he was, already settling down to idleness again.

'All the gold leaf in the churches.'

'It's often just paint, you know,' the priest murmured conciliatingly. He thought: yes, three days and I've done nothing, nothing, and he looked down at his feet elegantly shod in a pair of Mr Lehr's shoes, his legs in Mr Lehr's spare trousers. Mr Lehr said, 'He won't mind my speaking my mind. We're all Christians here.'

'Of course. I like to hear ...'

162

'It seems to me you people make a lot of fuss about inessentials.'

'Yes? You mean . . .'

'Fasting . . . fish on Friday . . .'

Yes, he remembered like something in his childhood that there had been a time when he had observed these rules. He said, 'After all, Mr Lehr, you're a German. A great military nation.'

'I was never a soldier. I disapprove . . .'

'Yes, of course, but still you understand – discipline is necessary. Drills may be no good in battle, but they form the character. Otherwise you get – well, people like me.' He looked down with sudden hatred at the shoes – they were like the badge of a deserter. 'People like me,' he repeated with fury.

There was a good deal of embarrassment; Miss Lehr began to say something, 'Why, father . . .', but Mr Lehr forestalled her, laying down the magazine and its load of well-shaved politicians. He said in his German–American voice with its guttural precision, 'Well, I guess it's time for a bath now. Will you be coming, father?' and the priest obediently followed him into their common bedroom. He took off Mr Lehr's clothes and put on Mr Lehr's mackintosh and followed Mr Lehr barefoot across the veranda and the field beyond. The day before he had asked apprehensively, 'Are there no snakes?' and Mr Lehr had grunted contemptuously that if there were any snakes they'd pretty soon get out of the way. Mr Lehr and his sister had combined to drive out savagery by simply ignoring anything that conflicted with an ordinary German–American homestead. It was, in its way, an admirable mode of life.

At the bottom of the field there was a little shallow stream running over brown pebbles. Mr Lehr took off his dressing-gown and lay down flat on his back. There was something upright and idealistic even in the thin elderly legs with their scrawny muscles. Tiny fishes played over his chest and made little tugs at his nipples undisturbed. This was the skeleton of the youth who had disapproved of militarism to the point of

163

flight. Presently he sat up and began carefully to soap his lean thighs. The priest afterwards took the soap and followed suit. He felt it was expected of him, though he couldn't help thinking it was a waste of time. Sweat cleaned you as effectively as water. But this was the race which had invented the proverb that cleanliness was next to godliness – cleanliness, not purity.

All the same, one did feel an enormous luxury lying there in a little cold stream while the sun sank ... He thought of the prison cell with the old man and the pious woman, the half-caste lying across the hut door, the dead child, and the abandoned station. He thought with shame of his daughter left to her knowledge and her ignorance by the rubbish-dump. He had no right to such luxury.

Mr Lehr said, 'Would you mind – the soap?'

He had heaved over on his face, and now he set to work on his back.

The priest said, 'I think perhaps I should tell you – tomorrow I am saying Mass in the village. Would you prefer me to leave your house? I do not wish to make trouble for you.'

Mr Lehr splashed seriously, cleaning himself. He said, 'Oh, they won't bother me. But you had better be careful. You know, of course, that it's against the law.'

'Yes,' the priest said. 'I know that.'

'A priest I knew was fined four hundred pesos. He couldn't pay and they sent him to prison for a week. What are you smiling at?'

'Only because it seems so ... peaceful here. Prison for a week!'

'Well, I've always heard you people get your own back when it comes to collections. Would you like the soap?'

'No, thank you. I have finished.'

'We'd better be drying ourselves then. Miss Lehr likes to have her bath before sunset.'

As they came back to the bungalow in single file they met Miss Lehr, very bulky under her dressing-gown. She asked mechanically, like a clock with a very gentle chime, 'Is the water nice today?' and her brother answered, as he must have

164

answered a thousand times, 'Pleasantly cool, dear,' and she slopped down across the grass in bedroom slippers, stooping slightly with short sight.

'If you wouldn't mind,' Mr Lehr said, shutting the bedroom door, 'staying in here till Miss Lehr comes back. One can see the stream – you understand – from the front of the house.' He began to dress, tall and bony and a little stiff. Two brass bedsteads, a single chair and a wardrobe – the room was monastic, except that there was no cross – no 'inessentials' as Mr Lehr would have put it. But there was a Bible. It lay on the floor beside one of the beds in a black oilskin cover. When the priest had finished dressing he opened it.

On the flyleaf there was a label which stated that the book was furnished by the Gideons. It went on: 'A Bible in every Hotel Guest Room. Winning Commercial Men for Christ. Good news.' There was then a list of texts. The priest read with some astonishment:

| | | |
|---|---|---|
| If you are in trouble | *read* | Psalm 34. |
| If trade is poor | | Psalm 37. |
| If very prosperous | | I Corinthians, x, 2. |
| If overcome and backsliding | | James I. Hosea xiv, 4–9. |
| If tired of sin | | Psalm 51. Luke xviii, 9–14. |
| If you desire peace, power and plenty | | John 14. |
| If you are lonesome and discouraged | | Psalms 23 and 27. |
| If you are losing confidence in men | | I Corinthians, xiii. |
| If you desire peaceful slumbers | | Psalm 121. |

He couldn't help wondering how it had got here – with its ugly type and its over-simple explanations – into a hacienda in Southern Mexico. Mr Lehr turned away from his mirror with a big coarse hairbrush in his hand and explained carefully, 'My sister ran a hotel once. For drummers. She sold it to join me when my wife died, and she brought one of those from the hotel. You wouldn't understand that, father. You don't like people to read the Bible.' He was on the defensive

165

all the time about his faith, as if he were perpetually conscious of some friction, like that of an ill-fitting shoe.

The priest asked, 'Is your wife buried here?'

'In the paddock,' Mr Lehr said bluntly. He stood listening, brush in hand, to the gentle footsteps outside. 'That's Miss Lehr,' he said, 'come up from her bath. We can go out now.'

The priest got off Mr Lehr's old horse when he reached the church and threw the rein over a bush. This was his first visit to the village since the night he collapsed beside the wall. The village ran down below him in the dusk: tin-roofed bungalows and mud huts faced each other over a single wide grass-grown street. A few lamps had been lit and fire was being carried round among the poorest huts. He walked slowly, conscious of peace and safety. The first man he saw took off his hat and knelt and kissed the priest's hand.

'What is your name?' the priest asked.

'Pedro, father.'

'Good night, Pedro.'

'Is there to be Mass in the morning, father?'

'Yes. There is to be Mass.'

He passed the rural school. The schoolmaster sat on the step: a plump young man with dark brown eyes and horn-rimmed glasses. When he saw the priest coming he looked ostentatiously away. He was the law-abiding element: he wouldn't recognize criminals. He began to talk pedantically and priggishly to someone behind him – something about the infant class. A woman kissed the priest's hand; it was odd to be wanted again, not to feel himself the carrier of death. She asked, 'Father, will you hear our confessions?'

He said, 'Yes. Yes. In Señor Lehr's barn. Before the Mass. I will be there at five. As soon as it is light.'

'There are so many of us, father . . .'

'Well tonight too then . . . At eight.'

'And, father, there are many children to be baptized. There has not been a priest for three years.'

'I am going to be here for two more days.'

'What will you charge, father?'

166

'Well – two pesos is the usual charge.' He thought: I must hire two mules and a guide. It will cost me fifty pesos to reach Las Casas. Five pesos for the Mass – that left forty-five.

'We are very poor here, father,' she haggled gently. 'I have four children myself. Eight pesos is a lot of money.'

'Four children are a lot of children – if the priest was here only three years ago.'

He could hear authority, the old parish intonation coming back into his voice, as if the last years had been a dream and he had never really been away from the Guilds, the Children of Mary, and the daily Mass. He asked sharply, 'How many children are there here – unbaptized?'

'Perhaps a hundred, father.'

He made calculations: there was no need to arrive in Las Casas then as a beggar; he could buy a decent suit of clothes, find a respectable lodging, settle down ... He said, 'You must pay one peso fifty a head.'

'One peso, father. We are very poor.'

'One peso fifty.' A voice from years back said firmly into his ear: they don't value what they don't pay for. It was the old priest he had succeeded at Concepción who had explained to him: 'They will always tell you they are poor, starving, but they will always have a little store of money buried somewhere, in a pot.' The priest said, 'You must bring the money – and the children – to Señor Lehr's barn tomorrow at two in the afternoon.'

She said, 'Yes, father.' She seemed quite satisfied; she had brought him down by fifty centavos a head. The priest walked on. Say a hundred children, he was thinking, that means a hundred and sixty pesos with tomorrow's Mass. Perhaps I can get the mules and the guide for forty pesos. Señor Lehr will give me food for three days. I shall have a hundred and twenty pesos left. After all these years, it was like wealth. He felt respect all the way up the street: men took off their hats as he passed: it was as if he had got back to the days before the persecution. He could feel the old life hardening round him like a habit, a stony cast which held his head high and

167

dictated the way he walked, and even formed his words. A voice from the cantina said, 'Father.'

The man was very fat, with three commercial chins: he wore a waistcoat in spite of the great heat, and a watch-chain. 'Yes?' the priest said. Behind the man's head stood bottles of mineral waters, beer, spirits ... The priest came in out of the dusty street to the heat of the lamp. He asked, 'What is it?' with his new-old manner of authority and impatience.

'I thought, father, you might be in need of a little sacramental wine.'

'Perhaps ... but you will have to give me credit.'

'A priest's credit, father, is always good enough for me. I am a religious man myself. This is a religious place. No doubt you will be holding a baptism.' He leant avidly forward with a respectful and impertinent manner, as if they were two people with the same ideas, educated men.

'Perhaps ...'

The man smiled understandingly. Between people like ourselves, he seemed to indicate, there is no need of anything explicit: we understand each other's thoughts. He said, 'In the old days, when the church was open, I was treasurer to the Guild of the Blessed Sacrament. Oh, I am a good Catholic, father. The people, of course, are very ignorant.' He asked, 'Would you perhaps honour me by taking a glass of brandy?' He was in his way quite sincere.

The priest said doubtfully, 'It is kind ...' The two glasses were already filled. He remembered the last drink he had had, sitting on the bed in the dark, listening to the Chief of Police, and seeing, as the light went on, the last wine drain away ... The memory was like a hand, pulling away the cast, exposing him. The smell of brandy dried his mouth. He thought: what a play-actor I am. I have no business here, among good people. He turned the glass in his hand, and all the other glasses turned too: he remembered the dentist talking of his children and Maria unearthing the bottle of spirits she had kept for him – the whisky priest.

He took a reluctant drink. 'It's good brandy, father,' the man said.

'Yes. Good brandy.'

'I could let you have a dozen bottles for sixty pesos.'

'Where would I find sixty pesos?' He thought that in some ways it was better over there, across the border. Fear and death were not the worst things. It was sometimes a mistake for life to go on.

'I wouldn't make a profit out of you, father. Fifty pesos.'

'Fifty, sixty. It's all the same to me.'

'Go on. Have another glass, father. It's good brandy.' The man leant engagingly forward across the counter and said, 'Why not half a dozen, father, for twenty-four pesos?' He said slyly, 'After all, father – there are the baptisms.'

It was appalling how easily one forgot and went back; he could still hear his own voice speaking in the street with the Concepción accent – unchanged by mortal sin and unrepentance and desertion. The brandy was musty on the tongue with his own corruption. God might forgive cowardice and passion, but was it possible to forgive the habit of piety? He remembered the woman in the prison and how impossible it had been to shake her complacency. It seemed to him that he was another of the same kind. He drank the brandy down like damnation: men like the half-caste could be saved, salvation could strike like lightning at the evil heart, but the habit of piety excluded everything but the evening prayer and the Guild meeting and the feel of humble lips on your gloved hand.

'Las Casas is a fine town, father. They say you can hear Mass every day.'

This was another pious person. There were a lot of them about in the world. He was pouring a little more brandy, but going carefully – not too much. He said, 'When you get there, father, look up a compadre of mine in Guadalupe Street. He has the cantina nearest the church – a good man. Treasurer of the Guild of the Blessed Sacrament – just like I was in this place in the good days. He'll see you get what you want cheap. Now, what about some bottles for the journey?'

The priest drank. There was no point in not drinking. He had the habit now – like piety and the parish voice. He said,

'Three bottles. For eleven pesos. Keep them for me here.'
He finished what was left and went back into the street; the
lamps were lit in windows and the wide street stretched like a
prairie in between. He stumbled in a hole and felt a hand
upon his sleeve. 'Ah, Pedro. That was the name wasn't it?
Thank you, Pedro.'

'At your service, father.'

The church stood in the darkness like a block of ice: it was
melting away in the heat. The roof had fallen in at one place,
a coign above the doorway had crumbled. The priest took a
quick sideways look at Pedro, holding his breath in case it
smelt of brandy, but he could see only the outlines of the face.
He said – with a feeling of cunning as though he were cheating
a greedy prompter inside his own heart – 'Tell the people,
Pedro, that I only want one peso for the baptisms . . .' There
would still be enough for the brandy then, even if he arrived
at Las Casas like a beggar. There was silence for as long as
two seconds and then the wily village voice began to answer
him, 'We are poor, father. One peso is a lot of money. I – for
example – I have three children. Say seventy-five centavos,
father.'

Miss Lehr stretched out her feet in their easy slippers and
the beetles came up over the veranda from the dark outside.
She said, 'In Pittsburgh once . . .' Her brother was asleep with
an ancient newspaper across his knee: the mail had come in.
The priest gave a little sympathetic giggle as in the old days;
it was a try-out which didn't come off. Miss Lehr stopped
and sniffed. 'Funny. I thought I smelt – spirits.'

The priest held his breath, leaning back in the rocking-
chair. He thought, how quiet it is, how safe. He remembered
townspeople who couldn't sleep in country places because of
the silence: silence can be like noise, dinning against the ear-
drums.

'What was I saying father?'

'In Pittsburgh once . . .'

'Of course. In Pittsburgh . . . I was waiting for the train.
You see I had nothing to read. Books are so expensive. So I

170

thought I'd buy a paper – any paper, the news is just the same. But when I opened it – it was called something like *Police News*. I never knew such dreadful things were printed. Of course, I didn't read more than a few lines. I think it was the most dreadful thing that's ever happened to me. It . . . well, it opened my eyes.'

'Yes.'

'I've never told Mr Lehr. He wouldn't think the same of me, I do believe, if he knew.'

'But there was nothing wrong . . .'

'It's knowing, isn't it . . .?'

Somewhere a long way off a bird of some kind called; the lamp on the table began to smoke, and Miss Lehr leant over and turned down the wick: it was as if the only light for miles around had been lowered. The brandy returned on his palate like the smell of ether that reminds a man of a recent operation before he's used to life: it tied him to another state of being. He didn't yet belong to this deep tranquillity. He told himself. In time it will be all right, I shall pull up, I only ordered three bottles this time. They will be the last I'll ever drink, I won't need drink there – he knew he lied. Mr Lehr woke suddenly and said, 'As I was saying . . .'

'You were saying nothing, dear. You were asleep.'

'Oh no, we were talking about that scoundrel Hoover.'

'I don't think so, dear. Not for a long while.'

'Well,' Mr Lehr said, 'it's been a long day. The father will be tired too . . . after all that confessing,' he added with slight distaste.

There had been a continuous stream of penitents from eight to ten – two hours of the worst evil a small place like this could produce after three years. It hadn't amounted to very much – a city would have made a better show – or would it? There isn't much a man can do. Drunkenness, adultery, uncleanness: he sat there tasting the brandy all the while, sitting on a rocking-chair in a horse-box, not looking at the face of the one who knelt at his side. The others had waited, kneeling in an empty stall – Mr Lehr's stable had been depopulated these last few years. He had only one old horse left, which blew windily in the dark as the sins came whimpering out.

'How many times?'

'Twelve, father. Perhaps more,' and the horse blew.

It is astonishing the sense of innocence that goes with sin –
only- the hard and careful man and the saint are free of it.
These people went out of the stable clean; he was the only
one left who hadn't repented, confessed, and been absolved.
He wanted to say to this man, 'Love is not wrong, but love
should be happy and open – it is only wrong when it is
secret, unhappy ... It can be more unhappy than anything
but the loss of God. It *is* the loss of God. You don't need a
penance, my child, you have suffered quite enough,' and to
this other, 'Lust is not the worst thing. It is because any day,
any time, lust may turn into love that we have to avoid it.
And when we love our sin then we are damned indeed.' But
the habit of the confessional reasserted itself: it was as if he
were back in the little stuffy wooden boxlike coffin in which
men bury their uncleanness with their priest. He said, 'Mortal
sin ... danger ... self-control,' as if those words meant anything at all. He said, 'Say three Our Fathers and three Hail
Marys.'

He whispered wearily, 'Drink is only the beginning ...'
He found he had no lesson he could draw against even that
common vice unless it was himself smelling of brandy in the
stable. He gave out the penance, quickly, harshly, mechanically. The man would go away, saying, 'A bad priest,' feeling
no encouragement, no interest ...

He said, 'Those laws were made for man. The Church
doesn't expect ... if you can't fast, you must eat, that's all.'
The old woman prattled on and on, while the penitents stirred
restlessly in the next stall and the horse whinnied, prattled of
abstinence days broken, of evening prayers curtailed. Suddenly, without warning, with an odd sense of homesickness,
he thought of the hostages in the prison yard, waiting at the
water-tap, not looking at him – the suffering and the endurance which went on everywhere the other side of the mountains. He interrupted the woman savagely, 'Why don't you
confess properly to me? I'm not interested in your fish supply

172

or in how sleepy you are at night ... remember your real sins.'

'But I'm a good woman, father,' she squeaked at him with astonishment.

'Then what are you doing here, keeping away the bad people?' He said, 'Have you any love for anyone but yourself?'

'I love God, father,' she said haughtily. He took a quick look at her in the light of the candle burning on the floor – the hard old raisin eyes under the black shawl – another of the pious – like himself.

'How do you know? Loving God isn't any different from loving a man – or a child. It's wanting to be with Him, to be near Him.' He made a hopeless gesture with his hands. 'It's wanting to protect Him from yourself.'

When the last penitent had gone away he walked back across the yard to the bungalow; he could see the lamp burning, and Miss Lehr knitting, and he could smell the grass in the paddock, wet with the first rains. It ought to be possible for a man to be happy here, if he were not so tied to fear and suffering – unhappiness too can become a habit like piety. Perhaps it was his duty to break it, his duty to discover peace. He felt an immense envy of all those people who had confessed to him and been absolved. In six days, he told himself, in Las Casas, I too. ... But he couldn't believe that anyone anywhere would rid him of his heavy heart. Even when he drank he felt bound to his sin by love. It was easier to get rid of hate.

Miss Lehr said, 'Sit down, father. You must be tired. I've never held, of course, with confession. Nor has Mr Lehr.'

'No?'

'I don't know how you can stand sitting there, listening to all the horrible things ... I remember in Pittsburgh once ...'

The two mules had been brought in overnight, so that he could start early immediately after Mass – the second that he had said in Mr Lehr's barn. His guide was sleeping somewhere, probably with the mules, a thin nervous creature, who

173

had never been to Las Casas; he simply knew the route by hearsay. Miss Lehr had insisted the night before that she must call him, although he woke of his own accord before it was light. He lay in bed and heard the alarm go off in another room – dinning like a telephone – and presently he heard the slop, slop of Miss Lehr's bedroom-slippers in the passage outside and a knock-knock on the door. Mr Lehr slept on undisturbed upon his back with the thin rectitude of a bishop upon a tomb.

The priest had lain down in his clothes and he opened the door before Miss Lehr had time to get away; she gave a small squeal of dismay, a bunchy figure in a hair-net.

'Excuse me.'

'Oh, it's quite all right. How long will Mass take, father?'

'There will be a great many communicants. Perhaps three-quarters of an hour.'

'I will have some coffee ready for you – and sandwiches.'

'You must not bother.'

'Oh, we can't send you away hungry.'

She followed him to the door, standing a little behind him, so as not to be seen by anything or anybody in the wide empty early world. The grey light uncurled across the pastures; at the gate the tulipán tree bloomed for yet another day; very far off, beyond the little stream where he had bathed, the people were walking up from the village on the way to Mr Lehr's barn – they were too small at that distance to be human. He had a sense of expectant happiness all round him, waiting for him to take part, like an audience of children at a cinema or a rodeo; he was aware of how happy he might have been if he had left nothing behind him across the range except a few bad memories. A man should always prefer peace to violence, and he was going towards peace.

'You have been very good to me, Miss Lehr.'

How odd it had seemed at first to be treated as a guest, not as a criminal or a bad priest. These were heretics – it never occurred to them that he was not a good man: they hadn't the prying insight of fellow Catholics.

'We've enjoyed having you, father. But you'll be glad to

174

be away. Las Casas is a fine city. A very moral place, as Mr Lehr always says. If you meet Father Quintana you must remember us to him – he was here three years ago.'

A bell began to ring. They had brought the church bell down from the tower and hung it outside Mr Lehr's barn; it was like any Sunday anywhere.

'I've sometimes wished,' Miss Lehr said, 'that I could go to church.'

'Why not?'

'Mr Lehr wouldn't like it. He's very strict. But it happens so seldom nowadays – I don't suppose there'll be another service now for another three years.'

'I will come back before then.'

'Oh no,' Miss Lehr said. 'You won't do that. It's a hard journey and Las Casas is a fine city. They have electric light in the streets: there are two hotels. Father Quintana promised to come back – but there are Christians everywhere, aren't there? Why should he come back here? It isn't even as if we were really badly off.'

A little group of Indians passed the gate, gnarled tiny creatures of the Stone Age. The men in short smocks walked with long poles, and the women with black plaits and knocked-about faces carried their babies on their backs. 'The Indians have heard you are here,' Miss Lehr said. 'They've walked fifty miles – I shouldn't be surprised.' They stopped at the gate and watched him; when he looked at them they went down on their knees and crossed themselves – the strange elaborate mosaic touching the nose and ears and chin. 'My brother gets so angry,' Miss Lehr said, 'if he sees somebody go on his knees to a priest, but I don't see that it does any harm.'

Round the corner of the house the mules were stamping – the guide must have brought them out to give them their maize. They were slow feeders, you had to give them a long start. It was time to begin Mass and be gone. He could smell the early morning. The world was still fresh and green, and in the village below the pastures a few dogs barked. The alarm clock tick-tocked in Miss Lehr's hand. He said, 'I must be

175

going now.' He felt an odd reluctance to leave Miss Lehr and the house and the brother sleeping in the inside room. He was aware of a mixture of tenderness and dependence. When a man wakes after a dangerous operation he puts a special value upon the first face he sees as the anaesthetic wears away.

He had no vestments, but the Masses in this village were nearer to the old parish days than any he had known in the last eight years – there was no fear of interruption, no hurried taking of the sacraments as the police approached. There was even an altar stone brought from the locked church. But because it was so peaceful he was all the more aware of his own sin as he prepared to take the Elements – 'Let not the participation of thy Body, O Lord Jesus Christ, which I, though unworthy, presume to receive, turn to my judgement and condemnation.' A virtuous man can almost cease to believe in Hell, but he carried Hell about with him. Sometimes at night he dreamed of it. *Domine, non sum dignus ... domine, non sum dignus. ...* Evil ran like malaria in his veins. He remembered a dream he had had of a big grassy arena lined with the statues of the saints – but the saints were alive, they turned their eyes this way and that, waiting for something. He waited, too, with an awful expectancy. Bearded Peters and Pauls, with Bibles pressed to their breasts, watched some entrance behind his back he couldn't see – it had the menace of a beast. Then a marimba began to play, tinkly and repetitive, a firework exploded, and Christ danced into the arena – danced and postured with a bleeding painted face, up and down, up and down, grimacing like a prostitute, smiling and suggestive. He woke with the sense of complete despair that a man might feel finding the only money he possessed was counterfeit.

'... and we saw his glory, the glory as of the only-begotten of the Father, full of grace and truth.' Mass was over.

In three days, he told himself, I shall be in Las Casas: I shall have confessed and been absolved, and the thought of the child on the rubbish-heap came automatically back to him with painful love. What was the good of confession when you loved the result of your crime?

The people knelt as he made his way down the barn. He saw the little group of Indians: women whose children he had baptized: Pedro: the man from the cantina was there too, kneeling with his face buried in his plump hands, a chain of beads falling between the fingers. He looked a good man: perhaps he was a good man. Perhaps, the priest thought, I have lost the faculty of judging – that woman in prison may have been the best person there. A horse cried in the early day, tethered to a tree, and all the freshness of the morning came in through the open door.

Two men waited beside the mules; the guide was adjusting a stirrup, and beside him, scratching under the arm-pit, awaiting his coming with a doubtful and defensive smile, stood the half-caste. He was like the small pain that reminds a man of his sickness, or perhaps like the unexpected memory which proves that love after all isn't dead. 'Well,' the priest said, 'I didn't expect you here.'

'No, father, of course not.' He scratched and smiled.

'Have you brought the soldiers with you?'

'What things you do say, father,' he protested with a callow giggle. Behind him, across the yard and through an open door, the priest could see Miss Lehr putting up his sandwiches. She had dressed, but she still wore her hair-net. She was wrapping the sandwiches carefully in grease-proof paper, and her sedate movements had a curious effect of unreality. It was the half-caste who was real. He said, 'What trick are you playing now?' Had he perhaps bribed his guide to lead him back across the border? He could believe almost anything of that man.

'You shouldn't say things like that, father.'

Miss Lehr passed out of sight, with the soundlessness of a dream.

'No?'

'I'm here, father,' the man seemed to take a long breath for his surprising stilted statement, 'on an errand of mercy.'

The guide finished with one mule and began on the next, shortening the already short Mexican stirrup; the priest giggled nervously. 'An errand of mercy?'

177

'Well, father, you're the only priest this side of Las Casas, and the man's dying . . .'

'What man?'

'The Yankee.'

'What are you talking about?'

'The one the police wanted. He robbed a bank. You know the one I mean.'

'He wouldn't need me,' the priest said impatiently, remembering the photograph on the peeling wall watching the first communion party.

'Oh, he's a good Catholic, father.' Scratching under his arm-pit, he didn't look at the priest. 'He's dying, and you and I wouldn't like to have on our conscience what that man . . .'

'We shall be lucky if we haven't worse.'

'What do you mean, father?'

The priest said, 'He only killed and robbed. He hasn't betrayed his friends.'

'Holy Mother of God, I've never . . .'

'We both have,' the priest said. He turned to the guide. 'Are the mules ready?'

'Yes, father.'

'We'll start then.' He had forgotten Miss Lehr completely; the other world had stretched a hand across the border, and he was again in the atmosphere of flight.

'Where are you going?' the half-caste said.

'To Las Casas.' He climbed stiffly on to his mule. The half-caste held on to his stirrup-leather, and he was reminded of their first meeting: there was the same mixture of complaint, appeal, abuse. 'You're a fine priest,' he wailed up to him. 'Your bishop ought to hear of this. A man's dying, wants to confess, and just because you want to get to the city . . .'

'Why do you think me such a fool?' the priest said. 'I know why you've come. You're the only one they've got who can recognize me, and they can't follow me into this state. Now if I ask you where this American is, you'll tell me – I know – you don't have to speak – that he's just the other side.'

178

'Oh no, father, you're wrong there. He's just this side.'

'A mile or two makes no difference.

'It's an awful thing, father,' the half-caste said, 'never to be believed. Just because once – well, I admit it – '

The priest kicked his mule into motion. They passed out of Mr Lehr's yard and turned south; the half-caste trotted at his stirrup.

'I remember,' the priest said, 'that you told me you'd never forget my face.'

'And I haven't,' the man put in triumphantly, 'or I wouldn't be here, would I? Listen, father, I'll admit a lot. You don't know how a reward will tempt a poor man like me. And when you wouldn't trust me, I thought, well, if that's how he feels – I'll show him. But I'm a good Catholic, father, and when a dying man wants a priest . . .'

They climbed the long slope of Mr Lehr's pastures which led to the next range of hills. The air was still fresh, at six in the morning, at three thousand feet; up there tonight it would be very cold – they had another six thousand feet to climb. The priest said uneasily, 'Why should I put my head in *your* noose?' It was too absurd.

'Look, father.' The half-caste was holding up a scrap of paper: the familiar writing caught the priest's attention – the large deliberate handwriting of a child. The paper had been used to wrap up food; it was smeared and greasy. He read, 'The Prince of Denmark is wondering whether he should kill himself or not, whether it is better to go on suffering all the doubts about his father, or by one blow . . .'

'Not that, father, on the other side. That's nothing.'

The priest turned the paper and read a single phrase written in English in blunt pencil: 'For Christ's sake, father . . .' The mule, unbeaten, lapsed into a slow heavy walk; the priest made no attempt to urge it on: this piece of paper left no doubt whatever.

He asked, 'How did this come to you?'

'It was this way, father. I was with the police when they shot him. It was in a village the other side. He picked up a child to act as a screen, but, of course, the soldiers didn't pay any attention. It was only an Indian. They were both shot, but he escaped.'

'Then how . . . ?'

'It was this way, father.' He positively prattled. It appeared that he was afraid of the lieutenant, who resented the fact that the priest had escaped, and so he planned to slip across the border, out of reach. He got his chance at night, and on the way – it was probably on this side of the state line, but who knew where one state began or another ended? – he came on the American. He had been shot in the stomach . . .

'How could he have escaped then?'

'Oh, father, he is a man of superhuman strength. He was dying, he wanted a priest . . .'

'How did he tell you that?'

'It only needed two words, father.' Then, to prove the story, the man had found enough strength to write this note, and so . . . the story had as many holes in it as a sieve. But what remained was this note, like a memorial stone you couldn't overlook.

The half-caste bridled angrily again. 'You don't trust me, father.'

'Oh no,' the priest said. 'I don't trust you.'

'You think I'm lying.'

'Most of it is lies.'

He pulled the mule up and sat thinking, facing south. He was quite certain that this was a trap – probably the half-caste had suggested it – but it was a fact that the American was there, dying. He thought of the deserted banana station where something had happened and the Indian child lay dead on the maize: there was no question at all that he was needed. A man with all that on his soul . . . The oddest thing of all was that he felt quite cheerful; he had never really believed in this peace. He had dreamed of it so often on the other side that now it meant no more to him than a dream. He began to whistle a tune – something he had heard somewhere once. 'I found a rose in my field': it was time he woke up. It wouldn't really have been a good dream – that confession in Las Casas when he would have had to admit, as well as everything else, that he had denied confession to a dying man.

He asked, 'Will the man still be alive?'

'I think so, father,' the half-caste caught him eagerly up.

'How far is it?'

'Four – five hours, father.'

'You can take it in turns to ride the other mule.'

The priest turned his mule back and called out to the guide. The man dismounted and stood inertly there, while he explained. The only remark he made was to the half-caste, motioning him into the saddle, 'Be careful of that saddle-bag. The father's brandy's there.'

They rode slowly back: Miss Lehr was at her gate. She said, 'You forgot the sandwiches, father.'

'Oh yes. Thank you.' He stole a quick look round – it didn't mean a thing to him. He said, 'Is Mr Lehr still asleep?'

'Shall I wake him?'

'No, no. But you will thank him for his hospitality?'

'Yes. And perhaps, father, in a few years we shall see you again? As you said.' She looked curiously at the half-caste, and he stared back through his yellow insulting eyes.

The priest said, 'It's possible,' glancing away with a sly secretive smile.

'Well, good-bye, father. You'd better be off, hadn't you? The sun's getting high.'

'Good-bye, my dear Miss Lehr.' The mestizo slashed impatiently at his mule and stirred it into action.

'Not that way, my man,' Miss Lehr called.

'I have to pay a visit first,' the priest explained, and breaking into an uncomfortable trot he bobbed down behind the mestizo's mule towards the village. They passed the white-washed church – that too belonged to a dream. Life didn't contain churches. The long untidy village street opened ahead of them. The schoolmaster was at his door and waved an ironic greeting, malicious and horn-rimmed. 'Well, father, off with your spoils?'

The priest stopped his mule. He said to the half-caste, 'Really . . . I had forgotten . . .'

'You did well out of the baptisms,' the schoolmaster said. 'It pays to wait a few years, doesn't it?'

'Come on, father,' the half-caste urged him. 'Don't listen to him.' He spat. 'He's a bad man.'

The priest said, 'You know the people here better than anyone. If I leave a gift, will you spend it on things that do no harm – I mean food, blankets – not books?'

'They need food more than books.'

'I have forty-five pesos here . . .'

The mestizo wailed, 'Father, what are you doing . . .?'

'Conscience money?' the schoolmaster said.

'Yes.'

'All the same, of course I thank you. It's good to see a priest with a conscience. It's a stage in evolution,' he said, his glasses flashing in the sunlight, a plump embittered figure in front of his tin-roofed shack, an exile.

They passed the last houses, the cemetery, and began to climb. 'Why, father, why?' the half-caste protested.

'He's not a bad man, he does his best, and I shan't need money again, shall I?' the priest asked, and for quite a while they rode without speaking, while the sun came blindingly out, and the mules' shoulders strained on the steep rocky paths, and the priest began to whistle again – 'I have a rose' – the only tune he knew. Once the half-caste started a complaint about something, 'The trouble with you, father, is . . .' but it petered out before it was defined because there wasn't really anything to complain about as they rode steadily north towards the border.

'Hungry?' the priest asked at last.

The half-caste muttered something that sounded angry or derisive.

'Take a sandwich,' the priest said, opening Miss Lehr's packet.

## Chapter 2

'THERE,' the half-caste said, with a sort of whinny of triumph, as though he had lain innocently all these seven hours under the suspicion of lying. He pointed across the barranca to a group of Indian huts on a peninsula of rock jutting out across the chasm. They were perhaps two hundred yards away, but it would take another hour at least to reach them, winding down a thousand feet and up another thousand.

The priest sat on his mule watching intently; he could see no movement anywhere. Even the look-out, the little platform of twigs built on a mound above the huts, was empty. He said, 'There doesn't seem to be anybody about.' He was back in the atmosphere of desertion.

'Well,' the half-caste said, 'you didn't expect anybody, did you? Except him. He's there. You'll soon find that.'

'Where are the Indians?'

'There you go again,' the man complained. 'Suspicion. Always suspicion. How should I know where the Indians are? I told you he was quite alone, didn't I?'

The priest dismounted. 'What are you doing now?' the half-caste cried despairingly.

'We shan't need the mules any more. They can be taken back.'

'Not need them? How are you going to get away from here?'

'Oh,' the priest said, 'I won't have to think about that, will I?' He counted out forty pesos and said to the muleteer, 'I hired you for Las Casas. Well, this is your good luck. Six days' pay.'

'You don't want me any more, father?'

'No, I think you'd better get away from here quickly. Leave you-know-what behind.'

The half-caste said excitedly, 'We can't walk all that way, father. Why, the man's dying.'

'We can go just as quickly on our own hooves. Now,

183

friend, be off.' The mestizo watched the mules pick their way along the narrow stony path with a look of wistful greed; they disappeared round a shoulder of rock – crack, crack, crack, the sound of their hooves contracted into silence.

'Now,' the priest said briskly, 'we won't delay any more,' and he started down the path, with a small sack slung over his shoulder. He could hear the half-caste panting after him: his wind was bad. They had probably let him have far too much beer in the capital, and the priest thought, with an odd touch of contemptuous affection, of how much had happened to them both since that first encounter in a village of which he didn't even know the name – the half-caste lying there in the hot noonday rocking his hammock with one naked yellow foot. If he had been asleep at that moment, this wouldn't have happened. It was really shocking bad luck for the poor devil that he was to be burdened with a sin of such magnitude. The priest took a quick look back and saw the big toes protruding like slugs out of the dirty gym shoes; the man picked his way down, muttering all the time – his perpetual grievance didn't help his wind. Poor man, the priest thought, he isn't really bad enough . . .

And he wasn't strong enough either for *this* journey. By the time the priest had reached the bottom of the barranca he was fifty yards behind. The priest sat down on a boulder and mopped his forehead, and the half-caste began to complain long before he was down to his level, 'There isn't so much hurry as all that.' It was almost as though the nearer he got to his treachery the greater the grievance against his victim became.

'Didn't you say he was dying?' the priest asked.

'Oh yes, dying, of course. But that can take a long time.'

'The longer the better for all of us,' the priest said. 'Perhaps you are right. I'll take a rest here.'

But now, like a contrary child, the half-caste wanted to start again. He said, 'You do nothing in moderation. Either you run or you sit.'

'Can I do nothing right?' the priest teased him, and then

he put in sharply and shrewdly, 'They will let me see him, I suppose?'

'Of course,' the half-caste said and immediately checked himself. 'They, they? Who are you talking about now? First you complain that the place is empty, and then you talk of "they".' He said with tears in his voice, 'You may be a good man, but why won't you talk plainly, so that a man can understand you? It's enough to make a man a bad Catholic.'

The priest said, 'You see this sack here. We don't want to carry that any farther. It's heavy. I think a little drink will do us both good. We both need courage, don't we?'

'Drink, father?' the half-caste asked with excitement, and watched the priest unpack a bottle. He never took his eyes away while the priest drank. His two fangs stuck greedily out, quivering slightly on the lower lip. Then he too fastened on the mouth. 'It's illegal, I suppose,' the priest said with a giggle, 'on this side of the border – if we are on this side.' He had another draw himself and handed it back: it was soon exhausted – he took the bottle and threw it at a rock and it exploded like shrapnel. The half-caste started. He said, 'Be careful. People might think you'd got a gun.'

'As for the rest,' the priest said, 'we won't need that.'

'You mean there's more of it?'

'Two more bottles – but we can't drink any more in this heat. We'd better leave it here.'

'Why didn't you say it was heavy, father? I'll carry it for you. You've only to ask me to do a thing. I'm willing. Only you just won't ask.'

They set off again uphill, the bottles clinking gently; the sun shone vertically down on the pair of them. It took them the best part of an hour to reach the top of the barranca. Then the watch-tower gaped over their path like an upper jaw and the tops of the huts appeared over the rocks above them. Indians do not build their settlements on a mule path; they prefer to stand aside and see who comes. The priest wondered how soon the police would appear; they were keeping very carefully hidden.

185

'This way, father.' The half-caste took the lead, scrambling away from the path up the rocks to the little plateau. He looked anxious, almost as if he had expected something to happen before this. There were about a dozen huts; they stood quiet, like tombs against the heavy sky. A storm was coming up.

The priest felt a nervous impatience; he had walked into this trap, the least they could do was to close it quickly, finish everything off. He wondered whether they would suddenly shoot him down from one of the huts. He had come to the very edge of time: soon there would be no tomorrow and no yesterday, just existence going on for ever. He began to wish he had taken a little more brandy. His voice broke uncertainly when he said, 'Well, we are here. Where is this Yankee?'

'Oh yes, the Yankee,' the half-caste said, jumping a little. It was as if for a moment he had forgotten the pretext. He stood there, gaping at the huts, wondering too. He said, 'He was over there when I left him.'

'Well, he couldn't have moved, could he?'

If it hadn't been for that letter he would have doubted the very existence of the American – and if he hadn't seen the dead child too, of course. He began to walk across the little silent clearing towards the hut: would they shoot him before he got to the entrance? It was like walking a plank blindfold: you didn't know at what point you would step off into space for ever. He hiccuped once and knotted his hands behind his back to stop them trembling. He had been glad in a way to turn from Miss Lehr's gate – he had never really believed that he would ever get back to parish work and the daily Mass and the careful appearances of piety, but all the same you needed to be a little drunk to die. He got to the door – not a sound anywhere; then a voice said, 'Father.'

He looked round. The mestizo stood in the clearing with his face contorted: the two fangs jumped and jumped; he looked frightened.

'Yes, what is it?'

'Nothing, father.'

'Why did you call me?'

'I said nothing,' he lied.

The priest turned and went in.

The American was there all right. Whether he was alive was another matter. He lay on a straw mat with his eyes closed and his mouth open and his hands on his belly, like a child with stomach-ache. Pain alters a face – or else successful crime has its own falsity like politics or piety. He was hardly recognizable from the news picture on the police station wall; that was tougher, arrogant, a man who had made good. This was just a tramp's face. Pain had exposed the nerves and given the face a kind of spurious intelligence.

The priest knelt down and put his face near the man's mouth, trying to hear the breathing. A heavy smell came up to him – a mixture of vomit and cigar smoke and stale drink; it would take more than a few lilies to hide this corruption. A very faint voice close to his ear said in English, 'Beat it, father.' Outside the door, in the stormy sunlight, the mestizo stood, staring towards the hut, a little loose about the knees.

'So you're alive, are you?' the priest said briskly. 'Better hurry. You haven't got long.'

'Beat it, father.'

'You wanted me, didn't you? You're a Catholic?'

'Beat it,' the voice whispered again, as if those were the only words it could remember of a lesson learnt some while ago.

'Come now,' the priest said. 'How long is it since you went to confession?'

The eyelids rolled up and astonished eyes looked up at him. The man said in a puzzled voice, 'Ten years, I guess. What are you doing here anyway?'

'You asked for a priest. Come now. Ten years is a long time.'

'You got to beat it, father,' the man said. He was remembering the lesson now; lying there flat on the mat with his hands folded on his stomach, any vitality that was left had accumulated in the brain: he was like a reptile crushed at one end. He said in a strange voice, 'That bastard . . .' The priest said furiously, 'What sort of a confession is this? I make a five hours' journey . . . and all I get out of you are evil words.'

187

It seemed to him horribly unfair that his uselessness should return with his danger – he couldn't do anything for a man like this.

'Listen, father . . .' the man said.

'I am listening.'

'You beat it out of here quick. I didn't know . . .'

'I haven't come all this way to talk about myself,' the priest said. 'The sooner your confession's done, the sooner I will be gone.'

'You don't need to trouble about me. I'm through.'

'You mean damned?' the priest said angrily.

'Sure. Damned,' the man replied, licking blood away from his lips.

'You listen to me,' the priest said, leaning closer to the stale and nauseating smell, 'I have come here to listen to your confession. Do you want to confess?'

'No.'

'Did you when you wrote that note . . . ?'

'Maybe.'

'I know what you want to tell me. I know it, do you understand? Let that be. Remember you are dying. Don't depend too much on God's mercy. He has given you this chance. He may not give you another. What sort of a life have you led all these years? Does it seem so grand now? You've killed a lot of people – that's about all. Anybody can do that for a while, and then he is killed too. Just as you are killed. Nothing left except pain.'

'Father.'

'Yes?' The priest gave an impatient sigh, leaning closer. He hoped for a moment that at last he had got the man started on some meagre train of sorrow.

'You take my gun, father. See what I mean? Under my arm.'

'I haven't any use for a gun.'

'Oh yes, you have.' The man detached one hand from his stomach and began to move it slowly up his body. So much effort: it was unbearable to watch. The priest said sharply, 'Lie still. It's not there.' He could see the holster empty under the arm-pit.

188

'Bastards,' the man said, and his hand lay wearily where it had got to, over his heart; he imitated the prudish attitude of a female statue, one hand over the breast and one upon the stomach. It was very hot in the hut; the heavy light of the storm lay over them.

'Listen, father . . .' The priest sat hopelessly at the man's side; nothing would shift that violent brain towards peace: once, hours ago perhaps, when he wrote that message – but the chance had come and gone. He was whispering now something about a knife. There was a legend believed by many criminals that dead eyes held the picture of what they had last seen – a Christian could believe that the soul did the same, held absolution and peace at the final moment, after a lifetime of the most hideous crime: or sometimes pious men died suddenly in brothels unabsolved and what had seemed a good life went out with the permanent stamp on it of impurity. He had heard men talk of the unfairness of a deathbed repentance – as if it was an easy thing to break the habit of a life whether to do good or evil. One suspected the good of the life that ended badly – or the viciousness that ended well. He made another desperate attempt. He said 'You believed once. Try and understand – this is your chance. At the last moment. Like the thief. You have murdered men – children perhaps,' he added, remembering the little black heap under the cross. 'But that need not be so important. It only belongs to this life, a few years – it's over already. You can drop it all here, in this hut, and go on for ever . . .' He felt sadness and longing at the vaguest idea of a life he couldn't lead himself . . . words like peace, glory, love.

'Father,' the voice said urgently, 'you let me be. You look after yourself. You take my knife . . .' The hand began its weary march again – this time towards the hip. The knees crooked up in an attempt to roll over, and then the whole body gave up the effort, the ghost, everything.

The priest hurriedly whispered the words of conditional absolution, in case, for one second before it crossed the border, the spirit had repented, but it was more likely that it had gone over still seeking its knife, bent on vicarious

189

violence. He prayed: 'O merciful God, after all he was thinking of me, it was for my sake ...' but he prayed without conviction. At the best, it was only one criminal trying to aid the escape of another – whichever way you looked, there wasn't much merit in either of them.

## Chapter 3

A VOICE said, 'Well, have you finished now?'

The priest got up and made a small scared gesture of assent. He recognized the police officer who had given him money at the prison, a dark smart figure in the doorway with the storm-light glinting on his leggings. He had one hand on his revolver and he frowned sourly in at the dead gunman. 'You didn't expect to see me,' he said.

'Oh, but I did,' the priest said. 'I must thank you. '

'Thank me, what for?'

'For letting me stay alone with him.'

'I am not a barbarian,' the officer said. 'Will you come out now, please? It's no use at all your trying to escape. You can see that,' he added, as the priest emerged and looked round at the dozen armed men who surrounded the hut.

'I've had enough of escaping,' he said. The half-caste was no longer in sight; the heavy clouds were piling up the sky: they made the real mountains look like little bright toys below them. He sighed and giggled nervously. 'What a lot of trouble I had getting across those mountains, and now ... here I am ...'

'I never believed you would return.'

'Oh well, lieutenant, you know how it is. Even a coward has a sense of duty.' The cool fresh wind which sometimes blows across before a storm breaks touched his skin. He said with badly-affected ease, 'Are you going to shoot me now?'

The lieutenant said again sharply, 'I am not a barbarian. You will be tried ... properly.'

'What for?'

'For treason.'

'I have to go all the way back there?'

'Yes. Unless you try to escape.' He kept his hand on his gun as if he didn't trust the priest a yard. He said, 'I could swear that somewhere . . .'

'Oh yes,' the priest said. 'You have seen me twice. When you took a hostage from my village . . . you asked my child: "Who is he?" She said: "My father," and you let me go.' Suddenly the mountains ceased to exist: it was as if somebody had dashed a handful of water into their faces.

'Quick,' the lieutenant said, 'into that hut.' He called out to one of the men. 'Bring us some boxes so that we can sit.'

The two of them joined the dead man in the hut as the storm came up all round them. A soldier dripping with rain carried in two packing-cases. 'A candle,' the lieutenant said. He sat down on one of the cases and took out his revolver. He said, 'Sit down, there, away from the door, where I can see you.' The soldier lit a candle and stuck it in its own wax on the hard earth floor, and the priest sat down, close to the American; huddled up in his attempt to get at his knife he gave an effect of wanting to reach his companion, to have a word or two in private. They looked two of a kind, dirty and unshaved: the lieutenant seemed to belong to a different class altogether. He said with contempt, 'So you have a child?'

'Yes,' the priest said.

'You – a priest?'

'You mustn't think they are all like me.' He watched the candlelight blink on the bright buttons. He said, 'There are good priests and bad priests. It is just that I am a bad priest.'

'Then perhaps we will be doing your Church a service . . .'

'Yes.'

The lieutenant looked sharply up as if he thought he was being mocked. He said, 'You told me twice. That I had seen you twice.'

'Yes, I was in prison. And you gave me money.'

191

'I remember.' He said furiously, 'What an appalling mockery. To have had you and then to let you go. Why, we lost two men looking for you. They'd be alive today . . .' The candle sizzled as the drops of rain came through the roof. 'This American wasn't worth two lives. He did no real harm.'

The rain poured ceaselessly down. They sat in silence. Suddenly the lieutenant said, 'Keep your hand away from your pocket.'

'I was only feeling for a pack of cards. I thought perhaps it would help to pass the time . . .'

'I don't play cards,' the lieutenant said harshly.

'No, no. Not a game. Just a few tricks I can show you. May I?'

'All right. If you wish to.'

Mr Lehr had given him an old pack of cards. The priest said, 'Here, you see, are three cards. The ace, the king, and the jack. Now,' he spread them fanwise out on the floor, 'tell me which is the ace.'

'This, of course,' the lieutenant said grudgingly, showing no interest.

'But you are wrong,' the priest said, turning it up. 'That is the jack.'

The lieutenant said contemptuously, 'A game for gamblers — or children.'

'There is another trick,' the priest said, 'called Fly-away Jack. I cut the pack into three — so. And I take this Jack of Hearts and I put it into the centre pack — so. Now I tap the three packs.' His face lit up as he spoke — it was such a long time since he had handled cards — he forgot the storm, the dead man and the stubborn unfriendly face opposite him. 'I say Fly-away Jack' — he cut the left-hand pack in half and disclosed the jack — 'and there he is.'

'Of course there are two jacks.'

'See for yourself.' Unwillingly the lieutenant leant forward and inspected the centre pack. He said, 'I suppose you tell the Indians that that is a miracle of God.'

'Oh no,' the priest giggled, 'I learnt it from an Indian. He was the richest man in the village. Do you wonder? with such a hand. No, I used to show the tricks at any entertainments we had in the parish – for the Guilds, you know.'

A look of physical disgust crossed the lieutenant's face. He said, 'I remember those Guilds.'

'When you were a boy?'

'I was old enough to know . . .'

'Yes?'

'The trickery.' He broke out furiously with one hand on his gun, as though it had crossed his mind that it would be better to eliminate this beast, now, at this instant, for ever. 'What an excuse it all was, what a fake. Sell all and give to the poor – that was the lesson, wasn't it? and Señora So-and-so, the druggist's wife, would say the family wasn't really deserving of charity, and Señor This, That and the Other would say that if they starved, what else did they deserve, they were Socialists anyway, and the priest – you – would notice who had done his Easter duty and paid his Easter offering.' His voice rose – a policeman looked into the hut anxiously and withdrew again through the lashing rain. 'The Church was poor, the priest was poor, therefore everyone should sell all and give to the Church.'

The priest said, 'You are so right.' He added quickly, 'Wrong too, of course.'

'How do you mean?' the lieutenant asked savagely. 'Right? Won't you even defend . . . ?'

'I felt at once that you were a good man when you gave me money at the prison.'

The lieutenant said, 'I only listen to you because you have no hope. No hope at all. Nothing you say will make any difference.'

'No.'

He had no intention of angering the police officer, but he had had very little practice the last eight years in talking to any but a few peasants and Indians. Now something in his tone infuriated the lieutenant. He said, 'You're a danger. That's why we kill you. I have nothing against you, you understand, as a man.'

'Of course not. It's God you're against. I'm the sort of man you shut up every day – and give money to.'

'No, I don't fight against a fiction.'

'But I'm not worth fighting, am I? You've said so. A liar, a drunkard. That man's worth a bullet more than I am.'

'It's your ideas.' The lieutenant sweated a little in the hot steamy air. He said, 'You are so cunning, you people. But tell me this – what have you ever done in Mexico for *us*? Have you ever told a landlord he shouldn't beat his peon – oh yes, I know, in the confessional perhaps, and it's your duty, isn't it, to forget it at once. You come out and have dinner with him and it's your duty not to know that he has murdered a peasant. That's all finished. He's left it behind in your box.'

'Go on,' the priest said. He sat on the packing-case with his hands on his knees and his head bent; he couldn't, though he tried, keep his mind on what the lieutenant was saying. He was thinking – forty-eight hours to the capital. Today is Sunday. Perhaps on Wednesday I shall be dead. He felt it as a treachery that he was more afraid of the pain of bullets than of what came after.

'Well, we have ideas too,' the lieutenant was saying. 'No more money for saying prayers, no more money for building places to say prayers in. We'll give people food instead, teach them to read, give them books. We'll see they don't suffer.'

'But if they want to suffer . . .'

'A man may want to rape a woman. Are we to allow it because he wants to? Suffering is wrong.'

'And you suffer all the time,' the priest commented, watching the sour Indian face behind the candle-flame. He said, 'It sounds fine, doesn't it? Does the jefe feel like that too?'

'Oh, we have our bad men.'

'And what happens afterwards? I mean after everybody has got enough to eat and can read the right books – the books you let them read?'

'Nothing. Death's a fact. We don't try to alter facts.'

'We agree about a lot of things,' the priest said, idly dealing out his cards. 'We have facts, too, we don't try to alter – that the world's unhappy whether you are rich or poor – unless you are a saint, and there aren't many of those. It's not worth bothering too much about a little pain here. There's one belief we both of us have – that we'll all be dead in a hundred years.' He fumbled, trying to shuffle, and bent the cards: his hands were not steady.

'All the same, you're worried now about a little pain,' the lieutenant said maliciously, watching his fingers.

'But I'm not a saint,' the priest said. 'I'm not even a brave man.' He looked up apprehensively: light was coming back: the candle was no longer necessary. It would soon be clear enough to start the long journey back. He felt a desire to go on talking, to delay even by a few minutes the decision to start. He said, 'That's another difference between us. It's no good your working for your end unless you're a good man yourself. And there won't always be good men in your party. Then you'll have all the old starvation, beating, get-rich-anyhow. But it doesn't matter so much my being a coward – and all the rest. I can put God into a man's mouth just the same – and I can give him God's pardon. It wouldn't make any difference to that if every priest in the Church was like me.'

'That's another thing I don't understand,' the lieutenant said, 'why you – of all people – should have stayed when the others ran.'

'They didn't all run,' the priest said.

'But why did you stay?'

'Once,' the priest said, 'I asked myself that. The fact is, a man isn't presented suddenly with two courses to follow: one good and one bad. He gets caught up. The first year – well, I didn't believe there was really any cause to run. Churches have been burnt before now. You know how often. It doesn't mean much. I thought I'd stay till next month, say, and see if things were better. Then – oh, you don't know how time can slip by.' It was quite light again now: the afternoon rain was over: life had to go on. A policeman passed the entrance of the hut and looked in curiously at the pair of them. 'Do you know I suddenly realized that I was the only priest left for miles around? The law which made priests marry finished them. They went: they were quite right to go. There was one

195

priest in particular – he had always disapproved of me. I have a tongue, you know, and it used to wag. He said – quite rightly – that I wasn't a firm character. He escaped. It felt – you'll laugh at this – just as it did at school when a bully I had been afraid of – for years – got too old for any more teaching and was turned out. You see, I didn't have to think about anybody's opinion any more. The people – they didn't worry me. They liked me.' He gave a weak smile, sideways, towards the humped Yankee.

'Go on,' the lieutenant said moodily.

'You'll know all there is to know about me at this rate,' the priest said, with a nervous giggle, 'by the time I get to, well, prison.'

'It's just as well. To know an enemy, I mean.'

'That other priest was right. It was when he left I began to go to pieces. One thing went after another. I got careless about my duties. I began to drink. It would have been much better, I think, if I had gone too. Because pride was at work all the time. Not love of God.' He sat bowed on the packing-case, a small plump man in Mr Lehr's cast-off clothes. He said, 'Pride was what made the angels fall. Pride's the worst thing of all. I thought I was a fine fellow to have stayed when the others had gone. And then I thought I was so grand I could make my own rules. I gave up fasting, daily Mass. I neglected my prayers – and one day because I was drunk and lonely – well, you know how it was, I got a child. It was all pride. Just pride because I'd stayed. I wasn't any use, but I stayed. At least, not much use. I'd got so that I didn't have a hundred communicants a month. If I'd gone I'd have given God to twelve times that number. It's a mistake one makes – to think just because a thing is difficult or dangerous . . .' He made a flapping motion with his hands.

The lieutenant said in a tone of fury, 'Well, you're going to be a martyr – you've got that satisfaction.'

'Oh no. Martyrs are not like me. They don't think all the time – if I had drunk more brandy I shouldn't be so afraid.'

The lieutenant said sharply to a man in the entrance, 'Well, what is it? What are you hanging round for?'

'The storm's over, lieutenant. We wondered when we were to start?'

'We start immediately.'

He got up and put back the pistol in his holster. He said, 'Get a horse ready for the prisoner. And have some men dig a grave quickly for the Yankee.'

The priest put the cards in his pocket and stood up. He said, 'You have listened very patiently . . .'

'I am not afraid,' the lieutenant said, 'of other people's ideas.'

Outside the ground was steaming after the rain: the mist rose nearly to their knees: the horses stood ready. The priest mounted, but before they had time to move a voice made the priest turn – the same sullen whine he had heard so often. 'Father.' It was the half-caste.

'Well, well,' the priest said. 'You again.'

'Oh, I know what you're thinking,' the half-caste said. 'There's not much charity in you, father. You thought all along I was going to betray you.'

'Go,' the lieutenant said sharply. 'You've done your job.'

'May I have one word, lieutenant?' the priest asked.

'You're a good man, father,' the mestizo cut quickly in, 'but you think the worst of people. I just want your blessing, that's all.'

'What is the good? You can't sell a blessing,' the priest said.

'It's just because we won't see each other again. And I didn't want you to go off there thinking ill things . . .'

'You are so superstitious,' the priest said. 'You think my blessing will be like a blinker over God's eyes. I can't stop him knowing all about it. Much better go home and pray. Then if he gives you grace to feel sorry, give away the money . . .'

'What money, father?' The half-caste shook his stirrup angrily. 'What money? There you go again . . .'

The priest sighed. He felt empty with the ordeal. Fear can be more tiring than a long monotonous ride. He said, 'I'll pray for you,' and beat his horse into position beside the lieutenant's.

197

'And I'll pray for you, father,' the half-caste announced complacently. Once the priest looked back as his horse poised for the steep descent between the rocks. The half-caste stood alone among the huts, his mouth a little open, showing the two long fangs. He might have been snapped in the act of shouting some complaint or some claim – that he was a good Catholic perhaps; one hand scratched under the arm-pit. The priest waved his hand; he bore no grudge because he expected nothing else of anything human and he had one cause at least for satisfaction – that yellow and unreliable face would be absent 'at the death'.

'You're a man of education,' the lieutenant said. He lay across the entrance of the hut with his head on his rolled cape and his revolver by his side. It was night, but neither man could sleep. The priest, when he shifted, groaned a little with stiffness and cramp. The lieutenant was in a hurry to get home, and they had ridden till midnight. They were down off the hills and in the marshy plain. Soon the whole State would be subdivided by swamp. The rains had really begun.

'I'm not that. My father was a storekeeper.'

'I mean, you've been abroad. You can talk like a Yankee. You've had schooling.'

'Yes.'

'I've had to think things out for myself. But there are some things which you don't have to learn in a school. That there are rich and poor.' He said in a low voice, 'I've shot three hostages because of you. Poor men. It made me hate you.'

'Yes,' the priest admitted, and tried to stand to ease the cramp in his right thigh. The lieutenant sat up quickly, gun in hand: 'What are you doing?'

'Nothing. Just cramp. That's all.' He lay down again with a groan.

The lieutenant said, 'Those men I shot. They were my own people. I wanted to give them the whole world.'

'Well, who knows? Perhaps that's what you did.'

The lieutenant spat suddenly, viciously, as if something unclean had got upon his tongue. He said, 'You always have answers which mean nothing.'

'I was never any good at books,' the priest said. 'I haven't any memory. But there was one thing always puzzled me about men like yourself. You hate the rich and love the poor. Isn't that right?'

'Yes.'

'Well, if I hated you, I wouldn't want to bring up my child to be like you. It's not sense.'

'That's just twisting...'

'Perhaps it is. I've never got your ideas straight. We've always said the poor are blessed and the rich are going to find it hard to get into heaven. Why should we make it hard for the poor man too? Oh, I know we are told to give to the poor, to see they are not hungry – hunger can make a man do evil just as much as money can. But why should we give the poor power? It's better to let him die in dirt and wake in heaven – so long as we don't push his face in the dirt.'

'I hate your reasons,' the lieutenant said. 'I don't want reasons. If you see somebody in pain, people like you reason and reason. You say – pain's a good thing, perhaps he'll be better for it one day. I want to let my heart speak.'

'At the end of a gun.'

'Yes. At the end of a gun.'

'Oh well, perhaps when you're my age you'll know the heart's an untrustworthy beast. The mind is too, but it doesn't talk about love. Love. And a girl puts her head under water or a child's strangled, and the heart all the time says love, love.'

They lay quiet for a while in the hut. The priest thought the lieutenant was asleep until he spoke again. 'You never talk straight. You say one thing to me – but to another man, or a woman, you say, "God is love." But you think that stuff won't go down with me, so you say different things. Things you think I'll agree with.'

'Oh,' the priest said, 'that's another thing altogether – God *is* love. I don't say the heart doesn't feel a taste of it, but what a taste. The smallest glass of love mixed with a pint pot of

199

ditch-water. We wouldn't recognize *that* love. It might even look like hate. It would be enough to scare us – God's love. It set fire to a bush in the desert, didn't it, and smashed open graves and set the dead walking in the dark. Oh, a man like me would run a mile to get away if he felt that love around.'

'You don't trust him much, do you? He doesn't seem a grateful kind of God. If a man served me as well as you've served him, well, I'd recommend him for promotion, see he got a good pension . . . if he was in pain, with cancer, I'd put a bullet through his head.'

'Listen,' the priest said earnestly, leaning forward in the dark, pressing on a cramped foot, 'I'm not as dishonest as you think I am. Why do you think I tell people out of the pulpit that they're in danger of damnation if death catches them unawares? I'm not telling them fairy stories I don't believe myself. I don't know a thing about the mercy of God: I don't know how awful the human heart looks to Him. But I do know this – that if there's ever been a single man in this state damned, then I'll be damned too.' He said slowly, 'I wouldn't want it to be any different. I just want justice, that's all.'

'We'll be in before dark,' the lieutenant said. Six men rode in front and six behind; sometimes, in the belts of forest between the arms of the river, they had to ride in single file. The lieutenant didn't speak much, and once, when two of his men struck up a song about a fat shopkeeper and his woman, he told them savagely to be silent. It wasn't a very triumphal procession. The priest rode with a weak grin fixed on his face; it was like a mask he had stuck on, so that he could think quietly without anyone noticing. What he thought about mostly was pain.

'I suppose,' the lieutenant said, scowling ahead, 'you're hoping for a miracle.'

'Excuse me. What did you say?'

'I said I suppose you're hoping for a miracle.'

'No.'

'You believe in them, don't you?'

'Yes. But not for me. I'm no more good to anyone, so why should God keep me alive?'

'I can't think how a man like you can believe in those things. The Indians, yes. Why, the first time they see an electric light they think it's a miracle.'

'And I dare say the first time you saw a man raised from the dead you might think so too.' He giggled unconvincingly behind the smiling mask. 'Oh, it's funny, isn't it? It isn't a case of miracles not happening — it's just a case of people calling them something else. Can't you see the doctors round the dead man? He isn't breathing any more, his pulse has stopped, his heart's not beating: he's dead. Then somebody gives him back his life, and they all — what's the expression? — reserve their opinion. They won't say it's a miracle, because that's a word they don't like. Then it happens again and again perhaps — because God's about on earth — and they say: these aren't miracles, it is simply that we have enlarged our conception of what life is. Now we know you can be alive without pulse, breath, heart-beats. And they invent a new word to describe that state of life, and they say science has disproved a miracle.' He giggled again. 'You can't get round them.'

They were out of the forest track on to a hard-beaten road, and the lieutenant dug in his spur and the whole cavalcade broke into a canter. They were nearly home now. The lieutenant said grudgingly, 'You aren't a bad fellow. If there's anything I can do for you . . .'

'If you would give permission for me to confess . . .'

The first houses came into sight, little hard-baked houses of earth falling into ruin, a few classical pillars just plaster over mud, and a dirty child playing in the rubble.

The lieutenant said, 'But there's no priest.'

'Padre José.'

'Oh, Padre José,' the lieutenant said with contempt, 'he's no good for you.'

'He's good enough for me. It's not likely I'd find a saint here, is it?'

The lieutenant rode on for a little while in silence; they

201

came to the cemetery, full of chipped angels, and passed the great portico with its black letters, 'Silencio'. He said, 'All right. You can have him.' He wouldn't look at the cemetery as they went by – there was the wall where prisoners were shot. The road went steeply downhill towards the river; on the right, where the cathedral had been, the iron swings stood empty in the hot afternoon. There was a sense of desolation everywhere, more of it than in the mountains because a lot of life had once existed here. The lieutenant thought: No pulse, no breath, no heart-beat, but it's still life – we've only got to find a name for it. A small boy watched them pass; he called out to the lieutenant, 'Lieutenant, have you got him?' and the lieutenant dimly remembered the face – one day in the plaza – a broken bottle, and he tried to smile back, an odd sour grimace, without triumph or hope. One had to begin again with that.

## Chapter 4

THE lieutenant waited till after dark and then he went himself. It would be dangerous to send another man because the news would be around the city in no time that Padre José had been permitted to carry out a religious duty in the prison. It was wiser not to let even the jefe know. One didn't trust one's superiors when one was more successful than they were. He knew the jefe wasn't pleased that he had brought the priest in – an escape would have been better from his point of view.

In the patio he could feel himself watched by a dozen eyes. The children clustered there ready to shout at Padre José if he appeared. He wished he had promised the priest nothing, but he was going to keep his word – because it would be a triumph for that old corrupt God-ridden world if it could show itself superior on any point – whether of courage, truthfulness, justice . . .

Nobody answered his knock; he stood darkly in the patio like a petitioner. Then he knocked again, and a voice called, 'A moment. A moment.'

Padre José put his face against the bars of his window and

asked, 'Who's there?' He seemed to be fumbling at something near the ground.

'Lieutenant of police.'

'Oh,' Padre José squeaked. 'Excuse me. It is my trousers. In the dark.' He seemed to heave at something and there was a sharp crack, as if his belt or braces had given way. Across the patio the children began to squeak, 'Padre José. Padre José.' When he came to the door he wouldn't look at them, muttering tenderly, 'The little devils.'

The lieutenant said, 'I want you to come to the police station.'

'But I've done nothing. Nothing. I've been so careful.'

'Padre José,' the children squeaked.

He said imploringly, 'If it's anything about a burial, you've been misinformed. I wouldn't even say a prayer.'

'Padre José. Padre José.'

The lieutenant turned and strode across the patio. He said furiously to the faces at the grid, 'Be quiet. Go to bed. At once. Do you hear me?' They dropped out of sight one by one, but immediately the lieutenant's back was turned, they were there again watching.

Padre José said, 'Nobody can do anything with those children.'

A woman's voice said, 'Where are you, José?'

'Here, my dear. It is the police.'

A huge woman in a white nightdress came billowing out at them. It wasn't much after seven; perhaps she lived, the lieutenant thought, in that dress – perhaps she lived in bed. He said, 'Your husband,' dwelling on the term with satisfaction, 'your husband is wanted at the station.'

'Who says so?'

'I do.'

'He's done nothing.'

'I was just saying, my dear . . .'

'Be quiet. Leave the talking to me.'

'You can both stop jabbering,' the lieutenant said. 'You're wanted at the station to see a man – a priest. He wants to confess.'

'To me?'

'Yes. There's no one else.'

'Poor man,' Padre José said. His little pink eyes swept the patio. 'Poor man.' He shifted uneasily, and took a quick furtive look at the sky where the constellations wheeled.

'You won't go,' the woman said.

'It's against the law, isn't it?' Padre José asked.

'You needn't trouble about that.'

'Oh, we needn't, eh?' the woman said. 'I can see through you. You don't want my husband to be let alone. You want to trick him. I know your work. You get people to ask him to say prayers – he's a kind man. But I'd have you remember this – he's a pensioner of the government.'

The lieutenant said slowly, 'This priest – he has been working for years secretly – for *your* Church. We've caught him and, of course, he'll be shot tomorrow. He's not a bad man, and I told him he could see you. He seems to think it will do him good.'

'I know him,' the woman interrupted, 'he's a drunkard. That's all he is.'

'Poor man,' Padre José said. 'He tried to hide here once.'

'I promise you,' the lieutenant said, 'nobody shall know.'

'Nobody know?' the woman cackled. 'Why, it will be all over town. Look at those children there. They never leave José alone.' She went on, 'There'll be no end of it – everybody will be wanting to confess, and the Governor will hear of it, and the pension will be stopped.'

'Perhaps, my dear,' José said, 'it's my duty . . .'

'You aren't a priest any more,' the woman said, 'you're my husband.' She used a coarse word. 'That's your duty now.'

The lieutenant listened to them with acid satisfaction. It was like rediscovering an old belief. He said, 'I can't wait here while you argue. Are you going to come with me?'

'He can't make you,' the woman said.

'My dear, it's only that . . . well . . . I *am* a priest.'

'A priest,' the woman cackled, 'you a priest.' She went off into a peal of laughter, which was taken up tentatively by the

204

children at the window. Padre José put his fingers up to his pink eyes as if they hurt. He said, 'My dear ...' and the laughter went on.

'Are you coming?'

Padre José made a despairing gesture – as much as to say, what does one more failure matter in a life like this? He said, 'I don't think it's – possible.'

'Very well,' the lieutenant said. He turned abruptly – he hadn't any more time to waste on mercy, and heard Padre José's voice speak imploringly, 'Tell him I shall pray.' The children had gained confidence; one of them called out sharply, 'Come to bed, José,' and the lieutenant laughed once – a poor unconvincing addition to the general laughter which now surrounded Padre José, chiming up all round towards the disciplined constellations he had once known by name.

The lieutenant opened the cell door. It was very dark inside. He shut the door carefully behind him and locked it, keeping his hand on his gun. He said, 'He won't come.'

A little bunched figure in the darkness was the priest. He crouched on the floor like a child playing. He said, 'You mean – not tonight?'

'I mean he won't come at all.'

There was silence for some while, if you could talk of silence where there was always the drill-drill of mosquitoes and the little crackling explosions of beetles against the wall. At last the priest said, 'He was afraid, I suppose ...'

'His wife wouldn't let him come.'

'Poor man.' He tried to giggle, but no sound could have been more miserable than the half-hearted attempt. His head drooped between his knees; he looked as if he had abandoned everything and been abandoned.

The lieutenant said, 'You had better know everything. You've been tried and found guilty.'

'Couldn't I have been present at my own trial?'

'It wouldn't have made any difference.'

'No.' He was silent, preparing an attitude. Then he asked

with a kind of false jauntiness, 'And when, if I may ask . . . ?'

'Tomorrow.' The promptness and brevity of the reply called his bluff. His head went down again and he seemed, as far as it was possible to see in the dark, to be biting his nails.

The lieutenant said, 'It's bad being alone on a night like this. If you would like to be transferred to the common cell . . .'

'No, no. I'd rather be alone. I've got plenty to do.' His voice failed, as though he had a heavy cold. He wheezed, 'So much to think about.'

'I should like to do something for you,' the lieutenant said. 'I've brought you some brandy.'

'Against the law?'

'Yes.'

'It's very good of you.' He took the small flask. 'You wouldn't need this, I dare say. But I've always been afraid of pain.'

'We have to die some time,' the lieutenant said. 'It doesn't seem to matter so much when.'

'You're a good man. You've got nothing to be afraid of.'

'You have such odd ideas,' the lieutenant complained. He said, 'Sometimes I feel you're just trying to talk me round.'

'Round to what?'

'Oh, to letting you escape perhaps – or to believing in the Holy Catholic Church, the communion of saints . . . how does that stuff go?'

'The forgiveness of sins.'

'You don't believe much in that, do you?'

'Oh yes, I believe,' the little man said obstinately.

'Then what are you worried about?'

'I'm not ignorant, you see. I've always known what I've been doing. And I can't absolve myself.'

'Would Father José coming here have made all that difference?'

He had to wait a long while for his answer, and then he didn't understand it when it came. 'Another man . . . it makes it easier . . .'

'Is there nothing more I can do for you?'

'No. Nothing.'

The lieutenant reopened the door; mechanically putting his hand again upon his revolver he felt moody, as though now the last priest was under lock and key, there was nothing left to think about. The spring of action seemed to be broken. He looked back on the weeks of hunting as a happy time which was over now for ever. He felt without a purpose, as if life had drained out of the world. He said with bitter kindness (he couldn't summon up any hate of the small hollow man), 'Try to sleep.'

He was closing the door when a scared voice spoke. 'Lieutenant.'

'Yes.'

'You've seen people shot. People like me.'

'Yes.'

'Does the pain go on – a long time?'

'No, no. A second,' he said roughly, and closed the door, and picked his way back across the whitewashed yard. He went into the office. The pictures of the priest and the gunman were still pinned up on the wall: he tore them down – they would never be wanted again. Then he sat at his desk and put his head upon his hands and fell asleep with utter weariness. He couldn't remember afterwards anything of his dreams except laughter, laughter all the time, and a long passage in which he could find no door.

The priest sat on the floor, holding the brandy-flask. Presently he unscrewed the cap and put his mouth to it. The spirit didn't do a thing to him – it might have been water. He put it down again and began some kind of a general confession, speaking in a whisper. He said, 'I have committed fornication.' The formal phrase meant nothing at all: it was like a sentence in a newspaper: you couldn't feel repentance over a thing like that. He started again, 'I have lain with a woman,' and tried to imagine the other priest asking him, 'How many times? Was she married?' 'No.' Without thinking what he was doing, he took another drink of brandy.

As the liquid touched his tongue he remembered his child,

coming in out of the glare: the sullen unhappy knowledgeable face. He said, 'Oh God, help her. Damn me, I deserve it, but let her live for ever.' This was the love he should have felt for every soul in the world: all the fear and the wish to save concentrated unjustly on the one child. He began to weep; it was as if he had to watch her from the shore drown slowly because he had forgotten how to swim. He thought: This is what I should feel all the time for everyone, and he tried to turn his brain away towards the half-caste, the lieutenant, even a dentist he had once sat with for a few minutes, the child at the banana station, calling up a long succession of faces, pushing at his attention as if it were a heavy door which wouldn't budge. For those were all in danger too. He prayed, 'God help them,' but in the moment of prayer he switched back to his child beside the rubbish-dump, and he knew it was for her only that he prayed. Another failure.

After a while he began again: 'I have been drunk – I don't know how many times; there isn't a duty I haven't neglected; I have been guilty of pride, lack of charity . . .' The words were becoming formal again, meaning nothing. He had no confessor to turn his mind away from the formula to the fact.

He took another drink of brandy, and getting up with pain because of his cramp he moved to the door and looked through the bars at the hot moony square. He could see the police asleep in their hammocks, and one man who couldn't sleep lazily rocking up and down, up and down. There was an odd silence everywhere, even in the other cells; it was as if the whole world had tactfully turned away to avoid seeing him die. He felt his way back along the wall to the farthest corner and sat down with the flask between his knees. He thought: If I hadn't been so useless, useless. . . . The eight hard hopeless years seemed to him to be only a caricature of service: a few communions, a few confessions, and an endless bad example. He thought: If I had only one soul to offer, so that I could say, Look what I've done. . . . People had died for him, they had deserved a saint, and a tinge of bitterness spread across his mind for their sake that God hadn't thought fit to send them one. Padre José and me, he thought, Padre

José and me, and he took a drink again from the brandy flask. He thought of the cold faces of the saints rejecting him.

The night was slower than the last he had spent in prison because he was alone. Only the brandy, which he finished about two in the morning, gave him any sleep at all. He felt sick with fear, his stomach ached, and his mouth was dry with the drink. He began to talk aloud to himself because he couldn't stand the silence any more. He complained miserably, 'It's all very well . . . for saints,' and later, 'How does he know it only lasts a second? How long's a second?' Then he began to cry, beating his head gently against the wall. They had given a chance to Padre José, but they had never given him a chance at all. Perhaps they had got it all wrong – just because he had escaped them for such a time. Perhaps they really thought he would refuse the conditions Padre José had accepted, that he would refuse to marry, that he was proud. Perhaps if he suggested it himself, he would escape yet. The hope calmed him for a while, and he fell asleep with his head against the wall.

He had a curious dream. He dreamed he was sitting at a café table in front of the high altar of the cathedral. About six dishes were spread before him, and he was eating hungrily. There was a smell of incense and an odd sense of elation. The dishes – like all food in dreams – did not taste of much, but he had a sense that when he had finished them, he would have the best dish of all. A priest passed to and fro before the altar saying Mass, but he took no notice: the service no longer seemed to concern him. At last the six plates were empty; someone out of sight rang the sanctus bell, and the serving priest knelt before he raised the Host. But *he* sat on, just waiting, paying no attention to the God over the altar, as though that were a God for other people and not for him. Then the glass by his plate began to fill with wine, and looking up he saw that the child from the banana station was serving him. She said, 'I got it from my father's room.'

'You didn't steal it?'

'Not exactly,' she said in her careful and precise voice.

He said, 'It is very good of you. I had forgotten the code – what did you call it?'

'Morse.'

'That was it. Morse. Three long taps and one short one,' and immediately the taps began: the priest by the altar tapped, a whole invisible congregation tapped along the aisles – three long and one short. He asked, 'What is it?'

'News,' the child said, watching him with a stern, responsible and interested gaze.

When he woke up it was dawn. He woke with a huge feeling of hope which suddenly and completely left him at the first sight of the prison yard. It was the morning of his death. He crouched on the floor with the empty brandy-flask in his hand trying to remember an Act of Contrition. 'O God, I am sorry and beg pardon for all my sins ... crucified ... worthy of thy dreadful punishments.' He was confused, his mind was on other things: it was not the good death for which one always prayed. He caught sight of his own shadow on the cell wall; it had a look of surprise and grotesque unimportance. What a fool he had been to think that he was strong enough to stay when others fled. What an impossible fellow I am, he thought, and how useless. I have done nothing for anybody. I might just as well have never lived. His parents were dead – soon he wouldn't even be a memory – perhaps after all he was not at the moment afraid of damnation – even the fear of pain was in the background. He felt only an immense disappointment because he had to go to God empty-handed, with nothing done at all. It seemed to him, at that moment, that it would have been quite easy to have been a saint. It would only have needed a little self-restraint and a little courage. He felt like someone who has missed happiness by seconds at an appointed place. He knew now that at the end there was only one thing that counted – to be a saint.

# PART FOUR

MRS FELLOWS lay in bed in the hot hotel room, listening to the siren of a boat on the river. She could see nothing because she had a handkerchief soaked in eau-de-Cologne over her eyes and forehead. She called sharply out, 'My dear. My dear,' but nobody replied. She felt that she had been prematurely buried in this big brass family tomb, all alone on two pillows, under a canopy. 'Dear,' she said again sharply, and waited.

'Yes, Trixy?' It was Captain Fellows. He said, 'I was asleep, dreaming . . .'

'Put some more Cologne on this handkerchief, dear. My head's splitting.'

'Yes, Trixy.'

He took the handkerchief away; he looked old and tired and bored – a man without a hobby, walking over to the dressing-table.

'Not too much, dear. It will be days before we can get any more.'

He didn't answer, and she said sharply, 'You heard what I said, dear, didn't you?'

'Yes.'

'You are so silent these days. You don't realize what it is to be ill and alone.'

'Well,' Captain Fellows said, 'you know how it is.'

'But we agreed, dear, didn't we, that it was better just to say nothing at all, ever. We mustn't be morbid.'

'No.'

'We've got our own life to lead.'

'Yes.'

He came across to the bed and laid the handkerchief over his wife's eyes. Then sitting down on a chair, he slipped his hand under the net and felt for her hand. They gave an odd effect of being children, lost in a strange town, without adult care.

211

'Have you got the tickets?' she asked.

'Yes, dear.'

'I must get up later and pack, but my head hurts so. Did you tell them to collect the boxes?'

'I forgot.'

'You really must try to think of things,' she said weakly and sullenly, 'there's no one else,' and they both sat silent at a phrase they should have avoided. He said suddenly, 'There's a lot of excitement in town.'

'Not a revolution?'

'Oh no. They caught a priest and he's being shot this morning, poor devil. I can't help wondering whether it's the man Coral – I mean the man we sheltered.'

'It's not likely.'

'No.'

'There are so many priests.'

He let go of her hand and going to the window looked out. Boats on the river, a small stony public garden with a bust and vultures everywhere.

Mrs Fellows said, 'It will be good to be back home. I sometimes thought I should die in this place.'

'Of course not, dear.'

'Well, people do.'

'Yes, they do,' he said glumly.

'Now, dear,' Mrs Fellows said sharply, 'your promise.' She gave a long sigh, 'My poor head.'

'Would you like some aspirin?'

'I don't know where I've put it. Somehow nothing is ever in its place.'

'Shall I go out and get you some more?'

'No, dear, I can't bear to be left alone.' She went on with dramatic brightness, 'I expect I shall be all right when we get home. I'll have a proper doctor then. I sometimes think it's more than a headache. Did I tell you that I'd heard from Norah?'

'No.'

'Get me my glasses, dear, and I'll read you – what concerns us.'

'They're on your bed.'

'So they are.' One of the sailing-boats cast off and began to drift down the wide sluggish stream, going towards the sea. She read with satisfaction, 'Dear Trix: how you have suffered. That scoundrel . . .' She broke abruptly off. 'Oh yes, and then she goes on: "Of course, you and Charles must stay with us for a while until you have found somewhere to live. If you don't mind semi-detached . . ."'

Captain Fellows said suddenly and harshly, 'I'm not going back.'

'"The rent is only fifty-six pounds a year, exclusive, and there's a maid's bathroom."'

'I'm staying.'

'"A cookanheat." What on earth are you saying, dear?'

'I'm not going back.'

'We've been over that so often, dear. You know it would kill me to stay.'

'You needn't stay.'

'But I couldn't go alone,' Mrs Fellows said. 'What on earth would Norah think? Besides – oh, it's absurd.'

'A man here can do a job of work.'

'Picking bananas,' Mrs Fellows said. She gave a little cold laugh. 'And you weren't much good at that.'

He turned furiously towards the bed. 'You don't mind,' he said, 'do you – running away and leaving *her* . . .'

'It wasn't my fault. If you'd been at home . . .' She began to cry hunched up under the mosquito-net. She said, 'I'll never get home alive.'

He came wearily over to the bed and took her hand again. It was no good. They had both been deserted. They had to stick together. 'You won't leave me alone, will you, dear?' she asked. The room reeked of eau-de-Cologne.

'No, dear.'

'You do realize how absurd it is?'

'Yes.'

They sat in silence for a long while, as the morning sun climbed outside and the room got stiflingly hot. Mrs Fellows said at last, 'A penny, dear. '

'What?'

'For your thoughts.'

'I was just thinking of that priest. A queer fellow. He drank. I wonder if it's him.'

'If it is, I expect he deserves all he gets.'

'But the odd thing is – the way she went on afterwards – as if he'd told her things.'

'Darling,' Mrs Fellows repeated, with harsh weakness from the bed, 'your promise.'

'Yes, I'm sorry. I was trying, but it seems to come up all the time.'

'We've got each other, dear,' Mrs Fellows said, and the letter from Norah rustled as she turned her head, swathed in handkerchief, away from the hard outdoor light.

Mr Tench bent over the enamel basin washing his hands with pink soap. He said in his bad Spanish, 'You don't need to be afraid. You can tell me directly it hurts.'

The jefe's room had been fixed up as a kind of temporary dentistry – at considerable expense, for it had entailed transporting not only Mr Tench himself but Mr Tench's cabinet, chair, and all sorts of mysterious packing-cases which seemed to contain little but straw and which were unlikely to return empty.

'I've had it for months,' the jefe said. 'You can't imagine the pain . . .'

'It was foolish of you not to call me in sooner. Your mouth's in a very bad state. You are lucky to have escaped pyorrhoea.'

He finished washing and suddenly stood, towel in hand, thinking of something. 'What's the matter?' the jefe asked. Mr Tench woke with a jump, and coming forward to his cabinet, began to lay out the drill needles in a little metallic row of pain. The jefe watched with apprehension. He said, 'Your hand is very jumpy. Are you quite sure you are well enough this morning?'

'It's indigestion,' Mr Tench said. 'Sometimes I have so many spots in front of my eyes I might be wearing a veil.'

He fitted a needle into the drill and bent the arm round. 'Now open your mouth very wide.' He began to stuff the jefe's mouth with plugs of cotton. He said, 'I've never seen a mouth as bad as yours – except once.'

The jefe struggled to speak. Only a dentist could have interpreted the muffled and uneasy question.

'He wasn't a patient. I expect someone cured him. You cure a lot of people in this country, don't you, with bullets?'

As he picked and picked at the tooth, he tried to keep up a running fire of conversation; that was how one did things at Southend. He said, 'An odd thing happened to me just before I came up the river. I got a letter from my wife. Hadn't so much as heard from her for – oh, twenty years. Then out of the blue she . . .' he leant closer and levered furiously with his pick: the jefe beat the air and grunted. 'Wash out your mouth,' Mr Tench said, and began grimly to fix his drill. He said, 'What was I talking about? Oh, the wife, wasn't it? Seems she had got religion of some kind. Some sort of a group – Oxford. What would she be doing in Oxford? Wrote to say that she had forgiven me and wanted to make things legal. Divorce, I mean. Forgiven *me*,' Mr Tench said, looking round the little hideous room, lost in thought, with his hand on the drill. He belched and put his other hand against his stomach, pressing, pressing, seeking an obscure pain which was nearly always there. The jefe leant back exhausted with his mouth wide open.

'It comes and goes,' Mr Tench said, losing the thread of his thought completely. 'Of course, it's nothing. Just indigestion. But it gets me locked.' He stared moodily into the mouth as though a crystal were concealed between the carious teeth. Then, as if he were exerting an awful effort of will, he leant forward, brought the arm of the drill round and began to pedal. Buzz and grate. Buzz and grate. The jefe stiffened all over and clutched the arms of the chair, and Mr Tench's foot went up and down, up and down. The jefe made odd sounds and waved his hands. 'Hold hard,' Mr Tench said, 'hold hard. There's just one tiny corner. Nearly finished. There she comes. There.' He stopped and said, 'Good God, what's that?'

215

He left the jefe altogether and went to the window. In the yard below a squad of police had just grounded their arms. With his hand on his stomach he protested, 'Not another revolution?'

The jefe levered himself upright and spat out a gag. 'Of course not,' he said. 'A man's being shot.'

'What for?'

'Treason.'

'I thought you generally did it,' Mr Tench said, 'up by the cemetery?' A horrid fascination kept him by the window: this was something he had never seen. He and the vultures looked down together on the little whitewashed courtyard.

'It was better not to this time. There might have been a demonstration. People are so ignorant.'

A small man came out of a side door: he was held up by two policemen, but you could tell that he was doing his best – it was only that his legs were not fully under his control. They paddled him across to the opposite wall; an officer tied a handkerchief round his eyes. Mr Tench thought: But I know him. Good God, one ought to do something. This was like seeing a neighbour shot.

The jefe said, 'What are you waiting for? The air gets into this tooth.'

Of course there was nothing to do. Everything went very quickly like a routine. The officer stepped aside, the rifles went up, and the little man suddenly made jerky movements with his arms. He was trying to say something: what was the phrase they were always supposed to use? That was routine too, but perhaps his mouth was too dry, because nothing came out except a word that sounded like 'Excuse'. The crash of the rifles shook Mr Tench: they seemed to vibrate inside his own guts: he felt sick and shut his eyes. Then there was a single shot, and opening them again he saw the officer stuffing his gun back into his holster, and the little man was a routine heap beside the wall – something unimportant which had to be cleared away. Two knock-kneed men approached quickly. This was an arena, and the bull was dead, and there was nothing more to wait for any more.

216

'Oh,' the jefe moaned from the chair, 'the pain, the pain.' He implored Mr Tench, 'Hurry,' but Mr Tench was lost in thought beside the window, one hand automatically seeking in his stomach for the hidden uneasiness. He remembered the little man rising bitterly and hopelessly from his chair that blinding afternoon to follow the child out of town; he remembered a green watering-can, the photo of the children, that cast he was making out of sand for a split palate.

'The filling,' the jefe pleaded, and Mr Tench's eyes went to the gold on the glass dish. Currency – he would insist on foreign currency: this time he was going to clear out, clear out for good. In the yard everything had been tidied away; a man was throwing sand out of a spade, as if he were filling a grave. But there was no grave: there was nobody there: an appalling sense of loneliness came over Mr Tench, doubling him with indigestion. The little fellow had spoken English and knew about his children. He felt deserted.

'And now,' the woman's voice swelled triumphantly, and the two little girls with beady eyes held their breath, 'the great testing day had come.' Even the boy showed interest, standing by the window, looking out into the dark curfew-emptied street – this was the last chapter, and in the last chapter things always happened violently. Perhaps all life was like that – dull and then a heroic flurry at the end.

'When the Chief of Police came to Juan's cell he found him on his knees, praying. He had not slept at all, but had spent his last night preparing for martyrdom. He was quite calm and happy, and smiling at the Chief of Police, he asked him if he had come to lead him to the banquet. Even that evil man, who had persecuted so many innocent people, was visibly moved.'

If only it would get on towards the shooting, the boy thought: the shooting never failed to excite him, and he always waited anxiously for the *coup de grâce*.

'They led him out into the prison yard. No need to bind those hands now busy with his beads. In that short walk to the wall of execution, did young Juan look back on those few, those happy years he had so bravely spent? Did he remember days in the seminary, the kindly rebukes of his elders, the moulding discipline, days, too, of frivolity when he acted Nero before the old bishop? Nero was here beside him, and this the Roman amphitheatre.'

The mother's voice was getting a little hoarse: she fingered the remaining pages rapidly: it wasn't worth while stopping now, and she raced more and more rapidly on.

'Reaching the wall, Juan turned and began to pray – not for himself, but for his enemies, for the squad of poor innocent Indian soldiers who faced him and even for the Chief of Police himself. He raised the crucifix at the end of his beads and prayed that God would forgive them, would enlighten their ignorance, and bring them at last – as Saul the persecutor was brought – into his eternal kingdom.'

'Had they loaded?' the boy asked.

'What do you mean – "had they loaded"?'

'Why didn't they fire and stop him?'

'Because God decided otherwise.' She coughed and went on: 'The officer gave the command to present arms. In that moment a smile of complete adoration and happiness passed over Juan's face. It was as if he could see the arms of God open to receive him. He had always told his mother and sisters that he had a premonition that he would be in heaven before them. He would say with a whimsical smile to his mother, the good but over-careful housewife: "I will have tidied everything up for you." Now the moment had come, the officer gave the order to fire, and – ' She had been reading too fast because it was past the little girls' bedtime and now she was thwarted by a fit of hiccups. 'Fire,' she repeated, 'and . . .'

The two little girls sat placidly side by side – they looked nearly asleep – this was the part of the book they never cared much about; they endured it for the sake of the amateur theatricals and the first communion, and of the sister who became a nun and paid a moving farewell to her family in the third chapter.

218

'Fire,' the mother tried again, 'and Juan, raising both arms above his head, called out in a strong brave voice to the soldiers and the levelled rifles, "Hail, Christ the King." Next moment he fell riddled with a dozen bullets and the officer, stooping over his body, put his revolver close to Juan's ear and pulled the trigger.'

A long sigh came from the window.

'No need to have fired another shot. The soul of the young hero had already left its earthly mansion, and the happy smile on the dead face told even those ignorant men where they would find Juan now. One of the men there that day was so moved by his bearing that he secretly soaked his handkerchief in the martyr's blood, and that handkerchief, cut into a hundred relics, found its way into many pious homes. And now,' the mother went rapidly on, clapping her hands, 'to bed.'

'And that one,' the boy said, 'they shot today. Was he a hero too?'

'Yes.'

'The one who stayed with us that time?'

'Yes. He was one of the martyrs of the Church.'

'He had a funny smell,' one of the little girls said.

'You must never say that again,' the mother said. 'He may be one of the saints.'

'Shall we pray to him then?'

The mother hesitated. 'It would do no harm. Of course, before we *know* he is a saint, there will have to be miracles ...'

'Did he call "*Viva el Cristo Rey*"?' the boy asked.

'Yes. He was one of the heroes of the faith.'

'And a handkerchief soaked in blood?' the boy went on. 'Did anyone do that?'

The mother said ponderously, 'I have reason to believe ... Señora Jiminez told me ... I think if your father will give me a little money, I shall be able to get a relic.'

'Does it cost money?'

'How else could it be managed? Everybody can't have a piece.'

'No.'

He squatted beside the window, staring out, and behind his back came the muffled sound of small girls going to bed. It brought it home to one – to have had a hero in the house, though it had only been for twenty-four hours. And he was the last. There were no more priests and no more heroes. He listened resentfully to the sound of booted feet coming up the pavement. Ordinary life pressed round him. He got down from the window-seat and picked up his candle – Zapata, Villa, Madero, and the rest, they were all dead, and it was people like the man out there who killed them. He felt deceived.

The lieutenant came along the pavement; there was something brisk and stubborn about his walk, as if he were saying at every step, 'I have done what I have done.' He looked in at the boy holding the candle with a look of indecisive recognition. He said to himself, 'I would do much more for him and them, more more; life is never going to be again for them what it was for me,' but the dynamic love which used to move his trigger-finger felt flat and dead. Of course, he told himself, it will come back. It was like love of a woman and went in cycles: he had satisfied himself that morning, that was all. This was satiety. He smiled painfully at the child through the window and said, '*Buenas noches.*' The boy was looking at his revolver-holster and he remembered an incident in the plaza when he had allowed a child to touch his gun – perhaps this boy. He smiled again and touched it too – to show he remembered, and the boy crinkled up his face and spat through the window bars, accurately, so that a little blob of spittle lay on the revolver-butt.

The boy went across the patio to bed. He had a little dark room with an iron bedstead that he shared with his father. He lay next to the wall and his father would lie on the outside, so that he could come to bed without waking his son. He took off his shoes and undressed glumly by candlelight. He could hear the whispering of prayers in the other room; he felt cheated and disappointed because he had missed something. Lying on his back in the heat he stared up at the

220

ceiling, and it seemed to him that there was nothing in the world but the store, his mother reading, and silly games in the plaza.

But very soon he went to sleep. He dreamed that the priest whom they had shot that morning was back in the house dressed in the clothes his father had lent him and laid out stiffly for burial. The boy sat beside the bed and his mother read out of a very long book all about how the priest had acted in front of the bishop the part of Julius Caesar: there was a fish basket at her feet, and the fish were bleeding, wrapped in her handkerchief. He was very bored and very tired and somebody was hammering nails into a coffin in the passage. Suddenly the dead priest winked at him – an unmistakable flicker of the eyelid, just like that.

He woke and there was the crack, crack on the knocker on the outer door. His father wasn't in bed and there was complete silence in the other room. Hours must have passed. He lay listening. He was frightened, but after a short interval the knocking began again, and nobody stirred anywhere in the house. Reluctantly, he put his feet on the ground – it might be only his father locked out; he lit the candle and wrapped a blanket round himself and stood listening again. His mother might hear it and go, but he knew very well that it was *his* duty. He was the only man in the house.

Slowly he made his way across the patio towards the outer door. Suppose it was the lieutenant come back to revenge himself for the spittle ... He unlocked the heavy iron door and swung it open. A stranger stood in the street, a tall pale thin man with a rather sour mouth, who carried a small suitcase. He named the boy's mother and asked if this were the señora's house. Yes, the boy said, but she was asleep. He began to shut the door, but a pointed shoe got in the way.

The stranger said, 'I have only just landed. I came up the river tonight. I thought perhaps ... I have an introduction for the señora from a great friend of hers.'

'She is asleep,' the boy repeated.

'If you would let me come in,' the man said with an odd

frightened smile, and suddenly lowering his voice he said to the boy, 'I am a priest.'

'You?' the boy exclaimed.

'Yes,' he said gently. 'My name is Father – ' But the boy had already swung the door open and put his lips to his hand before the other could give himself a name.

*The Heart of the Matter*
The terrifying depiction of a man's awe of the Church and Greene's ability to portray human motive and to convey such a depth of suffering make this one of his most enduring and tragic novels.    ISBN 0-14-018496-1

*Loser Takes All*
Greene offers up a tale of an unsuccessful accountant's second try at luck and love.    ISBN 0-14-018542-9

*The Man Within*
Themes of betrayal, pursuit, and the search for peace run through Greene's first published novel about a smuggler who takes refuge from his avengers.
ISBN 0-14-018530-5

*The Ministry of Fear*
This is a complex portrait of the shadowy inner landscape of Arthur Rowe, a man torn apart with guilt over mercifully murdering his sick wife.
ISBN 0-14-018536-4

*Our Man in Havana*
In this comic novel, Wormwold tries to keep his job as a secret agent in Havana by filing bogus reports and dreaming up military installations from vacuum-cleaner designs.    ISBN 0-14-018493-7

*The Power and the Glory*
Greene's masterpiece is a compelling depiction of a "whiskey priest" struggling to overcome physical and mortal cowardice and find redemption.
ISBN 0-14-243730-1

*Stamboul Train*
Set on the Orient Express, this suspense thriller involves the desperate affair between a pragmatic Jew and a naïve chorus girl.
ISBN 0-14-018532-1

*The Third Man and The Fallen Idol*
This edition pairs Greene's legendary thriller *The Third Man* with *The Fallen Idol*, in which a small boy discovers the deadly truths of the adult world.
ISBN 0-14-018533-X

*Travels with My Aunt*
Henry Pulling's dull suburban life is interrupted when his septuagenarian Aunt Augusta persuades him to travel the world with her in her own inimitable style.    ISBN 0-14-018501-1

# FOR THE BEST IN PAPERBACKS, LOOK FOR THE

In every corner of the world, on every subject under the sun, Penguin represents quality and variety—the very best in publishing today.

For complete information about books available from Penguin—including Penguin Classics, Penguin Compass, and Puffins—and how to order them, write to us at the appropriate address below. Please note that for copyright reasons the selection of books varies from country to country.

**In the United States:** Please write to *Penguin Group (USA), P.O. Box 12289 Dept. B, Newark, New Jersey 07101-5289* or call 1-800-788-6262.

**In the United Kingdom:** Please write to *Dept. EP, Penguin Books Ltd, Bath Road, Harmondsworth, West Drayton, Middlesex UB7 0DA.*

**In Canada:** Please write to *Penguin Books Canada Ltd, 90 Eglinton Avenue East, Suite 700, Toronto, Ontario M4P 2Y3.*

**In Australia:** Please write to *Penguin Books Australia Ltd, P.O. Box 257, Ringwood, Victoria 3134.*

**In New Zealand:** Please write to *Penguin Books (NZ) Ltd, Private Bag 102902, North Shore Mail Centre, Auckland 10.*

**In India:** Please write to *Penguin Books India Pvt Ltd, 11 Panchsheel Shopping Centre, Panchsheel Park, New Delhi 110 017.*

**In the Netherlands:** Please write to *Penguin Books Netherlands bv, Postbus 3507, NL-1001 AH Amsterdam.*

**In Germany:** Please write to *Penguin Books Deutschland GmbH, Metzlerstrasse 26, 60594 Frankfurt am Main.*

**In Spain:** Please write to *Penguin Books S. A., Bravo Murillo 19, 1° B, 28015 Madrid.*

**In Italy:** Please write to *Penguin Italia s.r.l., Via Benedetto Croce 2, 20094 Corsico, Milano.*

**In France:** Please write to *Penguin France, Le Carré Wilson, 62 rue Benjamin Baillaud, 31500 Toulouse.*

**In Japan:** Please write to *Penguin Books Japan Ltd, Kaneko Building, 2-3-25 Koraku, Bunkyo-Ku, Tokyo 112.*

**In South Africa:** Please write to *Penguin Books South Africa (Pty) Ltd, Private Bag X14, Parkview, 2122 Johannesburg.*